MYTH KEEPER

Also by Suneé le Roux

The Reverie Flash Fiction Series

A Spark of Reverie
A Flight of Reverie
A Song of Reverie
A Whisper of Reverie

Standalone Short Stories

Spirit Caller

The Mythical Menagerie Series

Keeper of Exotic Animals
Becoming Keeper

Myth Hunter
Myth Keeper
Myth Maker
Myth Bringer

MYTH
KEEPER

MYTHICAL MENAGERIE
SERIES BOOK 2

SUNEÉ LE ROUX

Strawberry Moon Press

Copyright © 2023 Suneé le Roux

All rights reserved.

Cover design: Covers by Tallulah

For permission requests, contact the author at contact@suneeleroux.com.

This book is a work of fiction. Names, characters, places, incidents and dialogues are used fictitiously. Any resemblance to actual people, living or deceased, is coincidental.

ISBN (Paperback): 978-0-6397-6207-4

Author's Note

The stories that make up the Mythical Menagerie series were written in serialised short-story form. Each story contains its own complete arc while contributing to the larger narrative of the series as a whole. Think of them as very large chapters in a single story.

This collection brings the episodes of the second series together into one continuous reading experience.

This novel makes use of UK English spelling and syntax.

TABLE OF CONTENTS

PART 6
BLOOD MOON'S LEGACY

"Come on, Ambrose!"

I glanced around Trafalgar Square to see if there was anyone around to witness this silliness. It was so late at night, it was almost early. The sky was a deep black, the crescent moon a silver sliver in the dark. Dots of yellow light from occasional lampposts and nearby buildings lit the square. Here and there, a homeless person settled into the shadows, while a group of boisterous teenagers hung out beside one of the fountains. They were laughing and smoking and splashing each other, hopefully too busy to pay any attention to us.

"I'm not sure this is such a good idea…" I said as I climbed up the base of one of the Landseer lions at the foot of Nelson's Column, ignoring the sign that expressly forbade people from doing so. The monumental bronze statue, much larger than a real lion, gazed out toward the second fountain; proud, serene, the master of all it surveyed.

"Oh, live a little!" Sarah laughed, already astride the statue, straddling the lion like it was the most natural thing in the world. For someone who had once charged into battle mounted on a centaur, it might well be. She held her hand out, inviting me up.

The back of my neck tingled and I hesitated. I turned around, sweeping my gaze across the square again. Experience had taught me to trust my instincts, and they were all shouting at me now that someone was watching me. And that the watcher's gaze wasn't friendly.

A shadow flickered in the corner of my eye

and I turned to stare at the columned façade of the National Gallery on the other side of the square. The building was aglow with floodlights, leaving little room for anyone to hide close to it. My eyes roved along its walls, searching for something, anything suspicious, but there was nothing. Probably just someone trying to find a sheltered spot for the night. Nothing to worry about.

Then why had it felt like someone was watching me?

"Ambrose?"

Sarah's voice tugged me back and I turned to see her smiling down at me, unaware of my unease. I shrugged. It was probably just my imagination.

I took Sarah's hand and let her help me up the surprisingly slippery side of the bronze statue. Ignoring the laughter coming from the kids below us, I scrambled up until I was perched behind Sarah on the lion's back. I wrapped my arms around her and she snuggled into my chest. Her signature citrusy scent wafted over me and I breathed deeply, savouring the moment.

Below us, the teenagers cheered and hooted. So much for going unnoticed. I winked at them, and two of the boys gave me a thumbs-up. One of them had sandy-blond hair like my own, the look on his face a mixture of amazement and envy. I didn't blame him. I hardly believed my luck either.

Thankfully, they lost interest in us soon enough. Someone must have realised how late it was – there was a sudden rush of activity as the teenagers grabbed their bags, took a few last selfies together, and handed out hugs. The sandy-haired boy strode off on his own in the direction of the museum while the rest of his friends were still saying their goodbyes. Perhaps it was his curfew calling an end to their party.

Finally. Now I could have some time alone with Sarah.

"Is this what it would feel like?" she asked, pulling away from me to sit up straight. I missed her warmth immediately. She flung her arms out to the sides, like she was a rich girl standing in the prow of a boat and me, Leonardo DiCaprio, behind her. "Is this what flying on a griffon would feel like?"

For a moment, I let myself be swept up in that fantasy. I closed my eyes and imagined myself soaring above the clouds, powerful eagle wings flapping on the wind, feline muscles bunching beneath me. A thrill of excitement shot through my veins.

I squished it down.

I was done with all of that now. Myths made flesh brought nothing but trouble. That world had split my family apart, made me believe my father was dead for more than four years, and had nearly cost me my life countless times. It wasn't worth the risk.

When Amari's last pay cheque had cleared about a week ago, I told her I would no longer accept assignments from the Elder Council. Or the Council for the Protection and Preservation of Cultural Creatures, as they preferred to be called. Whatever they named themselves, the Repository, and the things inside it, were no longer my concern.

In fact, I had an interview at my old firm tomorrow morning. A nice, normal job in a corner office with a view across the Thames was exactly what I needed. I'd have to get used to wearing a suit and tie again, but that would be a small price to pay to have a quiet life once more.

"I wonder how that baby griffon is doing now – the one you saved in Rome. What was his name again?" Sarah asked, pulling my thoughts back to the present.

"Caerus," I answered, my frown softening at the memory of that tiny ball of fluff, his eyes so wide and trusting. He would have been sold to the highest bidder if Amari hadn't sent me to intervene.

I suppose not all of it had been bad.

Truth be told, it had been fantastic to see living, breathing mythical creatures with my own eyes. My job as a Freelance Procurement Specialist had shown me things I would have never believed were real. Unicorns? Beautiful. Gargoyles? Shoulder-bruisingly solid. Leprechauns? Surprisingly good at playing squash.

They were all incredible.

And exceedingly dangerous, in their own way.

It had all started when I'd tried to save a girl from drowning in the lake at Hyde Park. As it turned out, that girl was an asrai, a water nymph with a taste for murder who had nearly frozen my heart. In return, I'd had her locked up in the Repository where she would never hurt anyone again.

But if it hadn't been for her, Sarah and I would never have met. Dating a detective inspector for the Metropolitan Police had been difficult at first, especially when I'd tried keeping it all a secret from her. But since the day we'd been kidnapped by a group of centaurs in Rome, almost three weeks ago, I'd had no choice but to lay all my cards on the table for her. It was the best thing that could have happened to us. We'd never been closer.

As if she could hear my thoughts, Sarah tilted her head towards me, those moss-green eyes filling my vision. My head dipped towards her lips.

A scream tore through the night.

I pulled away from Sarah, my gaze whipping

towards the sound. One of the teenage girls was standing at the foot of the stairs leading to the National Gallery's entrance, pointing at something lying on the ground. Her friends rushed towards her, gasping and wailing as they saw what she was staring at. One boy turned away from the group and vomited loudly.

I slid down the side of the lion and hit the ground running. My lucky white trainers smacked the cement as I sprinted up the steps leading to the museum. The kids were clumped together in a semi-circle. I pushed past them, dreading what I would find.

I swallowed back bile. Blood matted the sandy-blond hair of the boy laying crumpled at my feet, his grey eyes staring sightlessly into the dark. His jacket had been ripped to shreds. Bloody gashes covered his arms and torso. The metallic stench of blood seeped into my nose as I looked at a face that looked so much like my own, even Mother would have had trouble picking us apart in a lineup had I been a few years younger.

"Step aside." Sarah's voice was cool and professional as she joined me. The teenagers, clutching onto each other, shuffled around to make room for her. She knelt and pressed her fingers to the boy's neck, feeling for a pulse. After a few seconds, she sighed and shook her head, before pulling out her mobile phone and calling it in.

I looked at the kids surrounding the body of their dead friend. Tears streaked down pale faces as they clutched onto each other for support. They were too young for this. Hell, I was too young for this.

"Did any of you see what happened?" I asked, more to draw their attention away from the grisly sight than anything else.

Blank stares met my own, a headshake here and there. One boy opened his mouth, then closed it again, quickly looking away.

Sarah, her eyes narrowing behind her black-rimmed hipster glasses, didn't miss anything. "You saw something," she said. "What was it?"

The boy's face turned red as everyone's eyes were drawn to him. "Nothing," he stammered. "It's stupid. It doesn't matter."

"My friend's a police detective," I said. "She won't think you're stupid. Even something small might help her find the person who did this." I locked eyes with Sarah. Her jaw was clenched and there was something in her gaze that I didn't recognise.

The boy rubbed the back of his neck with one hand, his eyes everywhere but on the body by his feet. "I didn't see anything. But... I had a feeling." He looked around the group, as if daring his friends to mock him. A heaviness worked itself into my shoulders. I knew what this boy was going to say.

"What sort of feeling?" Sarah asked. "Can you describe it?"

The boy sighed. Then shrugged and said: "Like someone was watching me."

I felt the hair on the back of my neck stand on end. Unlike the dead boy, this one's mop of unruly curls was more red than yellow, but he had the lean build of a rugby fly-half and could easily have been my stunt double. Was it a coincidence that two of us had felt watched, and one of us was dead?

Sarah looked at me and I nodded slightly. Her eyes darted back to the boy, and then towards me again. Her eyes widened as she made the connection.

Blaring sirens and bright blue lights announced

the arrival of a police squad. Sarah turned to the kids and said: "An officer is going to take a statement from each of you. I don't want you to leave anything out, okay? No matter how silly it may sound. Anything you saw, smelled or felt, get it all down. Then phone your parents and get them to come pick you up. The streets aren't safe tonight. Alright?"

The teenagers nodded, subdued. Any bravado they had had earlier that evening was long gone now.

Sarah waved the oncoming officers over, before taking me aside and saying softly: "You felt someone watching you too earlier?" The space between her eyebrows creased.

"I thought it was just my overactive imagination."

Her scowl deepened. "I'd probably have said the same if we didn't have a dead boy on our hands right now." She took her glasses off and rubbed at her eyes, suppressing a yawn. When she put them on again, her expression had changed from tired to determined. "I'm going to be held up here for a while now, so you might as well go home." She pressed a finger against my lips as I started to protest. "No, you'll only be in the way. Sorry Ambrose, but there's nothing more you can do here now."

I nodded reluctantly. "You'll be alright if I leave you here?"

"I'll be fine," she said. "Whatever did this is gone now, and it's unlikely to attack a group of people anyway. I'm more worried about you. The resemblance…" I saw fear in her eyes and suddenly I wasn't sure if I wanted to go home on my own either. "Get into a cab, and make sure you lock the door of your apartment. I'll call you in the morning."

She hugged me tightly, as if afraid to let me go, and left to join her team, casting a last concerned glance my way.

I waved goodbye, trying to appear unworried, but fear was a dog gnawing at my bones. Every shadow, every unexpected sound had me on edge while I waited for the taxi to arrive. I stared out the window all the way home, trying to push the image of the dead teenager out of my mind.

The lights on my street were out when the taxi dropped me off. With only a thin slice of moon to light my way, I slammed the car door behind me and sprinted across the pavement. My fingers fumbled the keys to the front door and I dropped them. Swearing under my breath and casting furtive glances around me, I picked them up and jammed them into the lock. I thrust a hand into the house first, switching on the lights before I practically jumped through the door and slammed it shut behind me.

I stood there in my living room with my back to the door, panting. The fact that she'd said whatever instead of whoever haunted me almost as much as the fear in her eyes as she'd said it.

It was going to be a long night.

※※※

"I'm coming!" I shouted, wincing at the noise. My head pounded as I lugged myself out of bed. I grabbed the sword still tangled up in my bedsheets – just in case – and lurched towards the door. Whoever was outside hadn't heard me call out earlier and it seemed like they were trying to batter the door down with the knocker.

I flung the door open and nearly pulled Sarah off her feet before she let go of the brass door knocker. Relief and annoyance played across her face.

"Ambrose! Thank goodness," she said, wrapping her arms around me. I could feel her heart hammering against my chest. She pulled away from me, concern clouding her eyes. "Why haven't you answered any of my calls?"

"I've been asleep," I said, hiding a yawn behind my hand.

I'd lain awake most of the night, imagining every creak in the apartment to be someone – or something – coming to murder me in my bed. It took almost an entire bottle of red wine I'd found stashed in the back of the pantry to dull my nerves, but it was only after cuddling down with a stainless steel replica of Glamdring in my arms that sleep had finally claimed me.

"Asleep!" I winced at her tone as she pulled away from me. "You didn't even text to tell me you were home safe! What was I supposed to think?"

I rubbed at the back of my neck, staring sheepishly at her. It had been a while since someone other than my sister had cared enough to be worried about me. It felt… nice.

Sarah's eyes dropped to the sword in my hand and a smile tickled at her lips. "At least you're prepared for the worst."

"You know me," I mumbled. "Come in."

I ushered her inside, wishing that I'd used my sleepless hours last night to tidy the place up a bit. Sarah had never been in my apartment before and was looking around curiously. I wondered what her detective's eyes were noticing, and what it said about me.

I put the sword somewhere inconspicuous and turned back to her. "Want some tea?"

She checked her wristwatch and shook her head. "I'd better get back to the station. Just wanted to make sure you were alright. And tell you the news."

Apprehension stabbed icily through my heart. There must have been a reason for all those missed calls. "Did you learn something?"

"No," Sarah said, shaking her head. "The boy's body is still with the coroner. He'll call me when he's done with the post-mortem. What I wanted to tell you is that we found another one."

A sour taste filled my mouth. "What happened?"

"Taxi driver," Sarah said, her expression grave. "His car was still idling in the middle of the road when an irate motorist found him. His body was mangled. The same gashes across the torso that the boy had. Ambrose…" Her eyes had dark circles underneath them, not quite hidden by her glasses. She'd probably not slept all night. "I've seen my fair share of dead people over the years, but this… This isn't normal."

I swallowed, trying to work some moisture back into my mouth. Was it *my* taxi driver that had been murdered? Had the killer been after me and, having lost my trail, lashed out at someone else instead? My chest felt constricted and I pulled at the neck of my shirt to try to get some air.

It took a few seconds to register what Sarah had said. A lead ball settled in my stomach as I looked at her. "You think the killer is something… supernatural?"

"I don't know what to think," Sarah said, folding her arms across her body. "I know it sounds crazy, but now that I know there are things out there…" Her gaze drifted off into space and her jaw tightened. When her eyes met mine again, fear filled those green pools. "I don't know how to handle this."

I closed the space between us and wrapped her in my arms. I felt her tremble against my chest, and this, more than the two dead bodies and the murderer on the loose, scared me. Sarah was the bravest, most capable person I knew. Seeing her like this made my chest ache in a whole new way.

"We'll figure it out," I said. "We've managed up till now, and we didn't know about any of it then."

"Maybe it's better that way. Not knowing."

"It's easier. I don't know about better."

Sarah smiled wanly at me. Then she extricated herself from my arms. "Do you think you could... I don't know, talk to Amari about it? Ask around?" She paced around my living room, her eyes blazing. "There must be some local underground gang of creatures you can contact."

I laughed. "It's not like the books. I can't just waltz into a den of vampires and pump them for information. At least... I don't think so. I don't know any, in any event."

She grunted. "I know, I'm grasping at straws here. Also: vampires? Not making me feel any better."

"Sorry," I said, grimacing. "I do know someone I can ask, though. We'll get to the bottom of this, I promise. And who knows, it might just turn out to be normal murders." I flinched. "Not that I'm trying to say murder is normal."

"I know what you mean," Sarah laughed. Then she looked at her watch again. "I have to go. I'll let you know when I hear from the coroner. Promise me you'll be careful? Normal or supernatural, whoever did this might be after you. I'd prefer it if you didn't have a nametag on your toe the next time I see you."

I snorted. "I'd rather avoid that too."

She kissed me on the cheek and was out the door.

I ran a hand through my hair. The last thing I wanted was to get involved with the mythical world again. That part of my life was over now. If

I hurried, I could still make my interview.

Just then my mobile beeped. A text from Jake popped up. My old colleague would be my boss now and would sit in on the interview.

-- Crisis at the exchange. Can we reschedule? Same time tomorrow? --

Disappointment mixed with relief as I quickly typed a response. At least I had some time now to get my head clear first. One day to sort this mess out before everything goes back to normal again.

Off the top of my head, I could think of at least five creatures from English folklore that might be real and might be guilty of such violent murders, but why they'd be after me was a mystery.

Still, better safe than sorry. If something was hunting me, I'd should prepare for the worst. Maybe walking around with Glamdring strapped to my side wasn't such a crazy idea after all…

❊❊❊

After I'd had a shower and put some food in my belly, I went searching for answers. The sky was such a clear blue when I jogged up the steps of Westminster Tube station that it was almost difficult to believe that what had happened last night was real. The world seemed normal. People around me were going about their lives, oblivious of anything unusual going on. There wasn't even a telltale rainbow hanging over Big Ben today.

But there was a young woman with a shock of red hair standing underneath the clock tower, looking lost.

"Caitlynn!" I called, crossing the street and hurrying over to her.

Daniel's only sister looked so relieved it was

almost comical, but it was her incongruous appearance that made me smile. She wore a dress that looked straight out of a Jane Austen novel, all frills and organza. Her flaming hair was tied back in a demure style, but wisps of wild curls were already escaping their confinement.

"Ambrose! I'm so glad to see you," she said, clasping my hands with her gloved ones. "I didn't realise London was so big!" Her eyes were wide as she clutched onto me. "Daniel always talked about Big Ben, and I thought if I could just get to Big Ben, then finding Daniel would be easy, but this…" She swept one hand out to encompass the sea of people walking past us. "I didn't expect this," she finished in a small voice.

I squeezed the hands still tightly wedged into my own. "I guess London can be a bit overwhelming for newcomers," I admitted. "Are you here on your own? You're lucky I saw you." She sniffed, lifting an eyebrow at me. Talking to a leprechaun about luck was perhaps a bit on the nose. "Daniel's shop isn't far from here. I was just on my way there myself. Come, I'll take you."

I elbowed a way for us through the tourists and passers-by, while Caitlynn's eyes grew wider and wider with every step we took. Her gaze flitted from one sight to the next: Big Ben, the Houses of Parliament, statues of people long dead; all things I hardly noticed anymore.

"Normally, there would have been a rainbow to point the way for you," I said as we walked.

Beside me, Caitlynn gasped. "He flaunts it for everyone to see?"

I shrugged. "I've always been under the impression that he didn't have much control over it. It just seems to follow him around. Like a puppy." Caitlynn tutted and it occurred to me that there wasn't a rainbow shadowing her. "Where's yours?"

"Ambrose!" Caitlynn exclaimed. "You may be my brother's best friend, and I'm grateful for your help right now, but we're certainly not well enough acquainted for that kind of question." She looked so scandalised I had to suppress a chuckle.

"Here we are," I said as we reached Daniel's shop. Caitlynn's grip tightened as I put my hand on the doorknob. I looked at her. She was chewing her bottom lip in a way that made me want to tuck her hair behind her ear and tell her that everything will be alright.

She noticed me watching her and took a deep breath, before squaring her shoulders and nodding.

A bell jingled as I opened the door. Daniel looked up from behind a pile of shoes spread out on the countertop at the back. A warm light dangling from the ceiling illuminated his freckled face.

"Hey mate," he greeted me, but his smile faltered when he saw his sister following in my wake. "Caitlynn?"

"I'm sorry to arrive unannounced like this, Daniel," she said. Her voice was shaky, but she lifted her chin and straightened her back. "I hope it won't be too much of an inconvenience."

Daniel was off his chair and by his sister's side within seconds, wrapping his arms around her in a warm hug. Her stance softened as she let herself relax.

"You should have told me you were coming," he said. "I would have waited for you by the station. Hell, I would have fetched you from home myself and spared you the journey on your own."

"It's alright," she said. "It was… an adventure. And Ambrose found me just when I needed him." She smiled warmly at me and I couldn't help but grin back.

"He does have a knack for being at the right place at the right time," Daniel scoffed. "Here," he said, letting go of his sister and pulling his stool out from behind the counter for her. "Where's your suitcase? I can put it in the back for now."

Caitlynn's shoulders slumped. "I... lost it." Her cheeks turned rosy under our surprised stares. "There was a man... He offered to help me carry it up the stairs at the train station. It was so heavy, and there were so many stairs. I thought he was being gentlemanly."

"Well, that's London for you," I said, shrugging. "It could have been worse, I guess."

Caitlynn's face paled. I knew she'd led a sheltered life. Female leprechauns were rare – Daniel certainly had enough brothers to prove that point – and her parents had kept her safe by isolating her at their ancestral home in Ireland. She'd wiled away her hours by reading every book in the family's extensive library, which must have instilled in her a lust for adventure that, in her naivety, had led her here today. When we had met a few weeks ago, she'd begged me to help her escape the farm but, at the time, I'd thought it prudent not to go against her mother's wishes.

A thought suddenly occurred to me. "Does your mother know you're here?"

Caitlynn shook her head. "She would never have let me come."

Daniel whistled incredulously. "You're braver than I thought."

"You're not going to tell her, are you?" Caitlynn asked. "She won't let me stay. I didn't come all this way just to go back home on the evening train." Her fists were balled and some of the fire that had so intrigued me when I'd first met her was back in her eyes.

I might not agree with her mother's methods, but I could understand her reasons, at least. She just wanted to keep her only daughter safe. "You have to tell her you're here," I said, wincing as Caitlynn turned a heated gaze on me. "She'll be worried sick if you don't."

Her anger faded, but her hands were still clenched in defiance.

"I'll write to her," Daniel offered. He rubbed the back of his neck, probably dreading that conversation. "She's not going to like it, but I'll make her see reason. I knew she wouldn't be able to keep you cooped up on the farm much longer."

"Thank you." Caitlynn slumped onto the stool, her fire doused to simmering coals for now. She suddenly looked as fragile as a porcelain doll. It certainly didn't help that she was dressed like the heroine from a period drama.

"I know what you need," I said, struck by an idea. "I'll ask my sister to take you shopping and show you around a bit so you can find your feet."

Caitlynn's face lit up and Daniel said: "That's a great idea. I'll give you some money and you can get yourself clothes that will blend in a bit better here in the city."

"What about my – "

"We'll worry about that later," Daniel said as he walked towards the counter.

I quickly pulled out my mobile phone and texted my sister.

-- Are you busy today? Daniel's sister's in town and she needs to go shopping. --

Cassie's response came through immediately.

-- Any excuse to skip class will do. I'm on my way. --

I hesitated over a response, then thought better of it. Cassie was old enough to make her own decisions. Mother preached enough to her as it was.

Daniel and Caitlynn were hunched over a piece of paper spread out on the countertop, probably busy composing a letter to their mother. I smiled. I might have persuaded Daniel to try out the wonders of modern technology by giving him an old Nokia of mine, but the rest of his family certainly weren't as progressive yet. The slow correspondence would at least give Caitlynn a taste of the outside life she craved so much if she were forced to return home later. Watching her argue wording with Daniel, her cheeks flushed and her wild curls escaping their confinement, I couldn't help but feel a little protective of her. Surely she deserved her freedom as much as any of us did.

I nearly dropped the phone as it suddenly started ringing in my hand. Sarah.

"Cassie's coming," I said, heading for the door. With three people in there, Daniel's shop felt too crowded for whatever news I was about to receive. "Maybe we can all grab dinner tonight?" I asked as the bell jingled. "At that place I like near Tower Bridge?"

"Sounds good," Daniel called distractedly. "Thanks for your help, Ambrose."

I waved goodbye as I answered Sarah's call.

"I have the coroner's report in front of me," she said without preamble. "He found some DNA in the wounds. It's human... mostly."

"What?" I asked, and then walked straight into someone standing in the doorway. "Pardon me," I said, resisting the urge to rub my shoulder. The man was built like a brick wall, all hard planes and sharp angles. A snake-like tattoo crawled across one of his bulging biceps. He glared at me from beneath bushy eyebrows. What he was doing on Daniel's threshold was beyond me. His army-style boots were spotless.

I ducked out of the man's way and found a quiet spot next to the Thames. "What do you mean mostly? How can it be mostly human?"

"There were traces of something else mixed in."

It felt like someone had punched me in the gut. "Fox?" I joked weakly. I'd seen something on the telly about urban scavengers becoming increasingly bolder. I doubted they were aggressive enough to attack people, though.

"It's not a fox." She paused and I braced myself for what I feared was coming. "It's wolf DNA. He even narrowed it down to a very rare strain from a pack found in the Black Forest in Germany."

"Wolf?" I exhaled loudly, running a hand through my hair.

"Ambrose?" Sarah sounded worried. I pictured her pacing a hole in her office floor. "There was a werewolf in Rome. What happened to it?"

I shuddered at the memory. That monster had left a trail of blood in its wake during the night of the blood moon. It would definitely be capable of leaving a corpse in the state of the one we had found. But what would it be doing here, in London? As far as I knew, Amari and the Elder Council had captured all the mythical creatures that had been up for sale at the blood moon market and had taken them to the Repository.

"Ambrose?"

"Yes, sorry, I was just trying to repress some memories again. I'll talk to Amari. If that thing is here – and I sincerely hope it isn't – someone needs to capture it immediately." And it wasn't something I could expect the police to take care of.

I swallowed nervously. It felt like I had the entire Sahara in my mouth. "What about the human DNA?"

"Not someone on our database. I'm going to contact Interpol to see if they might have it on record, but I wanted to talk to you first."

"Right."

The hair on the back of my neck raised as that feeling of being watched crawled over me again. I glanced about me at the people walking past. If we were really dealing with a werewolf, any of them could be the murderer. I hadn't seen the beast in its human form at the Colosseum. It could be the tattooed guy coming out of Daniel's shop, or the man in the tracksuit pants who looked like he'd just come from the gym and could easily lift two hundred pounds. Hell, it could be that little old lady with her groceries in one hand, shuffling along with the cane. It could be anyone!

"Ambrose? What's going on? Are you alright?" Sarah's voice in my ear startled me back to my senses and I realised my breathing had turned short and ragged.

"Just… a little paranoid, I guess," I said. "Everything's fine." I wasn't fine. Visions of the dead boy floated in my mind's eye. The way his body had been mangled. The sharp smell of blood. The glint of moonlight on his staring eyes.

Moonlight! I did a little happy dance right there, ignoring the stares I attracted. "I just remembered! It's not even full moon yet. It can't be a werewolf. The coroner probably made a mistake."

"Okay…" Sarah sounded dubious. "Do me a favour and talk to Amari anyway. Let's make sure."

"Pfff," I scoffed. "I'm sure it's all coincidence. Just because we know there are unusual things out there doesn't mean the killer isn't anything other than some twisted psycho who happened to kill a boy who resembled me a little bit." And maybe my taxi driver, but I pushed that thought down. "There's no reason for anyone, or anything, to be after me. We're letting our imaginations get the best of us."

There was a short silence on the other end of the phone, before Sarah sighed. "Maybe you're right. Either way, be careful, Ambrose. I'll check in with you later. Talk to Amari. Let me know what you find out."

"Fine," I agreed, mostly to humour her. I ended the call, feeling like a weight had been lifted from my shoulders. I would talk to Amari, just to ease Sarah's worries, but I was confident there was a normal explanation for the murders. Who knows? Maybe they weren't even related at all.

Finding a discreet spot in the heart of London's tourist district was not an easy task. In the end, I had to duck into the public toilets in St James's Park before I blew the silent whistle hanging from a chord I still wore around my neck and tucked underneath my shirt. Some habits were hard to break.

The white light that announced Amari's arrival was blinding inside the small cubicle. The Keeper stumbled over the toilet and into my arms as the illumination faded.

"Ambrose!" she said as I steadied her. "What's this? Are we inside a loo?"

"It's the only private space I could find at short notice," I apologised.

She wrinkled her nose as she studied the graffiti on the stall's walls. "You want to talk to me here, or can we take this someplace a little more civilised?"

"By all means," I said. "Let's get out of here."

I closed my eyes as a Word from Amari swept

us away.

I always felt an immediate sense of belonging when I stepped into Amari's office. A fire was smouldering in the hearth, bathing the room in a warm glow, and the walls were lined with ancient books my fingers itched to touch. Amari stepped across the thick Persian carpet and sat down behind the large mahogany desk in the centre of the windowless room.

"What can I do for you, Ambrose?" she said, waving for me to take a seat opposite her. Her desk, usually spotlessly tidy, was covered in stacks of papers today. She looked at them, a small frown creasing her brows, then deliberately folded her arms and turned her gaze expectantly at me.

"I need to know if the werewolf could have escaped," I said, sinking down into the chair across from her.

Amari cocked her head to the side, frowning. "Werewolf? What werewolf?"

My palms were suddenly sweaty. "The one you captured during the blood moon market in Rome."

Amari's face was a blank. "We didn't acquire a werewolf that night. Or any other shapeshifters that I'm aware of." Her eyes widened. "Are you saying something escaped from the Colosseum?"

I swallowed and nodded glumly. I quickly told her about the bodies and what Sarah had learned from the coroner. "Sarah thinks the killer might be after me. I'm trying to find out if it's the werewolf."

"It's possible…" Amari said, leaning back in her chair and tapping a finger against her cheek in thought. "I've read they can be vindictive. It might have caught your scent that night and decided, for some reason, to track you down. If that's the case, then this is the perfect opportunity to apprehend it and get it into the Repository."

An incredulous laugh escaped my lips. "Your concern is touching," I said, half joking, half terrified. I still wasn't convinced it was the werewolf, but if it was... I rubbed my palms against my trousers, leaving damp streaks behind. "Who are you going to send after it?"

Amari waved my question away with one hand. "You're more than capable of handling it. Especially if you can catch it in its human form. Do you have something silver you can use to weaken it?"

"No." I shook my head. "Unless you want me to raid my mother's spoon drawer."

The corners of Amari's mouth lifted into a smile. "You see, resourceful. You'll be fine." She stood up from her chair, although I really wasn't as eager to get going. She seemed to have conveniently forgotten that I no longer worked for her. "Want to go see your father while you're here?"

I froze. "Father's here?"

The last I'd heard from him was about a week ago, saying he was going to be out of mobile signal for a while and not to worry about him. I had just assumed some new passion had taken hold of him and he was deeply entrenched in a library somewhere, up to his ears in musty old books chasing obscure references.

"Didn't he tell you he's my new assistant? Come, I think I saw him with the dryads earlier..."

I followed Amari out of her office and down the long corridor carved into the mountain that housed the Repository. She opened an iron door and we paused at the balcony overlooking the enclosures inside the main cave. My eyes darted to the compounds of the creatures I knew a little more personally. Una, the unicorn, was galloping across a sun-filled meadow. In an enclosure a few doors down, the griffon family were out hunting together, little Caerus pouncing on a startled rabbit while his parents watched proudly. In a darker corner of the cave, the asrai was sitting on a rock, her feet dipped into the pond, combing her pale shoulder-length hair.

"Where's Nessie?" I asked.

"You mean Kentigern Mor," Amari said sternly. "He's over there."

My gaze followed her pointed finger to a new enclosure a little apart from the rest where a great expanse of water, with a ruined castle brooding beside the lake, was visible. The sinuous blue dragon lay stretched out in a sunny spot on the pebbly shoreline. If I listened closely, I could hear him snoring.

"Apparently, he likes to sunbathe," Amari said, smiling fondly.

"No wonder he was always so cranky," I laughed, as we descended the steps. "He must be happy here, then. No tourists to hide from, no Scottish weather to contend with."

"Don't sound so surprised. I keep telling you the Repository is a haven. They're supposed to be happy."

"I know, I know," I said. "It's just…" I struggled to explain my reservations. "What if they wanted to leave? Would you let them?"

"You know they're safer here."

"But it's so easy to take advantage of them in a place like this."

Amari stopped and placed her hands on her hips, glaring at me. "Ambrose Davids, after all this time, don't you trust me?"

"Of course I do," I said hastily. "But you've admitted yourself that the Council might not have the pure intentions you do."

Amari's glare turned into a scowl. "These creatures are my responsibility and under my protection. No one will take advantage of them while I'm the Keeper. Not even the Council."

I believed her. Amari was a force of nature. I wouldn't want her as my enemy.

"I thought there'd be more new enclosures," I said as we reached the bottom of the stairs. "Where are you keeping the airavata?" The five-headed elephant had been one of the many creatures up for sale at the auction during that fateful night of the blood moon. The last time I'd seen it, it had been hurtling lightning at anyone trying to get too close to it.

"He's still in the holding pens with the rest," Amari replied, a weary sigh escaping her lips. "I've been drowning in bureaucracy the last few weeks. And here's the reason why..." she trailed off as a centaur wearing the red cloak of a Roman official trotted towards us.

"Miss Kerubo, a word if I may," the centaur said, barely sparing me a glance. "It's about the harpy enclosure. I'm not sure it should be so dark in there. The poor creatures barely get any sunlight."

Amari's jaw clenched and a vein thrummed at her temple. I knew her well enough by now to know that the clipped tones in which she answered held barely suppressed annoyance. "Of course, Flavius. Why don't we go talk to them to see what their thoughts are on the matter? Ambrose," she said, turning to me. "Your father's right over there. Call me when you're done and I'll send you back home." Then she stalked off and disappeared behind a corner, the centaur trotting after her.

I turned to see Father stepping out of an enclosure, locking the door behind him. He was humming the theme tune from Gladiator to himself, looking as happy as I'd ever seen him.

"Ambrose!" he said when he noticed me. "What a nice surprise! If I'd known you were here I'd have asked you to come have tea with us. The dryads do so love a bit of Earl Grey with their afternoon gossip."

"Why didn't you tell me you were working with Amari?" I asked as he slung an arm around my shoulder, hugging me closer.

"I wanted to see if it worked out first," he replied. "When the Chairman offered me the job, I wasn't sure if I was making the same mistake as I had with Marco, but so far this place seems like the real deal." His smile was infectious. I'd always thought he'd love the Repository.

"This must be a dream come true for you."

"Indeed," Father said, releasing me and walking over to the next enclosure. "I just wish Amari would give me access to the books in her study. I'm dying to get my hands on some of the tomes in there! Too delicate, she says. Like I don't know how to handle old books."

Father had been an academic most of his life and the thought of all that hidden knowledge, just out of his reach, must have been driving him insane. "I guess you'll just have to earn her trust first."

He shot me a sharp look. "Of course. I can be patient." He untangled a hosepipe and paused in front of the steel paddock door. "Want to help me clean out the cyclops cave? I've been watching him all week and I don't think he's going to do it himself. He might step on a shard of bone and cut his foot open."

"Actually, I was hoping you can tell me a little

more about werewolves," I said quickly. I did not want to go within arm's length of that creature, visually impaired or not. "Specifically, the one that was in Rome for the blood moon market."

"Well," Father said, scratching at his chin. "It was captured after I'd stopped cooperating, so I never had a chance to examine it. I overheard Marco saying it might make a good cage fighter, but I don't know what he had planned for it. Now that you mention it, I don't think I've seen it here in the holding pens…"

I shook my head. "Amari never even knew about it. It must have escaped from the Colosseum."

Father's eyes widened. "That's… probably not ideal. Have you encountered it?"

"Possibly. But only what it left behind." I grimaced. "I'm hoping to avoid the same fate."

He put the hose pipe down again. "Come, let's go have a look in my book. It's been a few years since I last did proper research on werewolves, and at the time I thought they really were just myths. Too mainstream to be real." He was practically bouncing on his feet as we headed back to the steps leading out of the cave. He took them two at a time and strode down the long corridor towards the residential wing.

I followed him into what I assumed was now his bedroom. It looked like a whirlwind had recently passed through. The four-poster bed was rumpled and unmade, and books and notes were strewn across every available surface, except for one spot on a desk in the corner where a little nest had been made from a straw fedora hat and scraps of torn cloth. A UV lamp was pointed at it, casting a warm glow across the nest. I peered inside.

The baby bird was a scraggly little thing. It had crimson feathers in patches, and a little golden crest on a head that looked too big for its ungainly body. It opened one eye, still completely black, and squinted back at me, making a strange clucking sound when I ran my forefinger along the back of its scruffy neck.

"Is this…?"

"The phoenix I rescued in Rome, yes," Father replied, while searching through the clutter. "I've named him Nusku."

"Let me guess…" I said. "God of Fire?"

"From…" Father prompted.

"Babylonia?" I hazarded.

"Close enough. Assyria. The phoenix myth occurs in various cultures from around the world: Greek, Egyptian, Persian, Slavic. It even has similarities with ancient Chinese and Japanese –"

"Does Amari know he's here?" I quickly interrupted. Knowing Father, this discussion could continue the entire day and I had more pressing concerns.

"If she suspects, she hasn't said anything yet. I doubt she'll mind, of course. The Repository is the best place for him, after all, and it's my job to help her look after the creatures now. He's too little to take care of himself. Maybe when he's older she'll show me how to build an enclosure for him. Ah, here it is."

I sat down on the bed as Father pulled his notebook from underneath a stack of scribbled-on papers and started paging through it. It took him only a few moments to find what he was looking for.

"Lycanthropy," he read. "The ability to shift from human into animal form, most often that of a wolf. Aided by a magical item. Vulnerable to silver weapons. Transformation during the full moon a popular notion originating from the twentieth century."

"What?" I blinked, feeling a heavy weight settle into my stomach. "A popular notion? Does that mean they don't need the full moon? They can transform at any time?"

Father put the book down. "Yes, the full moon myth was invented for dramatic effect during the early age of cinema. And, according to legend, most shifters had a piece of clothing, such as a belt or a cloak, that helped them change into a wolf – the normal kind, not the monsters we see in the movies today."

"So the killer isn't some crazy beast who can't control himself," I say, feeling my insides twist nervously. "It's someone who can change anytime he wants, and he's murdering people with his full wits about him." That idea left a bitter taste in my mouth. "But something doesn't add up," I continued, scratching at the stubble on my chin. "I have it on good authority that objects don't have any intrinsic magical properties. And the killer left wolf DNA behind, so he's not fully human either."

Father shrugged. "We both know the stories don't always get it right. Who's to know what's true and what's just old wives' tales. Why would a werewolf be vulnerable to silver? I can't think of any logical reason, and yet we all know they can only be killed with a silver bullet. But how old is the oldest werewolf myth, and when were bullets invented? The fact of the matter is, until we have a specimen to study, we won't know for sure what's true and what's not."

Well, shit.

Maybe Sarah was right. Maybe the killer was the werewolf. As much as I didn't want it to be true, perhaps it was time to face the facts. Perhaps there really was a mythical monster loose in London.

But why would it be after me? I didn't do

anything but stay the hell out of its way at the Colosseum.

I stood up, preparing to leave. I needed to tell Sarah what I'd learned. "I can't say I'm filled with confidence right now," I admitted. "But at least I have a better idea of what to expect. It was good to see you again, Father. I'll ask Amari if Cassie and I can come visit you from time to time."

"I'd like that," Father said as I headed for the door. "And here…" He slipped something into my hand. I looked down to see a silver letter opener nestled in my palm.

"I doubt the werewolf and I will correspond much…" I quipped.

"You never know, it might come in handy," Father replied, his academic fervour replaced by a worried frown. "It might be a good idea to find yourself some silver bullets. Just in case."

❉❉❉

Amari dropped me off in a secluded part of Hyde Park where I found an unoccupied bench and dialled Sarah.

"Ambrose, tell me you have good news." She sounded frazzled. I imagined her sitting by her desk, looking at pictures of the murder victims while chewing on the end of a pencil.

"I wish I could," I said, sighing. I quickly told her everything I had learned. "But what baffles me is why it would be after me. I'm not a threat. I'm not hunting it. Hell, no one would even have known it had escaped if it hadn't killed two people."

"Three," Sarah said, and my mouth went dry. "We found another body this afternoon. An older man, late fifties. Looked nothing like you, so perhaps it isn't after you at all."

I swallowed, trying to work some moisture back into my mouth. "Where?"

"In a stall in the public toilets at St James's Park."

It's a good thing I was already sitting down, because my knees suddenly turned to jelly. "I was there." On the other end of the line, I heard Sarah gasp. "I met Amari there. It must have followed me and then, frustrated when it didn't find me, lashed out at some innocent bystander." The bitter taste of guilt filled my mouth and I slumped down into the chair.

"It's not your fault, Ambrose," Sarah said, sighing. "Where are you now? If it's after you, then my best hope of catching it is to stay close to you."

I glanced around, wondering if I was being stalked right now. There were a few joggers running past, a couple with small kids chasing after the ducks at the edge of the lake, a young woman stretched out under a tree reading a book. It seemed safe enough.

"I think I lost it when I went to the Repository." I shivered as a cold wind ruffled through my hair. The sun was dipping towards the horizon. It had been a long day and I was tired from being on edge all the time. I needed to get my mind off things. "I'm supposed to meet the gang for dinner tonight," I said. "Come join us?"

"I'm not sure a public place – "

"It'll be perfect," I interrupted her. "It won't make a move with so many witnesses about. And besides, we both need a break. You sound exhausted." While I'd crashed and slept most of the morning away, Sarah had probably been at the precinct, doing paperwork and trying to track down a suspect that defied all her experience. I admired her tenacity, but working herself to death wasn't going to help anyone. "No excuses. Unless you want to go home and get some rest."

There was a brief pause while Sarah mulled it over. "No, I'll come with you. At least that way I'll know you're safe."

"And I'll feel better knowing I have my own private police protection," I joked. Hearing Sarah laugh in response eased some of the tension in my shoulders. "Meet me at Tower Bridge in twenty minutes."

"Okay," Sarah said. "I'll see you there."

※※※

Daniel was already waiting outside the restaurant when we arrived. "Finally!" he exclaimed when he saw us. "I'm famished. I could eat an entire roasted ox on my own! You must be Sarah," he said, grinning mischievously as he shook her hand. "Ambrose said you were easy on the eyes, but he didn't do you nearly enough justice."

Mortified, I glanced at Sarah to see how she'd respond.

"Oh, I like him," she said, her lips twitching into a smile. "Daniel, if I'm not mistaken?"

"Can't hide anything from a police detective," my friend joked, although I sensed some reserve to his usually carefree manner. There was a tightness about his eyes that made me think his good humour was a little forced.

Sarah didn't seem to notice. "Come on," she said. "I'll help you with that ox. I've had nothing but doughnuts all day."

I bit my lower lip, trying to hold back laughter. "Doughnuts? Seriously?"

Sarah rolled her eyes. "I'll admit it might be a little cliché," she replied, adjusting her glasses primly, "but after the day I've had…"

"Tell me about it!" Daniel said as he ushered us into the restaurant. "I could do with a pint or seven, myself."

We settled into a booth at the back. Daniel ordered the first round while Sarah excused herself to go to the ladies' room. When she was out of earshot, Daniel leaned in and asked quietly: "How much does she know?"

"She knows about Amari and the Repository, and she's seen some of the creatures for herself. She knows you were with me in Cardiff last week, and why we were there."

"What about me and my family?" All traces of his easy-going manner were gone as he held my gaze. His shoulders were tensed and his fists pressed into the table as he leaned forward towards me.

I shook my head. "Your secret is safe with me."

Daniel relaxed visibly and his smile flickered back into place. "Thank you. If it were just about me, then I'd take my chances, but with Caitlynn here…"

"Say no more, my friend. I understand."

The waitress arrived with our drinks. Daniel took a sip of his dark lager and sighed happily.

"Rough day?" I asked.

"You know it," he replied. "What with the family drama and the werewolf in my shop and Mrs Brown's entire collection of heels needing to be replaced –"

I choked on a sip of beer. "Werewolf?" I managed between coughs.

"You alright, mate?"

I waved for him to continue.

"Yeah. Mean-looking guy too. Not sure what he wanted. Came into the shop, sniffed around a bit, didn't say anything. I just wanted to get him out of there as soon as possible. His boots didn't even need mending."

I could feel my eyes bulging as I stared at my friend. "How do you know it was a werewolf?"

Daniel shrugged. "He had that air about him. Are you sure you're okay? You look very pale all of a sudden?"

"He does, doesn't he?" Sarah said as she sat down beside me again. "What have I missed?"

"Daniel says there was a werewolf in his shop today."

Sarah's body went rigid. "What did he look like?"

"Tall, muscular, brown hair," the redhead replied. "Oh, and he had a snake tattooed on his arm."

"I saw him," I said, my stomach twisting into a knot again. I was going to develop an ulcer if things kept up like this. "I bumped into him on my way out. Right before I went to St James'."

"Where we found the third victim," Sarah added, the blood draining from her face.

"Victim?" Daniel said, his eyes narrowing. "What victim? What's going on?"

Before Sarah or I could explain, my sister's cheerful voice interrupted us. "Sarah! I didn't know you'd be here too." Cassie pulled her into a hug, then turned to the girl standing next to her. "Have you met Caitlynn?"

My jaw dropped as Daniel's sister stepped out from behind Cassie. Gone was the tragic heroine haunting the moors. In her place stood a vibrant young woman dressed in jeans and a dark T-shirt. Her fiery hair hung in loose waves, framing a face that had been subtly made up to hide her freckles and accentuate her indigo eyes. Caitlynn smiled shyly at me, before shaking Sarah's hand in greeting. I closed my mouth, hoping she hadn't noticed my astonishment.

Daniel patted the chair next to him and beckoned his sister over. "You look grand," he said as she sat down beside him. "Ma wouldn't recognise you if you walked right past her on the street."

Caitlynn's cheeks turned rosy, but she beamed as she reached for the menu. "I've never had anything but a home-cooked meal."

Cassie plopped down beside her and pointed at one of the options. "You should try something outrageous then. Go for a curry. This one's Pavi's favourite."

While the two young women discussed Caitlynn's options, Sarah leaned in closer to me and whispered into my ear. "What's her story?"

"She's led a sheltered life," I explained. "Her parents have kept her cooped up on the family farm until she unexpectedly showed up at Daniel's doorstep this morning. Cassie's taken her under her wing and has been showing her around."

Sarah smiled. "I can't think of anyone better for the job."

I glanced at my sister. She was talking animatedly to the waitress, ordering another round of drinks for us all. My carefree sister enjoyed a bit of fun, but lately it seemed like she had trouble knowing when enough was enough. I should probably have a word with her before she took Caitlynn down a path the girl would be too naïve to resist.

"How are you finding London, Caitlynn?" Sarah asked, reaching for a complimentary bread roll as the waitress moved on to take Daniel's order.

"I love it!" she exclaimed, her eyes sparkling. "It was overwhelming at first, but there's just so much to see and do here. I don't think I'll ever be able to go back home now, knowing all this is here. I want to see everything!"

"Ah," Daniel said, sitting back and taking another sip of his beer as the waitress moved on to Sarah. "To be young and innocent again. Enjoy it while it lasts, sis. Soon, you'll be just as jaded and world-weary as the rest of us."

He grinned as Caitlynn elbowed him in the ribs. "Never! There's always something new to try. And I'm going to start with this!" She pointed at an item on the menu.

Daniel leaned over to have a look. "Sushi? Bold choice. Maybe start with something a little more familiar –" He cut off when he noticed Caitlynn glaring at him. "Okay, okay. Your choice. Just don't think I'm going to swap with you if you find out you don't care for raw squid."

"It's raw?" Caitlynn paused, considering. "What the hell. Let's try it."

I ordered a steak when it was my turn, remembering a time not too long ago when I couldn't afford a meal in a place as nice as this. Another thing the mythical world had changed. At least after tomorrow morning's interview, there was a good chance I'd have my old job back. And with Sarah by my side, life really wasn't too bad right now.

Apart from my murderous stalker, of course.

But that was tomorrow's worry. Tonight at least, I could pretend everything was fine and just enjoy the company of my friends.

I lifted my glass. "A toast. To friendship." Then, smiling at Caitlynn: "And new beginnings."

"Hear, hear!" Cassie cheered as we all clinked our glasses together.

The evening passed in a haze of happiness. The five of us chatted about everything under the sun, laughing at the expressions Caitlynn made

38

with each new drink she tried and each new taste she savoured. By the end of the night, her cheeks were flushed and her eyes were bright as stars. I doubted she'd ever be able to give up her freedom now.

When the time came to split the bill, Sarah squeezed my hand and gave me a kiss on the cheek. "Thanks for tonight, Ambrose. I needed this."

"Any time," I replied, handing her coat to her. "Want me to walk you home?"

She shook her head, and covered a yawn with one hand. "No, I'm too tired. I'm just going to get a cab. I think you should walk your sister instead."

She inclined her head at Cassie, who was giggling like a schoolgirl as she struggled to get up from her seat. I frowned, worried. She'd been so eager to have Caitlynn try out new things that she'd ordered every drink on the menu, downing the ones her new friend hadn't liked. The fact that she could still stand up at all was a miracle in itself.

Her eyes suddenly lit up and I followed her gaze to see a woman with long raven-black hair walk through the door. My sister's girlfriend was dressed in loose pants and a tank top with a lotus design printed on it. Cassie had once told me that Pavithra gave private yoga classes to celebrity clients. She'd probably come from a late-night session now.

"Pavi!" Cassie exclaimed, falling into the tawny-skinned woman's arms. "You're late."

"Sorry," Pavithra said, creasing the space between her brows where a small hollow circle with a thin vertical black line through it had been tattooed. She nodded a wordless greeting to the rest of us. "Looks like I missed all the fun." Her lips pursed as she put an arm around my sister to help keep her steady on her feet. I had a feeling she also didn't approve of Cassie's habit of over-indulging.

It was already dark when we exited the building. A thin fog veiled the empty streets, echoing our suddenly hushed words eerily back at us. The moon hid behind a blanket of clouds just as two headlights pierced the gloom.

"Here's my cab," Sarah said as the car pulled to a stop in front of us. "Anyone want to share it with me?" She cast a pointed look at Pavithra, who was stoically holding a giggling Cassie upright.

The woman shook her head. "The fresh air might do her some good."

Sarah nodded, then turned back to me. She brushed her lips against mine, before getting into the cab and slumping into the backseat, exhausted.

"I'll call you in the morning," I said, resisting the urge to climb in beside her. It wasn't that I didn't trust Pavithra to get Cassie home safely, but I'd feel better knowing she was alright if I walked with them.

Sarah nodded and I closed the cab door. She waved goodbye through the window as the car disappeared into the fog.

I turned back to the others. "I don't know about you, but I have an early appointment tomorrow morning and right now my bed is calling me. Shall we make this a brisk walk?"

Everyone muttered their agreement, all slowly fading after a long evening. We set off with Caitlynn and Daniel in front, the sister's arm hooked into her brother's to guide her somewhat unsteady steps, while the girls and I brought up the rear. Pavithra and I both had an arm around Cassie, who was more asleep than awake by this time.

We hadn't walked far when a howl split the quiet night. Everyone froze in shock. The hair on the back of my neck stood on end.

"What the hell was that?" Daniel asked. "Was that a wolf?" He looked at me, and whatever he saw in my face made all the colour seep from his.

"I didn't realise you had wolves in London…" Caitlynn said, a look of confusion painted across her face.

"We don't." Pavithra's words were clipped. I glanced at her. Her jaw was squared in a way that made me think she was more annoyed than frightened.

My sister straightened in my arms and blinked a few times. "What do we do now?"

"We take a shortcut," I replied. I extricated myself from Cassie's grip and peered into an alleyway passing between two tall buildings. If we could get through it before the werewolf found us, we'd cut ten minutes of walking off our journey. "This way," I said, ushering everyone into the alley.

We advanced carefully through the dim light, but impatience egged me on. We were moving too slowly.

Suddenly another howl echoed through the fog, much closer this time. Daniel swore loudly and I heard Cassie gasp as a dark shape loomed at the end of the alley, blocking our exit.

I fumbled in my jacket pocket and pulled out my mobile phone. I had to know what I was dealing with. I turned on the phone's torch, casting a beam of light towards the dark figure. My breath hitched in my throat as the werewolf was illuminated.

It was a thing of claws and teeth, a nightmare come to life. It was far bigger than the normal wolves I'd seen on the Discovery Channel; more muscular, more horrendous. Father was wrong. This looked exactly like the hairy monstrosities you'd see in a bad B-movie. It lifted itself up on its hindlegs and my knees turned to jelly.

Then it opened its jaws and howled again.

Caitlynn screamed, and the creature leaped at her.

Adrenaline spurted through my veins as I dove for her, pushing her and Daniel over. We toppled to the ground as the thing barrelled past us, its momentum carrying it forwards. Cassie shrieked and my blood ran cold. I looked up in time to see Pavithra push my sister to one side, sending her sprawling on the ground, while the dark-haired woman stood protectively over her.

"Ambrose!" Daniel hissed beside me. I glanced at him to see him cradling his sister in his arms. A thin trail of blood ran down her temple, where she'd been injured during the fall.

"Run," I said to him. His eyes widened, but he nodded and pulled Caitlynn to her feet. I barely heard their footsteps slapping against the pavement as I turned towards the werewolf again. It had its back to me, growling at Pavithra who was staring it down as if sheer force of will could overpower it.

Without thinking, I tossed my phone at the werewolf. It hit the thing in the back and fell to the ground. I winced as I heard it crack. The werewolf turned to me. Its top lip curled up into a snarl, revealing sharp fangs.

"Oh, shit," I muttered, scrambling away from it. Something sharp dug into my side. Father's letter opener! I yanked it out of my pocket and brandished it in front of me like a sword. The werewolf bounded towards me. I dodged a swipe from its curved claws and jabbed the little silver knife at it. The creature yowled as the sharp point dug into its ribs. It recoiled backwards, wrenching the letter opener from my grasp.

Behind the werewolf, I could see Pavithra

helping Cassie back onto her feet.

"Run!" I shouted at them, as the werewolf yanked the letter opener from its side and tossed it out of reach. The look it gave me was concentrated murder. Blood clotted the dark fur around the wound and a few drops spattered the ground. Good. It seems like it was vulnerable to silver weapons after all.

Too bad I didn't have any on me right now.

Time slowed to a crawl as the creature bunched its muscles, preparing to attack. I braced myself as the werewolf leaped at me, its jaws wide, going for my jugular. I lifted my hands to shield my face, knowing it was probably going to be the last thing I ever did.

"No!" I heard Cassie's voice, shrill in my ears. Then the monster crashed into me. It pushed me off my feet and I smacked my head against the wall. Stars blurred my vision as the scent of rotting meat washed over me. Someone was screaming. I heard Pavithra call out Cassie's name, and then the weight of the monster was off me. I shook my head to clear the fog.

The werewolf snarled and my vision returned just in time to be blinded again by a flash of pure white light. I heard the creature yelp, like a dog in pain, and then the sound of its claws scraping on the pavement as it scrambled away from me.

Was it fleeing?

"Cassie?" I cried out. The light faded and I blinked to adjust my eyes to the darkness of the alley. I could just make out the shape of someone hunching over a bundle lying on the ground.

"Ambrose!" The terror in Pavithra's voice was like ice slicing through my heart.

The figure on the ground was Cassie, crumpled in a pool of her own blood. Pavithra crouched next to her, her hand pressed against my sister's chest. Red oozed between her fingers.

"Cassie…" I stood transfixed, unable to believe my eyes. Pavithra was talking to me, but I couldn't hear her. My ears were ringing. All I could think of was how deep a shade of red it was, pooling underneath my sister's still frame. Not crimson. Not cherry. Definitely not rose. Mahogany. Or perhaps even that tint you see in a very old merlot.

"Ambrose!"

I tore my gaze from my sister's unmoving figure. Pavithra's face was pale, but her hands were steady and her eyes held a glint of steel. "There isn't much time," she said. "I need you to get an ambulance."

Her words made sense, in an abstract sort of way. But there was so much red. I couldn't stop staring at it.

"Now!" Pavithra barked, startling me into action.

I forced myself to look away from all the blood and scoured the ground, whooping when I found my mobile phone where it had fallen earlier. The screen was cracked, but it was still working. With trembling fingers, I dialled the number for emergency services.

※ ※ ※

I hated having to call Sarah at this hour, but I knew she would never forgive me if I didn't. Her phone rang a couple of times before she answered, and her voice sounded thick with sleep.

"Ambrose? Is everything alright?"

"No," I said, suddenly fighting a traitorous bottom lip. "It's Cassie. She's in ICU." Sarah gasped on the other end of the line. "You were right. It was a werewolf."

"I'm coming over."

"No, don't," I said quickly. I didn't know if I could keep it together in front of Sarah. I was having a hard enough time as it was. Exhaling loudly, I said: "I want you to get your rest, because tomorrow…" My teeth grinded so hard it hurt. "Tomorrow we're going to find the bastard who did this so I can make him pay."

"We'll find him, Ambrose," Sarah said, without a trace of doubt in her tone. "But you need to be careful. Revenge is never a good idea. Promise me you're not going to get into any more trouble?"

"Where is she? Where's my little girl?" Mother's anguished voice drove me to my feet as she barged into the waiting room, looking more dishevelled than I'd ever seen her. Her eyes were tinged red and she wasn't wearing any makeup. "Ambrose!" she wailed as she saw me.

"I have to go," I said to Sarah. "I'll call you again in the morning."

I barely had time to end the call and put my mobile away before Mother fell into my arms, sobbing. I clutched onto her, feeling the tears wrack her body. I had to bite back my own.

"She's going to be alright," I said softly. "She lost a lot of blood and the doctor said there's going to be a scar, but she'll live. She just needs rest now."

"What happened?" Mother pulled free and wiped at her eyes with the back of her hands.

My jaw clenched. "She got mugged. The guy had a knife." The lie tasted bitter in my mouth.

"What was she even doing out at night in a place where she could get mugged?"

"Mother," I said, my tone firm. "Now isn't the time."

Her lower lip trembled again. "You're right, Ambrose. You're right." She took a deep breath, trying to calm herself. "Where is she? Can I see her?"

I nodded my head at the door to Cassie's private hospital room. "Doctor said only one at a time. Father's with her now."

She balled her fists and I could see her working herself up for a fight, but then the door to the room opened and Father walked through. His face was grim.

"Jenna," he greeted Mother. "She's asleep, but you can go in."

All the fight left my mother's body. She squeezed my hand, before visibly steeling herself and entering the room. The door closed quietly behind her.

"How's she doing?" I asked.

"Not great," he replied. "But Cassie's a fighter. She'll get through this. I know it."

My eyes were stinging. "This is my fault."

"No, it's not." Father put his hand on my shoulder, trying awkwardly to comfort me. "You're not responsible for what that creature did."

"I let it escape in Rome," I said. "And it's here because of me."

"You don't know that." Amari entered the waiting room with two steaming cups of coffee in her hands. She gave one to my father before offering me the second. The scent was instantly soothing. "You don't know that it's here because of you, and you certainly couldn't have foreseen this happening in Rome. Don't beat yourself up about it, Ambrose." I tried to protest, but Amari cut me short. "You can't change what's happened, but you can prevent it from happening again."

"Amari's right, son," Father said, nodding. "You say it's after you – fine. But don't let it call the shots. It's time to turn the tables. Become the hunter instead of the hunted."

Amari nodded. "It's a predator. It won't expect that."

The thought of confronting that monster again sent a shiver down my spine, but one of anticipation, rather than dread. That thing had come to my city and had killed three innocent people. It had nearly killed my sister! I wouldn't let that happen again. I would find it and I would make sure it never had the chance to hurt anyone ever again.

My dad's smile was grim as he watched me come to a decision. "Good man," he said.

"Just don't kill it," Amari added. "Bring it to me and I'll make sure you don't have to worry about it ever again."

"Fine," I agreed. "But how do I catch it?"

Father started to say something, then stopped short and gave me a significant look. The scent of cloves filled the air and I turned around to see that Pavithra had returned, an overnight bag slung across her shoulder. The dark-haired woman looked around the room, as if hesitant to interrupt us.

"Pavi, you've met Amari," I said, waving her closer.

She nodded at the Keeper and then walked up to Father, holding her hand out in greeting. "You must be Mister Daniels," she said, shaking his hand.

"Just call me James," he replied. "Pavi, was it?"

"Pavithra," she replied. "It means 'purity' in Sanskrit. I'm afraid my mother had lofty ideals for me."

"I'm sure she's just as proud of you as I am of Ambrose and Cassie," Father replied. "My son tells me it was your cool head that saved my daughter's life. I don't know how to thank you."

"I'm just glad we got Cassie the help she needed in time."

"Well, I will light a candle in thanks to Banka-Mundi tonight."

Pavithra's eyes widened in surprise. "How did you..?"

"The combined tilaka and urna tattooed between your eyes – that's her sign, isn't it?" Father explained. "Goddess of the hunt, if I remember correctly."

"Yes," Pavithra stammered, her hand straying to her forehead before she resolutely wrapped her arms around herself. "She is not a well-known goddess. I'm surprised you've heard of her."

Father's chest puffed up a little bit. "I dedicated a few years of my life to studying the myths and legends of the Indian subcontinent. Fascinating, especially given the knowledge now that –"

"I'm sorry, James, but it's time for us to go," Amari interrupted, flashing him a warning look. I suppressed a relieved sigh. Father had almost said too much. If Pavithra hadn't been so startled, she might have been able to put two and two together. As it was, I still needed to discuss everything that had happened with her. She was surprisingly calm for someone who had faced off with a werewolf.

"Of course," Father said, realising his near mistake. "Keep an eye on your sister for me, Ambrose. Let me know if anything changes."

"I will."

After Father and Amari had left, I turned to Pavithra. "You're spending the night?" I asked, pointing at the bag she still held.

"For Cassie," she replied, dumping the bag into my arms. "A change of clothes in case she needs it. I figured her family would rather stay by her side tonight."

I shot her a grateful smile. "You're welcome to stay too, if you want. I'm sure Mother would like to meet you."

"I wouldn't want to impose. Besides, I'll need more courage than I have right now for that meeting," Pavithra said, a smile tugging at her lips.

I laughed with her. "Speaking of courage... What you did tonight –"

"Anyone would have done the same."

I shook my head. "No, you were braver than us all. When you faced that –" I hesitated.

Pavithra waved her hand dismissively. "India can be a dangerous place. I've seen my fair share of muggers. Most of them run away if you stand up to them."

I frowned. "Mugger?" I asked, suddenly not sure how to proceed. "You don't think it was... something else?" I finished lamely.

"It was dark and we were all tired and frightened," Pavithra said, shrugging. "It's easy to let your imagination carry you away." She glanced at the clock on the wall. "I'd better go. Call me when she wakes up?"

"Of course," I said.

She briefly gripped my hand in her own, her dark brown eyes holding my gaze for a moment as if she were trying to lend me some of her strength. Then she turned and left, leaving me alone in the cold and sterile waiting room.

Pavithra's casual dismissal of the truth grated at me. The lie I had told Mother had been one of necessity, but to hear Pavithra repeat it as if that was really what had happened bothered me more than I cared to admit. She'd been there. She'd stood up to it. If she couldn't believe her eyes then she should at least believe her ears. No mugger howled at his victims like some moon-crazed beast!

Perhaps she was in denial. Perhaps this was how she was coping with the trauma. It couldn't have been a werewolf, a monster from myths, so obviously it must have been fear and fatigue playing tricks with her mind.

I knew what had attacked us, and it hadn't been a figment of my imagination.

I flopped down in one of the hospital chairs. There was nothing for me to do now but wait. Wait and plot my revenge.

⁂

"Ambrose?"

I startled awake, nearly falling out of the chair next to Cassie's hospital bed. How long had I been asleep? My sister still looked the same as I had last seen her: pale and motionless. An angry scar ran across one side of her face, narrowly missing her left eye. I wanted to throttle the thing that did this to her.

Someone cleared their throat and my gaze whipped towards the doorway. Pavithra was wearing the same clothes she had had on last night. Her face looked tired and drawn.

"My turn to sit with her for a bit," she said. "Has she woken up yet?"

"No, but the doctor said we should give her time. Her body needs to rest and heal itself." I stood up and stretched the stiffness of spending the night sitting in a chair from my body. I glanced at my watch. Half past eight. I had an interview in thirty minutes.

Pavithra took my place beside Cassie, enveloping one of my sister's hands in her own. The woman's face was etched with worry and her eyes were red. Something told me she hadn't had much sleep last night.

"Are you sure you're up to it?" I asked. "No offence, but you look terrible."

Her smile was strained. "I had a rough night," she admitted. "But I'll be okay. I had a double espresso before coming here. Should keep me awake enough for a few hours at least."

I nodded, before kissing Cassie's cheek. Her skin was warm, feverish. The last thing I wanted to do was leave my sister's side, but I knew I couldn't be selfish with her time. Pavithra needed to be here too.

I picked up my phone from where it was lying on the bedside table. A light was flashing to show I had messages waiting. Probably Sarah. I hoped she had some news for me. I was about to leave when I remembered something I had wanted to talk to Pavithra about. "Do you know what that bright light was right after the… right after Cassie was attacked?"

Pavithra stared at me blankly. "I didn't see a light. You hit your head pretty hard, though. Maybe you need to see a doctor too?"

"No, no, I'm fine," I said. Could I have imagined it? "Probably just need some fresh air. I have something I need to do, anyway. Will you be all right here? Do you need anything?"

"Just go," she said, smiling. "I'll call you if something changes."

"Okay. I'll be back soon."

I stepped into the empty waiting room, closing the door to Cassie's room behind me, and looked at my phone. I did indeed have a missed call from Sarah. I quickly called her back.

"How's Cassie?" Sarah asked before I could say hello.

"Stable. Still resting. Pavi's with her now while I'm taking a break. Do you have any news for me?"

I heard Sarah sigh on the other end. "I do, but

I don't know what to make of it."

"Not another murder?"

"No, but an officer on patrol last night reported seeing someone dressed all in black lurking near the restaurant we were at last night. Said the suspect looked like they were looking for something. They were in that alley where you were attacked and then headed towards the river, but he lost them in the fog."

I swore. "Do you think it could be him?"

"More than likely," Sarah replied. "I'm afraid he could have come back to the scene to try and pick your scent up or something."

My insides clenched at the thought. "That means he could be coming here."

"I'm afraid so."

The soft squeak of rubber-soled shoes suddenly caught my attention. My eyes darted to the doorway as my body tensed. A nurse wearing an unflattering pair of Crocs walked in and I exhaled in relief as she looked at me and said with a bright smile: "Morning! Doctor should be here any minute now."

"What is it?" Sarah asked in my ear.

"Nothing, just a false alarm." I glanced at my watch again. I had fifteen minutes to get to the other side of the South Bank. I wasn't going to make it. "I need to make a quick call. Let me know if you find anything else."

"I will. Be careful."

"Always."

The nurse was scribbling on a chart outside my sister's room. She looked up at me and said: "I'll be right back. She'll want a top-up on her pain meds by now."

I nodded and hastily dialled my old colleague's number as she disappeared around the corner. I paced the room as I listened to the phone ringing.

"Ambrose!" Jake finally said. "I'll be right down."

"Sorry, Jake, I'm not going to make today's interview. Family emergency. Rain check?"

There was a long pause on the other end of the line. Then: "This is putting me in a difficult situation, my friend."

"I know, and I'll make it up to you. But I'm at St Thomas' right now and there's something really urgent I need to take care of."

"What could be more urgent than getting your job back?"

I frowned. Had he not heard me say I was at the hospital with a family emergency? "Look, Jake, I don't want to sound melodramatic, so please just trust me. Can we postpone again? Tomorrow?"

Jake huffed audibly. "Fine. But only because it's you, Ambrose. Don't let me down."

"I won't," I said, before ending the call.

"Well, I think you might."

I spun on my heels towards the sound of the voice. My mouth went dry. A sinuous tattoo slithered down the arm of the man standing in the doorway. He wore a bracelet made of sharp teeth at his wrist, and polished combat boots, but it was his predatory grin that scared me the most.

There was no doubt in my mind that the man standing in front of me was the werewolf that had attacked us last night.

"What do you want?" Thankfully, I didn't sound nearly as terrified as I felt.

"I want you dead."

I blinked. Straight to the point, I'll give him that. "I'm afraid I can't quite agree to that."

The man's grin widened. "The girl. Is she in there?" He nodded at the closed door behind me. My veins turned to ice.

"I won't let you get anywhere near her." I

plucked Amari's whistle out from underneath my shirt.

The man moved lightning fast. My back slammed against the wall as he pinned me to it, enormous bicep bulging as he forced my hand holding the whistle away from my lips. Stale breath assaulted me as he brought his face near mine, his bushy eyebrows drawn close together.

"You won't let me?" he drawled, amused.

There was a gasp and the sound of a stack of papers falling to the floor. I glanced away from the man and saw the nurse standing in the doorway, her face pale.

"Call security!" I yelled and heard the screech of her rubber shoes speeding down the hallway.

For an instant, the pressure on my arm relaxed, probably as my assailant debated whether or not to pursue the woman. Mustering all my strength, I shoved the whistle against the man's stubbly cheek. He roared and pulled away from me. The smell of burnt flesh hit my nostrils. More proof that werewolves and silver didn't go together.

While he was off guard, I lifted my mobile and snapped a picture of his face. I pressed 'Share' and sent it off to Sarah. I held the phone up for him to see. "Now the police know what you look like," I said.

A snarl contorted his face, a reddish welt puckering the side of it, and I gave a step backwards as he bunched his muscles, ready to attack. The sound of many footsteps running towards us reached my ears. The man heard it too. He breathed deeply, his nostrils flaring.

"Soon," he said ominously. "And tell that other hunter not to come looking for me again." Then he turned around and dashed out of the waiting room. Shouts sounded as someone else gave chase.

Other hunter?

I flopped into a chair, my knees suddenly weak. My mobile pinged. Sarah.

-- Backup team on the way. Are you safe? --

My fingers trembled as I answered her.

-- Rattled, but fine. Need someone to stand guard at Cassie's door. --

-- I'll handle it. --

I slumped back into the chair. That had been too close for comfort. I hadn't been prepared to face him and it had nearly cost me my life. Worse, it had put Cassie in danger again. I couldn't afford to let this happen again. I reached for my mobile.

-- Where can I get my hands on some silver bullets? --

Daniel's response was almost immediate.

-- I know a guy. Meet me at St Paul's in half an hour. --

✳✳✳

Daniel was sitting on the steps of the cathedral when I arrived. I had never seen my friend looking so serious before. His face was drawn and he stared at the ground in front of him, avoiding eye contact. He must have been out shopping when I called him, because there was a small Sainsbury's bag next to his feet.

"How's Cassie?" he asked as I sat down beside him.

"She's okay. Still sleeping. And now she has two burly policemen standing watch outside her door too."

Daniel's eyes widened as he finally looked at me. I quickly explained what had happened earlier. "I can't wait for him to come looking for me again, or use Cassie to get at me," I added. "I need to take the fight to him."

Daniel coughed and his freckled face turned a little redder than usual. "Ambrose, I'm sorry I left you like I did last night. It's just, with Caitlynn –"

"You don't need to apologise. I'm glad you got her out of there before she could get hurt too. I would have done exactly the same. Where is she now?"

"She's minding the shop for me." He scratched at his bearded chin, a frown wrinkling his forehead. "Honestly, I think she's finding the whole thing more exciting than scary. She wanted to come with me now. Said to give her a gun and, I quote: 'let her at him'. Apparently she thinks chasing foxes from the chicken coop and hunting murderous werewolves is the same thing."

I couldn't help but smile. "You're going to have your hands full with that one."

"Tell me about it," Daniel snorted. "Anyway, let's not waste any more time then. We're here to see Stan. Come on."

He picked up his shopping bag and started walking. To my surprise, he didn't head up the steps and towards St Paul's. For some reason I'd assumed the cathedral was our destination. The hallowed grounds where silver bullets were forged to kill an unholy monster, or something like that.

Instead, we crossed the road and ducked into a side street where Daniel pressed the buzzer next to an unremarkable brown door situated between a coffee shop and an electronics store. The door opened with a click and I followed Daniel down a dingy set of stairs. A lightbulb suspended from the ceiling provided just enough light to make the entire endeavour seem dodgy. The walls were stained and mouldy and I made sure not to touch anything. I had enough on my plate right now without adding some fungal disease into the mix.

Another door confronted us at the bottom of the stairs. This one meant business: it looked like solid steel reinforced by metal bars soldered lengthwise across it. No one was going to force their way through this door.

"Are we robbing a bank?" I asked, more in jest but secretly a little worried about the answer.

Daniel winked at me, before pressing the button on an intercom installed on the wall.

"Yes?" a gruff voice answered through the speaker.

"It's me," Daniel said, speaking into the system. "I have a tribute."

My blood ran cold. I trusted my friend, of course, but he lived fully in a strange and secret world that I only straddled. Who knew what he'd do to keep his sister safe?

A rattle sounded and the steel door swung open. Daniel walked through the doorway while I hesitated for a second, unsure of what I would find on the other side. Hell, it was too late to back down now. I clenched my fists and walked into the room.

I don't know what I'd expected, but it wasn't this.

Fluorescent lights bathed the room in a harsh bright light. The walls were lined with aluminium shelves and glass display cases, all stocked with random items, from guitars to motorcycle helmets to dollhouses. There were old boxy computers stacked in a corner next to a pile of National Geographic magazines that almost reached the ceiling. One wall held a creepy collection of porcelain dolls in various states of disrepair, and underneath them stood a set of dumbbells and a shiny treadmill that looked like it had hardly been used. The entire room reminded me of someone's overflowing attic, filled with a lifetime's worth of unwanted stuff. It was a hoarder's dream come true.

A guy in his late twenties with a chiselled jaw and a five o'clock shadow stood behind a counter towards the back of the room, where yet another steel door could be seen. Wavy brown hair spilled down the man's shoulders and his sculpted chest strained against his Billabong t-shirt. He looked like someone you'd expect on the beach clutching on to a surfboard, not locked up in an underground room surrounded by clutter.

When he spoke, it was with a thick Slavic accent. "Brady. What can I do for you today?"

Daniel nudged me closer. "Hey Stan. This is my friend, Ambrose Davids. He's looking for something special. Something from the room at the back."

"For back room, show tribute first. Then we talk."

Daniel reached into the Sainsbury's bag and placed a packet of whole-wheat digestive biscuits on the countertop. Stan grabbed the packet, his eyes lighting up as if Daniel had brought him treasure.

"This is acceptable," he said, bending down to hide the biscuits somewhere behind the counter. When he stood up again, his expression was a little friendlier than it had been before. He turned towards the second bolted door, punched a code into the security pad and waited for the door to unlock.

"Follow me," Stan said, leading the way.

I grabbed Daniel's sleeve. "What is this place?"

"It's a pawn shop, my friend," Daniel replied with a grin. "Or at least, that's the front. What goes on in the back is a little more interesting."

"More interesting than this guy's fetish for baked goods?"

Daniel shrugged. "He's a *domovoy*. They have a thing for bread."

I followed my friend into the back room. My jaw nearly dropped. It was a cave of wonders.

The walls of this room were lined with weapons of all sorts, from ancient broadswords, spears and javelins, to an assortment of modern automatic weapons, including something that looked like it belonged in Rambo's backpack. There were shelves covered in interesting artefacts: a silver weighing scale engraved with Egyptian hieroglyphics, two sets of winged boots, a bronze urn, a headless ragdoll, and three sets of bracelets stringed with sharp teeth. On a pedestal in one corner was a silver hammer I was pretty sure must be Mjolnir.

My eyes bulged as I looked around the room. "Is that... Is that Excalibur?" I asked, pointing at an elaborately engraved steel sword hanging on one wall.

Daniel glanced at it and shrugged.

"You want sword?" Stan asked, casting a disinterested glance its way. "I can make you good price."

I shook my head, laughing disbelievingly. What would a good price even be for that sword? "What I need is a gun that shoots silver bullets."

"Ah, you have trouble with werewolf," Stan said, nodding as if we were discussing something as common as an ant infestation. "I have what you need." He turned towards a glass display case and retrieved an antique revolver that glinted in the fluorescent light. It looked like it was made from silver itself. Stan handed it to me.

It was surprisingly light in my hand, almost like an expensive toy gun, something that was more for show than shooting. "You sure this will do the job?"

Stan shrugged. "You want gun with silver bullets, I give you gun with silver bullets. But…" He hesitated.

"What's the catch, Stan?" Daniel asked.

"No catch. But…" He took the revolver from me and opened the cylinder. My heart sank. "I only have three silver bullets."

"Three will be enough," Daniel said confidently. I stared at him and he shrugged. "If you miss the first time, it's too late, isn't it?"

I gulped. "Fair enough."

I'd been to a shooting range once before as part of a team building session with my old company. I wasn't a bad shot, but it had been a few years since I'd last held a gun in my hand, and never with the aim of shooting anything other than a stationary target.

"How much?"

Stan gave a price that made my eyes water, but what choice did I have? Surprisingly, he had a credit card machine at the ready.

"You need to up your game," I said to Daniel as the pawnbroker swiped my Visa.

Daniel grinned. "What can I say? I like the feel of money in my hands, even if it is only bits of paper these days."

Of course he does.

While I waited for the slip to print, my eyes roved around the room again until they locked onto the bracelets I had spotted earlier. They were similar to the one the werewolf wore.

"What are those?" I asked, pointing them out.

Stan glanced at the bracelets. "Is werewolf

amulet. You bring me when you kill it."

I frowned. "Does this help them change into wolves?" I turned towards Daniel. "I thought you said objects didn't have any intrinsic magical properties?"

"They don't," my friend replied. "To you and me that bracelet is nothing more than decoration. But in the hands of a werewolf it's something more. They can only shapeshift voluntarily if they have one of these bracelets. Without one, they're bound to the moon's cycle and the change is forced on them during the full moon. And they won't be able to change any other time."

I scratched at the stubble on my cheek. "So if I can get his bracelet from him, I'd effectively prevent him from turning into the creature? He'd be human?"

"Yes," Daniel said. "Well, almost human. He's still a werewolf. He'll be faster and stronger than you'd expect him to be."

"Swell." That explained the deviance in the man's DNA. I'd have to keep that in mind when it was time to confront him again.

I felt like a new man when we exited the nondescript door leading down to Stan's shop. St Paul's towered above me and pedestrians swarmed around us. The world was the same as it had been an hour ago, and yet everything had changed. With a silver gun in my pocket, I was ready to take on a werewolf.

"What do you say we get some practice in?" I asked Daniel. "If I only have three shots, I'd better make them count."

"Good idea," my friend agreed. "I know a place."

"Take twenty millilitres four times a day for two days, then the same amount twice for two days." The pharmacist, an older lady with her greying hair tied back in a severe bun, looked at me like I had looked at the mould growing on the walls leading down to Stan's shop. I wanted to tell her not to judge me, that I had a specific reason for buying something which all the health websites I'd googled warned 'lacked sound scientific evidence' and 'wasn't safe or effective for treating any disease or condition'. It was perfect for what I had in mind.

"Can I get a syringe with that?" I asked. "One with a sturdy needle, please."

Her eyebrows almost reached her hairline, but she pursed her lips and added it to the rest. I swiped my card and hotfooted it out of there, a brown paper bag filled with medically dubious contents tucked into my jacket pocket.

I nodded at the two men standing guard in the waiting room outside Cassie's door. I was relieved to see my sister still sleeping peacefully, unaware of the threat waiting somewhere outside these sterile hospital walls. Cassie's face was as pale as the sheet tucking her in, but the machine next to her beeped a regular heartbeat.

I looked around the room. Where was Pavi? How could she have left Cassie on her own like this?

I stepped around the bed towards the chair I had slept in last night, but stopped short when I saw my sister's girlfriend on the floor, balancing in some sort of yoga pose. Both her legs were in the air, extended sideways and wrapped around the single arm with which she was keeping her body balanced, while her other arm was stretched out to the side. Her face was serene, her eyes glazed and staring into the distance, a single bead of sweat rolling down her temple the only indication of the effort it took to hold herself in place like that.

My gaze swept across her toned body, only now noticing how defined her biceps were, the lean musculature of her back and the curves of her powerful legs. Cassie had told me that they'd met when Pavithra had modelled for an art class, and I'd always thought of the long-haired beauty as someone who wouldn't be out of place on a catwalk in Milan or in front of Bollywood cameras. How strong must her core be to get into a position like this? And hold it for so long! Maybe I should dust off my old gym membership again…

Her vision focussed and she untangled herself, coming back up to her feet in one fluid motion, her palms together, raised above her head, then slowly lowered down to her chest. She inhaled deeply and then exhaled loudly. Then she turned to me, her expression unreadable.

"You'll have to teach me how to do that some time," I said. "Very impressive."

A small smile tucked at Pavithra's lips. She was always so serious, but the thought of me doing yoga must have finally tickled her sense of humour. "It helps to keep the body active while focussing the mind."

"Right…" I said, wondering if she knew about my lapsed gym membership. I turned back to Cassie. "Any change?"

Pavithra shook her head. "The doctor's been to see her again. He says just to be patient and let her rest. She'll wake up when she's ready."

I exhaled loudly, frustrated. The doctor didn't know that Cassie's injuries had been caused by a werewolf, a creature known to pass its curse on with a bite. What if she'd been infected? What if her body wasn't recovering from the attack, but rather preparing for the ordeal that was to come – where she would change into a werewolf too?

I clenched my jaw as I stared at my sister, contemplating that grim possibility.

Pavithra quickly gathered her things, before leaning over and kissing Cassie softly on the cheek. She smoothed my sister's hair and I could see the affection Pavithra held for her in every move she made. Finally, she turned to me and placed a hand on my arm. "Don't worry, Ambrose," she said. "She'll be alright."

I sighed. "How can you be so sure?"

"I just know. Call me when she wakes up." And then she was out the door, leaving only a hint of cloves hanging behind in the air.

I flopped down into the chair beside the bed just as my phone pinged. A message from Sarah.

-- DNA match found, and I verified the image on file with the one you sent me. His name is Sean Norton. Ex-military. Assumed dead a year ago after going missing on a hunting trip in Germany. --

Shit. Not only was I dealing with a vicious shapeshifter, but he'd had military training as well. That's not the kind of thing you wanted to hear when your gun only had three bullets in it.

My phone pinged again.

-- My shift's ending in 5 minutes. Are you at the hospital? I'll bring you some tea. --

-- That would be great, thanks. --

I nearly dropped my phone as Cassie murmured something in her sleep. I shifted the chair closer and took her hand in mine. She wasn't feverishly hot anymore. I moved to put my hand across her forehead, but stopped suddenly as I noticed that the scar running across her face was hardly visible anymore. Instead, a tiny symbol was engraved into the skin beside her left eye, thin silver lines so faint I wouldn't have noticed it if I hadn't been so close. It looked like a word written in a strange alphabet. I peered at it so long that my eyes started blurring.

What the hell was this? How long had it been there?

Suddenly, it was all I could do to keep the tears from welling up in my eyes. "I'll fix this, Cassie," I whispered fiercely. "I'll make sure he can never do this to you, or to anyone else, again."

※※※

I felt eyes on me the moment I stepped out of St Thomas' main entrance.

It was past midnight, but there were always people coming and going at all hours at a hospital. I quickly surveyed my surroundings. There! The man with the snake-like tattoo sat on the steps of the footpath leading up to street level. He smiled when our eyes locked.

I squared my shoulders and slipped my hand into my jacket pocket, feeling more confident as I gripped the cool metal handle of the silver gun. It took everything I had in me to walk up to the man, and step past him to ascend the stairs.

The night bus arrived exactly on time and I was first on it, taking a seat right at the front. I watched nervously as a few other passengers filed in. The last one on was Sean Norton, the werewolf. He walked past me, grinning in that predatory way, and I turned around to watch him take a seat right at the back. When I turned to face the front again, I could still feel his eyes on me.

The ten-minute ride felt like a lifetime, and when the bus reached the stop I had been waiting for, I was out the door as soon as it opened. The road was deserted. My lucky white trainers slapped against the pavement as I sprinted away from the bus stop, hearing footsteps following me. It wasn't very far to Trafalgar Square, but my heart was racing by the time I reached its dubious safety.

As my luck would have it, it was empty. Nothing but the murmur of fountains filled the night's stillness. Had the footsteps following me stopped?

I glanced over my shoulder just in time to see fangs and fur leaping at me. The full force of the werewolf's weight struck me from behind. I toppled to the ground, stretching my hands out just in time to prevent my face from smacking against the pavement.

A growl rumbled in my ear and hot breath assailed the back of my neck. I flinched, expecting pain to rip through me any second.

Instead, the weight suddenly lifted off me.

I scrambled onto my feet and spun around. The werewolf was on its back, clawing at the end of a whip wrapped around its neck. At the other end was a figure with the lithe build and curves of a woman, dressed in black from head to toe. The bottom half of her face was masked and dark eyes stared at me from the shadows cast by a hood.

The other hunter!

She pulled on the whip, dragging the werewolf towards her. The creature thrashed around wildly, and suddenly the cord snapped. The woman took a step backwards, regaining her balance. She lashed the whip at the werewolf again as it rushed towards her. It grabbed it with one claw and yanked her off her feet. She fell and rolled smoothly back onto her feet, and ducked as the monster leaped at her. It soared over her, twisting and clawing, but she somersaulted backwards out of its reach.

I gaped at the spectacle. I was clearly being out-classed here. But at least I had a gun.

I pulled the silver revolver out of my pocket. When the monster skidded to a halt, I aimed and pulled the trigger.

The shot struck the werewolf in the shoulder. It fell to the ground, yelping. I watched, fascinated, as the pelt of thick black hair around the wound receded, revealing human flesh. Blood poured from the wound, filling the air with a thick metallic stench.

I took a step towards the injured creature. The black-clad woman thrust a hand into the air, stopping me in my tracks. As I watched, the bald patch where the bullet had hit the werewolf started sprouting hair again. The creature rolled up onto its hind feet. It glared at me, then lifted its muzzle into a howl that pierced the still air and sent a shiver of fear down my spine.

Two bullets left. Make them count.

I lifted the gun and pulled the trigger.

Click.

Nothing happened.

I tried again. Nothing! The gun was jammed.

Shit!

I looked at the werewolf. Its muzzle was twisted into a toothy grin that made my insides squirm. It knew exactly what had happened.

I spun around and ran!

Shoving the useless revolver back into my pocket, I sprinted towards the statue of King George astride his horse. I looked over my shoulder and wished I hadn't. The werewolf was hot on my heels.

It nearly yanked me off my feet as it hooked a

claw into my jacket. Wrenching my shoulder, I pulled free from its grasp, hearing the tweed rip as the jacket's arm tore loose. Ignoring the death of my favourite piece of clothing, I scrambled up the base of the statue. The werewolf's claws scraped against stone as I pulled my feet out of reach.

The crack of a whip sounded. I clutched onto the horse's bronze legs and turned around to see the huntress gracefully launching herself away from the werewolf again. She was much lighter and faster on her feet than it was. When it lunged right, she ducked left. When it went for her throat, it found empty air. When it swiped for her feet, she rewarded it with a nip from her whip.

I wrenched my gaze away from the fight and pulled the revolver out again to inspect it. I opened the barrel and swore. Both remaining bullets had crept out of their shell casing and had been bent askew, jamming up the cylinder. It was completely unusable now.

Not that it mattered much. When the silver bullet had hit the creature, the patch around the wound had reverted back to human state for a few seconds, but then the change had stopped and it had turned back into the wolf. Perhaps it would have worked if I could have shot it full of silver, but three bullets were never going to be enough.

Time for Plan B.

Below me, the woman and the werewolf were still fighting. I slipped down from the pedestal and stuck my hand into my other jacket pocket, gripping the syringe I had bought earlier. I'd need to get in close to the werewolf to use it. Perhaps if she could keep it occupied…

I took a tentative step towards the creature. Suddenly, it growled and jumped backwards, away from the sting of the woman's whip. It collided with me, sending me sprawling. I dropped the syringe. It rolled into a shadow and I lost sight of it.

I heard the woman cry out, and then a splash as something tumbled into a fountain. When I looked up, the werewolf was crouched in the pool, but there was no sign of the huntress. Water splashed around its shaggy form. It must be holding her under!

Scanning the ground, I searched for the syringe again. There! My heart skipped a beat as I spotted the syringe rolling towards a grate in the ground.

Swearing, I scrambled towards it on my hands and knees. My hand clamped around the syringe just before it fell into the sewer. I bounded to my feet again and lunged at the creature, sticking the needle into the softer flesh of its armpit.

The werewolf yowled and lurched away from me.

I jumped into the water and grabbed the woman's arm. She spluttered as I dragged her out of the fountain. She let go of me as soon as we were on dry land again, gasping and coughing behind her mask.

I turned to the werewolf again and watched in fascination as the nanoparticles of colloidal silver I had injected into its bloodstream did the job. The fur receded from its body, the claws on its hands and feet shortened into fingers, the head contorted back into human shape, until Sean Norton stood before us, his bare chest heaving in what I assumed must be gasps of pain after the shift. The gunshot wound in his shoulder was an ugly crimson mess against his smooth skin.

His eyes fixed on mine, his bushy eyebrows drawing together in a scowl.

Uh oh. I'd been so focused on getting the werewolf into human form that I hadn't considered what I'd do if I managed it. There was no Plan C.

Norton stormed at me, a feral growl rumbling across his lips. I braced myself for the impact, clenching my fists. I wasn't going to go down without a fight.

"Luck," I breathed, and luck came to my rescue.

Norton stepped into a puddle made by the huntress as she had stood recovering from her near drowning. His foot slipped out from under him and he fell, smacking his head on the edge of the fountain's pool. He grunted and lay motionless in a heap on the ground.

Cautiously, I moved closer. His chest was still moving. I prodded his side with my toe. Nothing. I bent down and checked the side of his head. There was no blood, but I could already see a bump forming. He was going to have one hell of a headache in the morning.

"He's out cold," I said, turning to the huntress. She was nowhere to be seen. How had she disappeared without my notice? There weren't even any wet footprints to show which way she'd gone.

"Fine," I muttered, pulling out the silver whistle.

Even though it was long past midnight, Amari was fully dressed when she stepped out of the beam of white light. "I'd hoped I'd hear from you tonight," she said, eyeing the comatose man at my feet. "Is that our werewolf?"

"Yeah," I replied. "Let's get him out of here before he wakes up."

Amari nodded, and then the world turned white again.

※※※

"I'll take his feet. You grab him by the shoulders," the Keeper instructed as soon as we arrived in her office. I did as she asked and helped her carry Norton out the door and down a corridor I hadn't seen before. He was surprisingly heavy and I was relieved when we finally reached a barred door at the start of another long passage.

Amari unlocked the door and then helped me dump Norton onto a pallet in one corner of an otherwise empty room. Unconscious, he looked like a normal guy, maybe one who'd had one too many pints at his local and was sleeping it off now. I knew better. I bent down and pulled the bracelet made of sharp teeth from his wrist. That should keep him out of trouble, and make life a little easier for the Keeper. Amari held her hand out and I deposited the amulet in it. She pocketed it while I followed her out of the cell. She locked the door behind us.

"What's this?" I asked as I finally noticed where we were. The rest of the corridor was lined with more cell doors and I could hear noises coming from the closest ones. I peered past the bars into the cell next to Norton's and saw a three-headed dog asleep on its pallet, snoring like three very competitive lumberjacks.

"Holding cells," Amari replied. "Oh, don't look so perturbed," she said when she noticed my expression. "It's just a temporary place to keep creatures while I sort out their long-term enclosures."

"But these are all full!" I exclaimed, peering into some of the other nearby cells. All this time the Keeper had assured me the Repository was a haven for mythical creatures. If Daniel was right and it really was just a prison, then I was going to have trouble with my conscience for a very long time.

"Blame the centaurs," Amari huffed. "They've been blocking my every move and making my life a bureaucratic nightmare." She took a deep breath, visibly calming herself down. Then she sighed. "Don't worry, they'll all be housed much more comfortably as soon as possible."

"And him?" I asked, nodding at the comatose werewolf. "He's murdered at least three people that we know of. If he were fully human, he'd be standing trial for his life right now."

"The Council will have to decide on that. It's unlikely they'd send him to the scaffold, and it's my job to ensure he's safe here in the Repository." A small smile tugged at her lips. "But not necessarily comfortable."

A groan came from Norton's cell. The man was coming to his senses. He pushed himself upright, shaking his head. He looked around his room, his bushy eyebrows drawing together in a scowl. When he noticed us watching him, he climbed to his feet and walked up to the bars of the cell door.

"You have no right to keep me locked up here," he growled.

"You nearly killed my sister," I hissed. "You deserve much worse than this."

Norton grunted. "It's not often I see a man hide behind his sister in the face of danger. You have no one but yourself to blame for her injuries."

I gritted my teeth, itching to punch his face. Werewolf or not, I wanted nothing more than to step inside that cell and kick him where it hurts.

"Why did you attack Ambrose?" Amari asked, her voice as calm as if she interrogated murderous monsters on a daily basis.

"Do I need a reason?" the man drawled. "Just look at that face. Don't you just want to slap him?"

I bristled, but Amari only said: "Answer the question."

Norton growled. "To cover my tracks. He saw me in Rome, and I couldn't leave any witnesses alive. I have no intention of being locked up like that again."

"Well, then you should be a little disappointed right about now," I said.

"This?" the man scoffed, gripping the bars of the cell door. "This is just a temporary setback. I wouldn't sleep too soundly if I were you. Ambrose." He lifted his head and howled, a feral sound that set all the animals in the cells around us into a frenzy. "Or you, pretty lady," he leered at the Keeper.

Unimpressed, Amari lifted an eyebrow at him. "I've neutered scarier things than you." Then she turned her back on him. "Come on, Ambrose. I've got things to do."

Norton banged against the bars of his cell door as we walked away, shouting curses at us. Neither of us looked back.

✕✕✕

Sarah was opening the curtains, letting the early morning sunshine stream in through the window, when I walked into Cassie's hospital room. With the warm glow of the sun shining on her, my sister looked so much better than when I had last seen her. Her face was no longer pale and clammy and there were no traces of scarring that I could detect.

"Is he…?" Sarah asked when she saw me. She came in for a hug and I wrapped my arms around her, breathing in her citrusy scent.

"Locked up where he won't bother anyone again," I confirmed.

I felt the tension seep from her body as she relaxed against me. "Thank goodness. The case will never be solved, but I'll sleep better at night."

"I won't."

Sarah pulled away from me. Her eyes were large behind her black-rimmed hipster glasses.

"That thing came here to find me after it escaped from the Colosseum. I didn't set it free that night, but I may as well have. It got away, and because of me, three people are dead and Cassie is in hospital." Sarah started to object, but I interrupted her. "Who knows what else is out there? Who knows what's lurking in the shadows, preying on innocent people, because of me?"

Sarah squeezed my hand. "You're going to go look for them?"

"I have to. Do you remember what the Chairman said in Rome? He said: 'Where myth and the mundane collide, there's bound to be bloodshed'. I can't let that happen. Not again."

My phone suddenly started ringing. I pulled it out of my tattered jacket's pocket and glanced at the cracked display. It was Jake. I was already ten minutes late for my interview. I swiped to cancel the call and put the phone on silent.

"Ambrose?"

Startled, I turned towards Cassie. Her eyes were open, and she was looking around her in a dazed and confused manner. "Where am I?"

"You're in the hospital," I replied, moving to her side. "But you're going to be alright."

"What happened?"

"You saved my life," I said. "You almost got killed."

Cassie's eyes focussed on my own and her lips curved into a smile. "You're welcome."

"Don't make a habit of it." I grinned, feeling relief wash over me. Everything was going to be alright.

I knew what I had to do now. It had taken me a long time to admit it, and I knew I wasn't ready for it, but that wouldn't stop me anymore. I would do what needed to be done. I was going to make the world safe again.

I was finally ready to become the hunter.

PART 7

CHIMAERA'S FALL

C louds hung low across the Thames, drenching London in an unnerving darkness. Rain lashed down as if someone somewhere had just finished building an ark. I thrust my hands deep into the pockets of my black leather jacket. My hair clung to my scalp and rivulets of water flowed across my face. I should have brought an umbrella.

I should have stayed in bed.

The deaths of two people had dragged me here instead.

Sarah hadn't given me much to go on. They'd found the bodies two nights in a row, both waterlogged and dumped at the foot of the ramps leading up to the Millennium Bridge. Both had been gnawed on. And since most murderers rarely nibble on their victims, I took it upon myself to come investigate. Sarah would have tried to talk me out of it, so I hadn't told her of my plan. Besides, the police weren't equipped to deal with monsters – if that was indeed what I was looking for. Hopefully, I'd be able to see what we were dealing with and prevent another death.

My footsteps squelched as I walked across the bridge, all my senses on high alert. Tonight, I was both hunter and bait, a tactic that had made sense in the comfort of my own home when I'd decided to come here alone, but now seemed both reckless and arrogant.

Through the downpour, I could just make out the domed silhouette of St Paul's on the far side of the river. Beneath me, the black waters of the Thames churned, murky and ominous. It was some time after midnight. Everyone with any sense was inside right now.

And here I was, hunting monsters, hoping luck was on my side.

I froze as a strange sound reached my ears. Clack-clack-clack. Like someone drumming their fingernails on metal. A soft swooshing followed it, and then a snorting snuffle, the kind that would have had Mother thrusting a handkerchief at me if I had been the one to make it.

I squinted into the darkness, unable to see anything but the faint lights of the city blurring in the downpour. Just for once, I'd like to do this in the daylight.

I jumped as something growled right beside me, ducking sideways just in time to avoid sharp teeth grinding together as the thing's jaws clamped down on the bridge's handrailing. My heart lurched into my throat as I scampered out of its reach, slipping on the wet surface. My breath was suddenly ragged in my ears.

Wiping rain out of my eyes, I gaped at the monster in front of me, feeling hope fade as I recognised one of the three possible candidates I had narrowed the murderer down to.

The creature was on its hind legs, hunched over like a man carrying a heavy burden. Thick scaly ridges covered its body, except for a patch of matted brown fur clinging to its back and the bridge of its elongated snout. Its head was a monstrous mashup of crocodile and beaver, with two large front teeth and a row of sharp fangs to the sides. I shuddered at the thought of this thing chomping on human flesh.

It was an afanc, a creature known for preying upon anyone foolish enough to wade into its waters. According to legend – and a quick Google search last night – only the voice of a maiden could lull it into submission.

Unfortunately, I hadn't brought any maidens with me.

Too late I saw the afanc's scaled tail swiping towards me. It knocked me off my feet and I fell to the ground, gasping for breath. The creature grunted and lunged at me with its webbed claws.

I rolled aside and scrambled back onto my feet, narrowly avoiding snapping jaws, its front teeth inches away from my throat. The creature's breath stank of rotting meat. I shied away from it. It had already eaten two people. I really didn't want to be the third.

I retreated until I felt the bridge's handrailing against my back. The afanc opened its mouth in a toothy grin. It knew I was cornered. There was nowhere else to go.

Damn. Why wasn't I more prepared? If I'd brought an umbrella, I could have at least used it as a weapon. Now I had nothing but my bare hands with which to fend off a cold-blooded killer. What had I been thinking coming here tonight? That I was some kind of hero? That I could take care of this monster all by myself? Had I thought I could reason with it? Make it see the error of its ways? I'd been a fool.

The afanc snorted, probably thinking the same thing. It lurched towards me.

Adrenaline spurted through my veins, and the next thing I knew I had vaulted across the railing and grabbed onto one of the horizontal beams of the outer railing that gave the Millennium Bridge its distinctive shape. My arms burned as I dangled in the air. I looked down into the inky waters below me, gulping. Face the afanc on the bridge, or drop into the Thames?

I winced. I'd rather get eaten.

Claws scraped on metal, setting my teeth on

edge. I glanced over my shoulder. The afanc was climbing the inner railing, its beady eyes trained on me. A black tongue lolled out of the side of its mouth, dripping saliva that fell in gooey strings into the river below.

Palms sweating, I heaved myself forward by another rung. My shoulders ached as I struggled to hold on, wet fingers slipping on wet railing. I gritted my teeth and moved forward again. With a Herculean effort, I swung myself over to the fourth and last horizontal bar. As my hand closed around the railing, my fingers slipped and I cried out, clutching on for dear life with only one hand.

Heart racing, I looked over my shoulder again. The afanc was astride the inner railing now. Any minute now it would leap across at me, either sinking its teeth into my flesh or dropping me down into the deep. I'd be just another statistic, another missing person, mysteriously disappeared, or washed up at Dead Man's Hole. I'd been so fired up at the thought of protecting the world from these monsters, from preventing anyone else from getting hurt like Cassie had been, that I hadn't even thought about what could happen to me.

Grunting, I swung my free arm upward and grabbed hold of the railing again. I twisted my body around so I could see the creature. What the hell?

It was just sitting there, its head cocked to one side as if listening to something.

I could hear nothing but the rain, but the bridge's outer railing was wobbling slightly, as if someone was walking on it. I tightened my grip and shook my head to clear the water from my eyes.

Then I heard it too. A haunting melody hummed through the rain's relentless patter, coming closer with every breath. A woman, singing!

I wanted to cry out, to warn her to turn back and run for her life, but then a familiar dark-clad figure stepped into view. I clamped my mouth shut. The woman's skin-tight black leather outfit creaked as she walked across the railing, nimble as an acrobat. A veil obscured her face, but I could feel her brown eyes on me as she came to a stop on the beam across from me, still humming.

The huntress.

I grinned up at her, sheepishly. She must think I'm a complete amateur.

The woman looked at me, disdainfully shaking her head, before turning to the afanc and increasing the volume of her song. I stared at the creature. It was utterly mesmerised, swaying slightly back and forth in time to her tune.

Damn it. If I'd known that all it would take was a woman singing, I could probably have charmed it with something from the playlist on my phone. I had enough Taylor Swift songs on there to keep it spellbound for at least a day or two.

Still humming, the huntress slowly unwrapped a length of chain from around her waist.

I rolled my eyes. Well, at least she had come prepared.

She tiptoed across the supporting beam until she stood right beside the afanc. Never letting her song waiver, she wrapped the creature in the chain. It stood as if frozen, its beady eyes glazed and its mouth slowly opening and closing as if it were trying to sing along with her in some bizarre bestial attempt at karaoke. She pinned its arms against its body and then slapped a padlock onto the end of the chain.

With one hand holding onto the captured afanc, the woman lifted her other hand into the air. My eyes widened as she drew a strange symbol, sparkling in the night air like a trail of fireflies. She glanced at me, and then the symbol exploded in a bright flash of light. I blinked, trying to clear my vision. When I could see again, the woman and the afanc were both gone.

I gaped at the empty space where they had stood a moment before. Who was that woman? And where had she taken the afanc?

But more importantly, how was I going to get off this bridge? My shoulders were screaming at me by now, and it felt like an elephant was dangling from my fingers. I looked down at the Thames again, swallowing loudly.

Nope. Not an option.

Swearing under my breath, I inched my hands towards the nearest supporting beam. Now that the adrenaline rush had faded, my arms were shaking with exhaustion. When I got close enough, I wrapped a leg around the beam and used it to manoeuvre myself into an upright position, still clutching onto the horizontal bars. I took a moment to catch my breath, wiping either rain or sweat from my face. When I'd worked up enough courage, I lunged for the bridge's inner railing. It was slick with rain, but fear tightened my grip and I scrambled across it and back onto the safety of the walkway.

Breathing heavily, I stood there for a moment, wondering what to do next. The area was safe again, no thanks to me, but a quick glance at my watch confirmed that it was too late to tell anyone about it right now. Neither Sarah nor Amari would thank me for waking them up at this ungodly hour.

I thrust my hands into the pockets of my leather jacket and started walking toward the nearest Tube station.

My mood was dour. Even though I had gone looking for trouble, I'd been woefully unprepared.

And I had nothing to show for it apart from aching arms and an acute sense of inadequacy. Not only had I not apprehended the afanc, but it had nearly caught me instead. If the huntress hadn't saved my life – again – I'd have been the next corpse dredged up from the river.

My luck could only last so long. I needed to up my game, or it could be game over all too soon.

✳✳✳

"A symbol, you say?" Amari frowned as she leaned back in her chair, casting her eyes up at the stone ceiling in contemplation. "And then she disappeared?"

"Like it had all been my imagination," I confirmed. "Like it was magic."

Amari's eyes darted back towards me. Even though it was mid-morning, the fire in her study was crackling happily in the hearth, and Amari had the tired air about her of someone who'd had little sleep lately. I could probably have called on her earlier this morning. She'd most likely been awake then. As if confirming my theory, she hid a small yawn behind one of her hands.

"There is very little magic left in the world," she said. "A few Words, and whatever unsanctioned bits and pieces of mythical creatures are traded by unscrupulous people. Like that unicorn blood you found." She tapped a finger against her cheek, thoughtful. "I've never heard of symbols being used. I guess it could be a written Word. Did you hear her say anything?"

"No. She was busy singing to keep the afanc mesmerised. Unless her song concealed the Word, but I don't think so. It was the symbol she drew in the air that made them disappear."

"Interesting." Her tired eyes suddenly lit up.

"Do you think you can replicate it? Can you draw it?"

I nodded, lifting my finger into the air, and then hesitated. As if she could read my mind, Amari pushed a blank piece of paper towards me across her enormous mahogany desk.

"Here," she said, handing me a fountain pen. "Let's be careful about this. We don't know what it will do."

I took the pen and slowly, deliberately, drew the symbol I had seen the huntress make in the air onto the paper. Amari gasped.

"A Symbol!" she said, the capitalisation of the word clearly audible this time. She jumped from her chair and strode over to a bookshelf on the wall behind her desk. It took her only a moment to find what she was looking for: a small leather-bound journal. She sat back down at her desk and quickly flipped through the book. I leaned in to have a closer look. An archaic, although immaculate, handwriting with very few flourishes or embellishments covered the pages. A practical hand.

"This is Diana's diary," Amari said distractedly, her finger trailing across a page covered in strange ciphers. I glanced up at the painting of the legendary Keeper hanging on the wall behind Amari's desk, a stern-faced Victorian woman who looked like she would brook no nonsense. Exactly the type of woman I could picture this handwriting belonging to.

"This!" Amari said, pointing at something in the book. "Is this it?"

I peered at the list of strange symbols covering the yellowing page. I recognised the one just above the Keeper's finger, although it wasn't from any alphabet I could identify.

"That's it, yes. What does it mean?"

"It's the Word I use to travel with," Amari said, her eyes sparkling. "All this time we thought the power lay in the sound, but if this mysterious woman of yours only had to draw it... That opens up a world of possibilities!"

"But how does it work?" I asked. "You've told me before that certain words have power, but what makes the magic happen?" I twiddled my fingers at her in my best impression of a mighty sorcerer. Amari lifted an eyebrow, and I dropped my hand into my lap.

"We only have a few remnants of the First Language available to us," she said, tracing her fingers across the rest of the symbols on the page. "Diana dedicated her life to searching for them and learning how they worked. I've gleaned what I could from her diary, but I'm afraid much is still lost."

"Will you teach it to me?" I asked, feeling my pulse quicken. This was it. This was how I finally became the hero. And this was the power I needed to make the world a safer place.

An indelicate sound escaped Amari's lips. "Not likely."

I swallowed down the bitter taste of disappointment and tried again. "Come on, Amari," I wheedled. "I already know the Symbol. I've heard you speak the Word many times. It's only a matter of time before I figure it out myself. Do you really want me to experiment on my own?"

Amari frowned. She opened her mouth as if to say something, then closed it abruptly again. She stared at me until it took effort to hold her gaze. Finally, she nodded. "Fine. Just this one." I felt like pumping my fists into the air. "And mostly because I don't want you to get yourself into trouble with it."

"Me?" I asked innocently, wondering if I

should tell her I'd already learned a Word from her and that I'd avoided trouble successfully so far. I decided not to push my luck.

Amari's lips didn't so much as twitch. "Listen to me, Ambrose," she said, her expression alarmingly serious. "Words of Wonder can be dangerous in the wrong hands. You must promise me you will not share this knowledge with anyone, understood?"

"Of course," I said easily, unable to keep a triumphant grin from slipping across my face.

"And that includes your father."

I paused for a second. I could understand why Amari wouldn't want to share her knowledge with him. He had spent years working, quite willingly, for the enemy. He'd have to win her trust first.

"Agreed," I said.

Amari relaxed visibly, and a small smile tucked at the corner of her lips. "At least this way I won't have to be at your beck and call every time you need to go somewhere anymore."

Suddenly my thoughts raced with possibilities. No more waiting for the train to arrive! No more long-haul flights to bucket list destinations. I could have breakfast in Sydney and lunch in New York. I could even go back to France without worrying about passport control. This thought excited me so much that I missed what Amari was saying until I realised she was looking at me expectantly. "I'm sorry, what?"

"I want you to say the Word and see what happens," she repeated patiently.

"Oh." I blinked, suddenly a little unsure of myself. "What if I...?"

"Yes?"

I laughed nervously. "What if I make a mistake and cut myself off?"

"Cut yourself off?" Amari looked confused.

"You know, leave a limb behind. Or arrive on the other side inside out."

Both of Amari's eyebrows shot up into her hairline. "This is not Star Trek, Ambrose," she said in a withering tone. "And it isn't science. Nobody's going to make a mistake while beaming you up."

I nodded, feeling sheepish. Then I took a deep breath. "Okay, here goes." I stood up and took a few steps away from Amari's desk, swinging and stretching my arms, still stiff from last night's exertion, as if I were loosening up for some physical activity. I rolled my neck and took a few deep breaths. Then, noticing Amari's amused expression, I clenched my fists and braced myself.

I said the Word and half closed my eyes against the bright light that always accompanied a visit from Amari, but nothing happened. I blinked. "Did I say it wrong?"

"No." Amari's chair creaked as she leaned back, studying me. "Your pronunciation was perfect, but that's not all there is to it. The Word has power, yes, but in this case, it is the speaker's intent that gives it meaning."

Understanding dawned on me. "So you mean I need to picture where I want to be when I do this?"

"If that helps, yes."

"But then, how do you know where to go when I call you? I've summoned you from Paris and Loch Ness and Rome, and somehow you always knew exactly where I was."

Amari gave me a pointed look.

Of course. "The whistle…"

"I'm a little disappointed you didn't realise it sooner," Amari said, smiling to take the sting out of her words. "The whistle acts as a beacon. I can do the same with GPS coordinates."

I stared at her for a moment before I realised

my jaw had dropped and I clamped it firmly shut. Squaring my shoulders, I formed an image of my apartment in my mind. I pictured the leather sofa in front of the TV, Glamdring hanging against the wall, my bookshelf filled with fantasy novels. I took a deep breath and said the Word.

Nothing.

My shoulders slumped in defeat.

"Never mind, Ambrose."

Amari beckoned for me to come sit down again, and I flopped down into the chair opposite her, crestfallen. Perhaps this wasn't it, after all.

"Don't look so discouraged," Amari said. "I'd have been very impressed if you'd managed it so easily. Besides, there's something I haven't told you yet."

"What's that?"

"The Repository has a powerful Word of protection over it. Only the Keeper can travel in and out of the mountain using a Word. Everyone else needs more conventional means."

"Oh…" I said, feeling optimism spark again. Maybe there was still hope for me.

Amari stood up. "Come, I'll go show you where the West Gate is. Maybe you'll have better luck there."

A chime sounded, and Amari stopped mid-stride. She pulled a mobile phone out of her pocket. "Ah, I need to take this," she said, glancing at the caller ID. "Why don't you go see James while I'm busy here? He should be almost done with the morning rounds by now."

I nodded, closing the heavy oak door of Amari's study behind me, and went looking for my father. I found him just as he stepped out of an enclosure, a small bottle clutched in one hand. There were scrapings of wood bark in the bottle.

"Morning," I said as I walked up to him.

Father startled, whipping the bottle behind his back, and then exhaled loudly when he saw me. "Ambrose!" he exclaimed, placing a hand across his heart. "This is not the type of place to creep up on people."

"If Amari finds out you're harvesting nymphs…"

"I know, I know," Father said, looking around furtively. "Keep your voice down."

I folded my arms, barring his way. Heat flushed through my body. If he was still doing Marco's work by exploiting these creatures…

Father's jaw clenched. "You needn't look so righteous," he said sharply. "This is from the dryad that was captured in Rome. Look." He held up the bottle and I peered at the blackened bark inside it. "This is where Amari had set her alight. It's not healing. I took some scrapings so I could study it a little closer and see if I can come up with a salve or a poultice of some sort."

Embarrassment washed over me. Of course he was trying to help the nymph. That's exactly what Father would do. "I'm sorry," I apologised, dropping my arms to my sides. "I should have known."

He grunted. "Yes, you should have. Nevertheless, let's keep it quiet, shall we? Amari is very adamant about creature parts. Even if only for personal study."

"Fine," I agreed as he tucked the bottle into the pocket of his trousers. It looked like I was going to have to keep everybody's secrets today.

"How's your sister doing?" Father asked as he walked over to a cart standing in the corridor between enclosures. He picked up a pitchfork and started attacking the hay stacked in it.

"Surprisingly well, actually," I replied. "There's no outward sign of the attack anymore, and no more internal bleeding. The doctor sent her home yesterday. Said all Cassie needs now is rest. She's probably driving Pavi up the walls by now."

Father grunted as he transferred hay from the cart into a trough beside another compound door. I looked for a sign to show what was inside the enclosure, but couldn't see anything. Judging by the choice of feed, this might be the lone unicorn's encampment. Amari had once said that Una had been living in the Repository longer than all its current residents. I wondered if she missed the outside world at all.

"I like that girl," Father said, putting the pitchfork down and wiping his brow. "She seems very... capable."

"Indeed." If anyone could keep Cassie in line while she was recovering, it was Pavi. At least this left me free to hunt down anything that might try to hurt my sister again. There were several things out there that the world could happily do without, if you asked me. Which reminded me: "How's the werewolf?"

Father scowled, clenching his fists. "Disagreeable. If I hadn't known Amari would disapprove, I'd add a sedative to his food just to keep him quiet. The man's a menace. The world might just be better off without him in it."

I nodded grimly as Father echoed my thoughts. Amari wanted me to bring creatures to the Repository for their protection, but I was beginning to think she might have it wrong. Most people were blissfully unaware of what was out there, what could be stalking them in the dark. I for one would sleep better at night knowing fewer monsters roamed the streets, and that they were all safely locked up here inside the mountain.

"There you are." I turned to see Amari striding into view. "Ah, morning, James. I'm glad I found you both. I have a feeling you might know more about this one than I do, James."

My heart lurched. "You've found something else that escaped from the Colosseum?"

"Possibly." Amari grimaced. "One of my retired Specialists just contacted me. There's a chimaera on the loose in Croatia."

"Oh yes," Father said, his eyes widening. "A fearsome beast, that one. We caught it while it was asleep in a cave somewhere in the foothills outside of Athens. It's probably trying to find its way back home now."

Amari huffed before turning to me. "Can I count on you, Ambrose?"

My pulse quickened. I'd seen the chimaera in Rome, and the thought of having to confront it, without the protection of sturdy steel between us, sent a shiver of fear down my spine. It was a thing of teeth and claws. I imagined the devastation the monster was leaving in its wake as it travelled through the countryside. Who knew how many innocents it was killing along the way? I clenched my fists. "Of course. Just tell me where and when."

"Good man," Father said, clapping me on the shoulder. "History's most famous chimaera slayer was Bellerophon, and the legends say he had a lead-tipped spear and the help of Pegasus when he killed his monster. What do you have in mind?"

"I don't want it killed," Amari interrupted before I could answer. "Just capture it, Ambrose. I'll find a nice spot for it here in the Repository." She suddenly scowled. "If the bureaucrats will allow it."

"Is the centaur still giving you grief?" Father asked.

"Yes," Amari growled. "He's in Rome now, giving feedback to the Army. My hands are tied until he comes back with their approval." She turned to me again. "I'll take you home again so you can gather what you want to take with you, and then I'll drop you off at the meeting point. We'd better not keep Nadiya waiting. She might take things into her own hands."

I barely had time to say goodbye to Father before Amari bustled me up the steps and back towards her office. When I asked her more about the retired Specialist I was about to meet, Amari just shook her head and pursed her lips, refusing to say anything more.

I suddenly wondered who I should be more wary of – the chimaera, or this Nadiya?

✳✳✳

When the white light faded, I found myself high in a tower overlooking an ancient walled town. Stone buildings gleamed golden in the early morning sun as I gazed out over a city of orange-tiled roofs, enveloped within thick fortress walls. I turned to see the cerulean waters of the Adriatic Sea lapping lazily in a harbour dotted with hundreds of little white sailboats.

"So, this is Dubrovnik," I said aloud, for the moment forgetting about my mission and basking in the beauty of the Old Town spread out below me. It was still shoulder season – before the hordes of tourists would descend and trample anyone getting in the way of their sightseeing checklist – and only a few people milled about with the wandering aimlessness of holidaymakers. It didn't look like a city being harassed by a mythical monster. Perhaps if I could capture the chimaera quickly, I'd have a few days to myself to relax and soak up the sun before I returned to London.

"*Sveti Josip!* Are you just going to stand there staring?"

I spun around at the sound of the lightly accented voice to see a woman glaring at me, her hands on her hips. Frown lines seemed permanently etched into her forehead and her shoulder length flaxen hair was streaked with strands of grey. I'd straightened my spine and started tucking my shirt before I caught myself.

"You must be Nadiya Telep," I said, extending a hand in greeting. "Ambrose Davids."

The woman ignored my hand, the lines around her eyes deepening as she looked me over. I felt like a piece of meat being sized up by a butcher. I let my hand drop to my side.

"What are you, a skilled martial artist? Fighter of some sorts?"

"No…"

"Know many Words of power?"

"Afraid not."

"Then what makes you special enough that Amari would send you to come catch this monster?"

I shrugged, not letting the woman intimidate me. "I'm willing? Oh, and I'm lucky. Sort of."

Nadiya snorted. "Lucky," she repeated, her tone leaving little doubt what she thought of that. "What good is luck to me?"

I didn't know how to answer that.

Her eyes bored into my own for what felt like ages, until she finally shrugged and said: "Come on, then. I guess I'll have to make do with what I've got."

I picked up my duffle bag and trotted behind her down the steel steps of the tower. Nadiya walked with a noticeable limp in her left leg, but it didn't slow her down at all. We exited the building just as the bells started chiming. I stopped for a moment, listening to them echoing through the square, as they must have done for hundreds of years.

Nadiya grabbed my arm. "You think you're on holiday? Maybe you want to go visit a museum too? Or go for a swim in the ocean?"

"I can't swim," I replied automatically, cursing under my breath as Nadiya's scowl turned into a sneer.

"Then it's time you learn," she said in a no-nonsense tone that brooked no argument.

Still holding onto my arm, she pulled me towards a large arch in the city's imposing walls. I shrugged her off, earning a wry grin, and followed her into the harbour. She led me along a stone footpath running along the city walls until we came to the end of a stone pier jutting out into the turquoise ocean. Benches were scattered around a red lamppost where weary tourists could sit and appreciate the view of the bay and a small island in the distance. A set of steps led down into the gently lapping water.

Nadiya jutted her chin towards the greenery in the distance. "Swim to Lokrum Island," she said bullishly.

I laughed. Surely she was joking. "I told you I can't swim."

"And I told you it was time you learned." Her voice was steely. "How do you expect to capture a monster if you're afraid of water?"

"Are you kidding me? A chimaera isn't aquatic. It's probably the most land-bound animal I can think of," I shot back. "Besides, I didn't bring my swimming shorts."

"Then do it naked, for all I care," came the reply. "Are you going to stop to put on a swimsuit if a monster drags you into the ocean? Are you going to tell it you can't swim? No." She folded her arms across her chest. "Swim to Lokrum Island." Each word was a nail slamming into my coffin.

"Fine," I said, trying hard not to sound like a sulky child. Besides, she had a point. I yanked my cloverleaf trainers off and put them on top of my duffle bag, next to a bench. "Keep an eye on those. I'll need them when I get back." If Nadiya heard, she gave no response. She sat down on the bench, watching me procrastinate with pursed lips. I pulled my phone out of my jeans' pocket and tucked it into a shoe – I'd just had the screen fixed and I wouldn't risk it getting water damage now. I pulled my shirt over my head and tossed it into my bag, along with Amari's whistle, suddenly conscious of how pale my body was compared to Nadiya's sun-kissed skin. I considered taking my jeans off too, but with Nadiya's vulture-eyed gaze on me, decided against it.

Finally, taking a deep breath to calm my rising heart rate, I stepped gingerly into the lukewarm water. My feet slipped on pebbles as I waded in, moving forward carefully, hesitantly, until the water reached my hips.

My breathing was coming hard and fast. All I could think of was cold, clammy hands on my skin. Of a girl's cruel smile as she pulled me in deeper. Of bubbles rising in the darkness. The cold inevitability of death.

The sound of laughter brought me back from the brink.

I glanced around. All I could see was the clear blue waters of the Adriatic and the island I was aiming for, closer than I'd thought. I looked over my shoulder to see why Nadiya had been laughing at me, but she was playing on her phone, not even looking in my direction. There was a surprising amount of water between me and the pier. Maybe it didn't get any deeper than this. Maybe I *could* walk all the way to the island.

Two more steps and that option was gone as I stumbled into a deeper section, the water suddenly up to my neck. I gasped as a small wave splashed into my face, flailing my arms and straining to keep my head above water. Another step and my foot found nothing to tread on. I was in the deep.

Panic was a kraken rising to the surface.

Laughter tinkled just outside my field of vision again. Like a swan with a broken wing, I floundered around in circles, trying to see where the sound was coming from.

Blue water, blue skies, green island.

The island. The sooner I reached the island, the sooner this ordeal would be over.

Kicking furiously, I somehow managed to propel myself forward in a swimming style that could only be described as 'nearly drowning dog'. I spat salty water from my mouth. The sun, directly overhead, was blindingly bright, my exposed skin burning a shade of pink I knew would turn hazmat red by this evening.

I splashed and thrashed and flailed, but the island stayed frustratingly far away.

And then something grabbed my leg and pulled me under the water.

Blinking the salty sting of the ocean away, I opened my eyes to see a girl hovering beside me. Her lips were blue and her skin so pale it was almost translucent. She looked all but dead, but her grip on me was like a vice. When her grey eyes met my own, I felt that same tug of forced enamour that the asrai had had on me.

That's when I knew Nadiya had sent me here to die.

Memories of another watery girl bubbled into my mind's eye, of a siren who had decided to save rather than kill me. She had seen my past written across my face: touch of frost, breath of fire. Perhaps this one would too?

"Look at me!" I said, the words effervescing around us. Did she even understand English? I had no more oxygen left to plead my case. All I could do was hope and trust the luck.

But the girl did look at me. In fact, she pulled me back up to the surface and, as I gasped for air, she studied me like I was the strange creature to be gaped at. She traced a droplet of water running down my cheek, her finger as cold as winter's frost against my sunbathed skin and said: *"Poglavičina suza."*

"I don't understand," I said. Travelling by Word didn't really provide an opportunity for studying a phrase book. "Do you speak English?"

"Yes, a little," she surprised me by saying. Her voice, although a little hoarse like she had a scratchy throat, susurrated like a murmuring brook. "Why are you here?"

The question caught me off guard. Wasn't I supposed to ask her that? She was right, though. Of the two of us, I was clearly the one out of his element. I shrugged and flashed her a lopsided grin. "I'm supposed to be learning how to swim."

"You're very bad at it," she replied, no hint of malice in her voice, just stating the truth. "I will teach you."

Before I could protest, she tilted me into a horizontal position, making slight corrections as I struggled to stay afloat. She was surprisingly strong for such a wispy creature. The girl showed how my arms and legs should move, and how I should hold my head so I could catch a breath in between strokes. I swallowed more of the Adriatic Sea than I'd care to admit, but eventually it became less of a struggle and more exhilarating as my body tore through the water like a slightly dull knife through butter. With her swimming beside me to help when I faltered, I eventually reached the island's rocky shore.

Dripping in my soggy jeans, I stumbled along the shingles until I found a suitable spot where I lay down on my back and stared up at the blue sky above. My arms ached from the unusual exertion and my eyes stung from the salty water, but I couldn't wipe the smile off my face.

The girl cast a quick shadow as she sat down beside me.

I pushed myself onto my elbows. "Thank you," I said simply. She could have killed me, but instead she'd given me a gift.

The girl's smile was like water gently lapping on the shore. She leaned over and brushed her lips against mine. Then she stood up and walked back into the sea, her pale translucent figure disappearing beneath the water before the tingle had faded from my lips.

※※※

I emerged from the water like some sea beast from the deep, dripping and glaring.

Although there were a handful of people occupying the benches scattered along the pier – glancing my way, but apparently a half-naked nutball surfacing from the sea wasn't all that interesting – Nadiya was nowhere in sight. Fortunately, my bag and my shoes were exactly where she had left them. Why bother to keep my things safe? After all, she hadn't expected me to return.

I rummaged in my bag until I found my travel towel and gingerly dried myself off. My skin was tingling and had a distinct reddish cast to it, the brush of my shirt against my back a promise of the discomfort to come. Probably best to stay out of the sun for the next few days.

I tramped back towards the city with the vague idea of finding a hotel when I spotted Nadiya sitting at an outdoor table of a restaurant beside the harbour. I dumped my bag by her feet and flopped down into a chair opposite her.

The older woman's eyes widened, but she showed no other hint of either surprise or remorse. She picked up her glass, swirling the white wine around for a second, then asked: "How did you overcome the rusalka?"

Ha! So she *had* known what she was sending me to. "I talked to her."

Nadiya coughed as the sip she'd taken went down the wrong way. "You did what?" she spluttered. She grabbed the napkin I offered, dabbing at the spilled wine on the table. "You don't talk to these creatures!" she hissed. "You kill them!" She cleared her throat and visibly calmed herself down. "Or capture them, at the very least. Do you know how dangerous a rusalka is?"

"She can't be *that* dangerous if you sent me into her arms knowingly without warning." I watched the former Specialist closely, but there was still no trace of guilt in her eyes. "Fortunately, she's a good swimming coach. I would never have made it to the island and back without her help." I leaned back in the chair, lifting my hands behind my head. "Not a bad kisser either."

"Unbelievable," Nadiya muttered, shaking her head.

"By the way, what does *poglavičina suza* mean?"

Nadiya hesitated. "Chieftain's tear," she finally said, suspiciously. "Why?"

I chuckled. Father had said that nymphs enjoyed gossiping. Every naiad, nereid and oceanid from here to Scotland must have been wagging their tongues for a rusalka to recognise me, like I was a celebrity of the mythological world. Nadiya couldn't have foreseen my complicated history with water nymphs. The woman was formidable, but she didn't have all the answers. "No reason."

"You think you're clever, don't you?" Nadiya said. "You think because you survived my test that I should trust you? That I should entrust all these people's lives to you?" She swept the hand still holding the napkin outwards, encompassing everyone sitting at the restaurant as well as the city beyond the walls.

"Amari does."

That gave Nadiya some pause. "Well." She put her empty glass down and stood up. "We'll see." She turned on her heel and walked away. I stared after her. She took a few steps and turned back, frowning at me. "Come on then. What are you waiting for?"

I jumped to my feet, grabbed my duffle bag, and followed her. She led me back into the old city, through a maze of alleyways paved in white limestone, past tightly packed sandstone buildings with shuttered wooden windows, and up a set of stone stairs where she finally stopped in front of a green door. She unlocked it and ushered me in.

A modest living room and an open-plan kitchen greeted me. The furnishings were spartan and in shades of grey and the white walls were unadorned. It was minimalism taken to the extreme.

I followed Nadiya up the stairs, past a bedroom and a bathroom on the second floor, and up into an attic room sparsely furnished with a steel frame single bed and a washbasin with a mirror in the corner next to a small dresser. Dust specks floated in the light falling in from a narrow window in the slanted roof, casting a line of sunshine on the bare wooden floor. I had a feeling Nadiya didn't entertain many visitors.

"Here's the spare key," she said, reluctantly placing it on the dresser. "I want it back when this is over, of course."

"Of course." She sure knew how to make a guy feel welcome.

"Meals are your own responsibility. This isn't a B&B."

"Noted," I replied, wondering if I shouldn't have found myself a nice hotel instead. "When are we going to discuss the reason you asked for help?"

"Tomorrow. I have an appointment this evening. Find a way to keep yourself out of trouble until I return," she said before leaving, her footsteps echoing as she descended the stairs.

I tossed my duffle bag into a corner – no use in making myself at home by unpacking – I clearly wasn't welcome here – and fell onto the bed. Exhaustion overtook me. Every muscle in my upper body ached from my unexpected swimming lesson. I closed my eyes – just for a moment – and fell into a deep, deep sleep.

※※※

I woke up with a start. It felt like a high-speed train had run me over. Everything ached. A staccato beat pounded inside my skull, and my sunburnt skin was painful to touch. I stared up at the ceiling, moaning and feeling sorry for myself. This would never have happened if I'd just stayed in London. It wasn't even like Nadiya wanted me here.

Nadiya. What kind of person could send someone off to get killed like that without even blinking, anyway? The woman was a menace. I had half a mind to let her confront the chimaera on her own. Except that it was my fault it was here in the first place.

But I should definitely go down and shout at her.

After I've borrowed her sunburn lotion.

I plodded down the stairs, looking for my hostess, but the house was empty. I didn't feel comfortable rummaging around her cupboards, so I grabbed my phone and did a quick Google search for the nearest pharmacy. There was one not too far from here, apparently inside a museum. Too touristy. I plotted a route to another nearby health shop instead.

The sun was dipping towards the horizon outside. I must really have been exhausted to have nodded off for that long. Would the pharmacy still be open at this time of night? I hastened my steps, past clusters of stone houses and through cluttered back alleys, and came to a stop in front of the pharmacy just as the woman was locking the door.

"Excuse me," I said. "I just need some sunburn cream. Please." I was desperate. My tender British skin hadn't been prepared for the full force of an Adriatic sun.

The woman said something in a language I didn't understand. Where was a Babel fish when you needed one? I pointed at my pinkish arms and she nodded in understanding, mercifully unlocking the door again.

Inside, the shop was cool and smelled of disinfectant. The woman took a tube off a shelf and rang it up on the till. I swiped my credit card, trusting that she knew what I needed. I thanked her profusely as she ushered me out of the pharmacy. She must have been eager to get home, but not as eager as I was for relief.

I slumped down on the cool tiled floor outside the shop and looked at my purchase. Fortunately, the label was in English, and I quickly layered my arms and face in the blue goo that proclaimed to be after-burn lotion. My skin tingled, but I instantly felt better.

With my immediate discomfort eased, perhaps it was time for a little sightseeing. I ambled in the museum's direction. What could possibly be interesting enough about an old pharmacy that tourists would flock to it?

It took me a few turns to find the entrance hidden inside a narrow alley. The sign on the door said it was a Franciscan monastery's old apothecary shop, founded in 1317, and that it was already closed for the evening.

Sudden disappointment washed over me. Strangely enough, that *did* sound fascinating. It must be filled with all sorts of ancient home remedies, potions, ointments and cure-alls. Who knew what kind of unexpected concoctions were still being brewed behind these cloistered walls? This sounded like the kind of place you'd come to if you'd been afflicted by an asrai's frosty touch.

My mind was still full of possibilities when the door handle rattled, setting my pulse to racing. I dashed out of the alley and darted into the closest shop, feeling like I'd trespassed and not wanting to be caught. I looked through the window to see Nadiya coming out of the alley carrying a long walking stick, a dark hoodie casting her face in shadow. She glanced around, almost furtively, before striding off.

What was she up to?

I stepped out of the shop. Nadiya was moving quickly. I'd have to hurry if I didn't want to lose her in this warren of streets. Luckily her route turned out to be straight and for a moment I felt foolish, thinking I was trailing her back to her house, but she kept going and only turned when she'd nearly reached the harbour. She followed a path that led us underneath the Old Town walls and out onto a more modern street that ran between the houses on the coastline.

There were fewer pedestrians here, so I kept a fair distance between us, afraid she might look over her shoulder and see me shadowing her, but she never looked back.

I glanced at my watch. We'd been walking for nearly fifteen minutes. It would be typical of my luck if she were just out visiting friends, but I somehow doubted it. I might have felt guilty back in that alley, but she'd looked it.

When I raised my eyes again, Nadiya was gone.

I swore under my breath and jogged towards the place I'd last seen her. There was a gap in the hip-high stone wall running along the pedestrian walkway. A rocky footpath led through the brush in the sea's direction. I pushed past the greenery and bit a yelp back as I skid to a stop on the edge of a cliff, the water twinkling far below me in the fading light.

I scanned the area and saw a rope tied to the base of a tree, the rest of it dangling down the cliff. Did Nadiya go this way? Maybe she was a mountain climber, practicing her abseiling…

A roar from below suddenly split the air, followed by a brief scream. A woman's voice. Nadiya!

I grabbed the rope, but paused at the edge of the cliff, looking down. It was a sheer drop to the water below and I could just see the rim of a pebbly beach sticking out. There must be a cave underneath this overhang. My hands trembled and I swallowed loudly as I contemplated the drop.

A bleating sound rose from below and my heart lurched into my throat. A lion's roar and a goat's bleat. The chimaera was down there!

And so was Nadiya.

I clutched onto the rope and prayed for luck as I propelled myself off the cliff.

The rapid movement blurred my vision and I cried out as my hands slid along the rope, friction rubbing my palms raw. Then there was no more rope to hold on to and I felt myself free-falling the rest of the distance. I closed my eyes, expecting the bone-breaking crunch of the pebbles below, but instead I landed on something relatively soft that gave way beneath my weight.

My eyes popped open and widened at the scene confronting me.

I was in a rocky alcove opening up to the ocean. Nadiya was sprawled out on the ground, her left leg twisted at an unnatural angle at the knee. A spear lay a few feet from her, beyond reach. She grimaced at me; I wasn't sure whether in pain or surprise, but probably both.

Beside me, the chimaera was pushing itself back up after I'd knocked it off its feet.

I gaped at the monster. With nothing between me and it but crisp evening air, it seemed so much larger than I remembered. At first, all I could see was its feline body, the reddish mane of a male lion, and its snarling black lips pulled back to reveal jagged fangs. Then it shifted its weight and the bearded goat's head became visible, its short horns glinting razor sharp in the fading light, and its silky black neck horribly merging into the lion's back. The thing's tail lashed to the side, and I shuddered as the scaly head of a snake opened its maw and hissed at me.

Perhaps I should have stayed in Finance after all.

The monster's powerful leg muscles bunched together, ready to leap at me, and then a fist-sized pebble hit the goat's head from the side. Nadiya, still on the ground, shouted something and the chimaera swivelled back towards her. It snarled as she tried to scramble away from it, her broken leg dragging uselessly through the gravel.

I surged to my feet, adrenaline racing. The monster was between me and the spear, its snake head darting towards me, a single needle-sharp fang dripping with venom. I did the only thing I could think of. I grabbed my bottle of after-burn lotion and squeezed it into the snake's face. The serpent recoiled as blue goo spurted down its throat, and I ducked past it and slammed my still-stinging palm against the chimaera's flank. Light blinded me as a Word tumbled from my lips.

The next thing I knew, the monster and I stood on the beach at Lokrum Island where the rusalka had kissed me.

The creature roared, spittle flying from the lion's jaws. Then it lowered its head and rushed towards me. I turned and ran, diving into the lukewarm sea just as flames ignited above my head. Swearing inwardly as the saltwater stung my palms, I kicked my legs and swam with what little newfound skill I had, murmuring a thank you to the nymph who'd cured me of my fear.

When I realised I didn't hear any splashing but my own, I stopped and turned around, treading water. The chimaera stood at the edge of the beach, snarling at the rippling sea. I laughed in relief. I'd hoped a fire-breathing creature would be hesitant to follow me.

I'd probably have to find a way to contain it or otherwise dozens of people would have a nasty surprise tomorrow as soon as they stepped off the ferry, but it could wait. I needed to go see if

Nadiya was alright.

I said the Word, expecting to land up at the cove where I'd left her, but nothing happened.

I tried again. Nothing, not even so much as a fizzle.

The chimaera paced along the water's edge, all three of its heads watching me. There was no way I could go back to the island if, for some reason, I needed to be on dry land for the Word to work. I'd have to swim for it.

I turned back towards the far coast, sighing as I saw the secluded cave in the distance. Familiar panic clutched at my throat at the sight of all that water between me and the shore, but I pushed it down. It was either swim or get eaten. The chimaera bleated forlornly as I propelled myself forward.

Stars were twinkling above when I finally reached the shore where Nadiya was waiting for me. She sat on the shingles with her legs pulled up against her body, her chin resting on her knees. The walking stick she'd carried earlier was stuck upright into the rocks beside her, but there was no sign of the spear I'd seen during the fight.

"Are you alright?" I asked as I emerged, dripping like a wet dog, and stumbled up to her. "Your leg…"

"It's fine," she said, holding a hand out so I could help her up. I pulled her to her feet, and she leaned on the stick as she regarded me, her left leg seeming perfectly healed now. "You took a long time coming back." The question hung unspoken in the air.

I shrugged, pretending indifference. "I was hot. The swim cooled me off nicely." I wasn't sure I trusted her with the truth. Especially since she was clearly keeping her own secrets.

Nadiya pressed her mouth into a thin line.

"What did you do with the creature?"

I stooped down to pick up the half-empty bottle of after-burn lotion I'd dropped earlier. It had come in handier than I'd expected, and I might need it again. Besides, I wasn't a litterbug. I tucked it into the pocket of my jeans. "Dropped it off on the island. It was the best I could come up with under the circumstances."

She nodded. "Not ideal, but it will do, for now. Can you…" I followed her gaze to where the rope was still dangling, just out of reach. "… Get us back to the city?"

I knew what she was asking, but even if it did work, I had no intention of using a Word without the roar of a monster to prevent her from overhearing it. "I'll give you a boost."

The woman nodded. She tucked the stick into her belt loop and grabbed the rope as I hoisted her into the air. With surprising strength and agility, she started pulling herself up along the rope. I was just wondering how I was going to get back up there myself when she reached down and offered me a hand.

I jumped, clasping onto her, and then, arm muscles protesting loudly, I heaved myself onto the rope too, wincing as my sore hands touched its coarse surface. The rope swung wildly for a few seconds before Nadiya started climbing again. I glanced down at the floor and then back up at her ascending legs. Rope climbing was the thing I'd hated most about gym class in school.

Still, I wasn't going to back down now. I'd outwitted a chimaera and swam the length of a strait. I wouldn't let a stupid rope get the best of me now.

Sweat was running down the side of my face when I finally grabbed onto Nadiya's hand again, letting her pull me over the lip of the cave. I collapsed in the dirt, breathing hard and wincing as the ache in my arms settled in.

Nadiya sat down beside me, her legs hanging over the edge of the cave's mouth. "You are weak, Ambrose," she said. "You must be lucky to still be alive."

I nodded, too tired to feel insulted.

"But you have a good heart," she continued, surprising me. Even more astonishing was the look of remorse in her eyes. "I... apologise for sending you to the rusalka without warning."

I grunted. "That was not cool."

A smile tucked at her lips. "No, it wasn't. But I will make it up to you. Tomorrow, I will train you," she said in a tone that brooked no arguments.

I groaned. Couldn't I just spend the day sleeping instead?

"Look," she said, the smile gone now.

Grimacing, I lifted myself up onto my elbows and looked at where she was pointing. The chimaera was in the water, halfway between the island and the shore. It didn't look like it was heading back towards the cave.

"It will find another lair now," Nadiya said. "We'll have to track it down again."

"Not now, I hope," I blurted out.

"No, not now," Nadiya said, smiling again. "Come." She used her walking stick to push herself to her feet. I struggled up like a man twice my age, my back suddenly killing me too. "Let's go home and get some rest. We've both earned it tonight."

✖✖✖

The sun was barely up before Nadiya was stomping up the stairs to my loft room. "Get up!" she shouted as she pulled the covers off my bed.

"Ten laps around the city walls. You want to do it before the tourists arrive or the sun is too high in the sky."

"I don't remember signing up for boot camp," I grumbled as I flopped out of bed. All I wanted to do was roll over and sleep some more. Or, better yet, book myself into a spa and have someone rub hot oil into my sore muscles, preferably with soothing music in the background and a cup of tea close by.

Apparently Nadiya had ears like a bat, because her face now resembled a thundercloud. "You think you're on holiday? You think just because you got lucky last night, you're fit to fight a chimaera? This! This is what a chimaera can do!" She pulled the left leg of her trousers up, and my eyes widened. The bottom half of her leg was gone, replaced by a steel prosthetic attached to her knee. So, this was the accident that had forced her to retire. And this is why her 'broken' leg had been so easily healed last night.

"What happened?" I asked, trying my best to keep the sympathy from my voice. She wouldn't want my pity.

"I was too slow," she said simply. There was no trace of sadness in her eyes. Her voice sounded bitter and the lines in her face deepened as her eyes glazed with memory. "Too sure of myself. I lost a leg, and three people died before I killed the monster. Do you want that to happen to you too?"

"No," I admitted, pulling a fresh shirt on. "And I appreciate what you're trying to do. I know I can learn a lot from you."

The woman's face softened a little. "Amari was right to send you. You have potential. But if you face that thing on your own, you will die."

I grimaced. I knew she was right. "Let's try to avoid that, shall we?"

The first round along the walls of Dubrovnik was tough, but exhilarating. My feet pounded on the stone walkways, my tummy rumbling as the smell of fresh pastries wafted on the early morning air. The rising sun blazed across the Old Town's orange rooftops, and the cerulean waters of the Adriatic Sea sparkled across my horizon. I was in love with the city before my second lap was complete.

By the third lap, however, I understood why Nadiya had advised me to come early. I was drenched in sweat, and the people thronging along the walls were getting in my way. My knees wobbled as I descended the slippery stone steps down towards the ground level, nodding at the guy in the ticketing booth smirking at me like I was the funniest thing he'd seen this week. I pushed my way past the tourists milling around the Pile Gate, staring at their maps and fanning themselves with their Lonely Planet guides, and dipped my entire head underneath the spout of the fountain in the centre of the little square. The icy cold spring water was just what I needed to revive myself again.

Shaking the droplets out of my hair, I pushed myself into a slow jog again. I was going to do this, even if it took me all day.

※※※

Nadiya was waiting for me by the fountain when I stumbled down the steps after the last lap around the walls. She looked up at the sky. The sun was already high. I could feel my nose and the back of my neck tingling again.

"Took you long enough," she said, offering me

a tube of sunburn lotion. I must have done something right for her to show such kindness. I took it gratefully, rubbing it liberally across every bit of exposed skin.

"What's next?" I asked, handing the lotion back to her before gulping down some more of the refreshing fountain water. When I'd drunk my fill, I flopped down onto the floor and sat with my back against the cool marble of the fountain.

Nadiya's gaze was inscrutable as she studied me. Finally, she said: "Go rest, have some lunch. Weapons training at two o'clock. Don't be late." Then she turned on her heels and strode off.

Weapons training? I groaned. I was too tired to even wipe the sweat off my brow. The chimaera might not get a chance to kill me. Nadiya's boot camp would.

Still, I had to admit that tired as I was, the exercise and the sense of accomplishment of completing the challenge had left me feeling buoyant. And now I had a few precious hours of freedom to explore this gorgeous city. I'd be a fool to let this opportunity pass me by.

I climbed to my feet and followed my nose, wandering through Dubrovnik's maze-like streets until I reached an open-air market where I bought a fish sandwich that tasted much better than it smelled. I gobbled it up while sitting on the bench from which Nadiya had sent me swimming yesterday. Looking out across the water towards Lokrum Island, the distance amazed me, and I could hardly believe I had swum there and back all on my own. Twice.

Perhaps I should try taking the quick way again.

I glanced around. Although people had been jostling for seats at the many restaurants dotting the Old Town while I was looking for lunch, the pier was mostly deserted. The only other people visible were a young couple sitting with their feet in the water, closer to the town walls. They were staring so deeply into each other's eyes, I doubted they even knew I existed.

I looked back at the island. Focus. Amari had said I needed intent, and I'd certainly been bent on removing the chimaera from the cave last night, even though I hadn't exactly had time to think it through.

I pictured the rocky beach I'd visited twice now, letting my imagination fill all my senses. I breathed in the scent of the pine trees in the air. I tasted the salt on my lips.

And then I said the Word.

Again, nothing happened. Was my pronunciation off?

I tried again, this time tracing the lines of the Symbol I had seen the huntress use. My pulse quickened as the Symbol sparkled to life with a white energy, but then it fizzled out and I was left standing exactly where I was. Disappointment tasted bitter in my mouth.

My phone suddenly rang and my heart lifted as the caller ID flashed across the screen.

"Tell me you're jumping on a plane and meeting me here for a wild weekend of fun in the sun?" I said, smiling as I sat down on the bench again, stretching my tired legs out to the water.

Sarah laughed on the other end of the line. "I wish! I have so much paperwork to do, I'm not even sure I'll be able to go home tonight. Even if tonight hadn't been a full moon."

"Tonight's the full moon?" I asked, frowning. "But the —" I glanced towards the love-struck couple and lowered my voice. "Norton's been taken care of. Why would the full moon be a problem?"

"It often is," Sarah replied, sighing. "Something about that shining orb in the sky sets the crazies off. The normal ones, I mean, not the ones you have to deal with. Ambrose..." Sarah hesitated. "Have you talked to Cassie? You know, after what happened, and with the full moon tonight..."

"You're afraid she might turn?" The thought gripped my heart like a vice.

"I don't know. Aren't you?"

I thought about it for a few seconds. I never did have a chance to ask Norton how he became a werewolf. He probably wouldn't have told me the truth, anyway.

"I'll call her and find out. Thank you for reminding me."

"Let me know, okay? If she needs any help, I'll be there. Even if I have to bring my handcuffs."

I grimaced. "Let's hope that won't be necessary."

"How are things going in Dubrovnik?" she asked. "Have you seen the chimaera yet?"

I quickly filled her in on everything that had happened so far. "I have weapons training with Nadiya in a few minutes. I don't know if I should be excited or scared," I quipped.

"Be careful, Ambrose." Sarah sounded worried. "This woman sounds unstable. I'm not so sure you should trust her."

"She's a hard-boiled badass, no doubt about that, but I think she means well. I'll get on her good side yet."

"Just... be careful. I miss you."

I never wanted that bloody Word to work more than right then. "I'll be back soon," I said, swallowing down the unexpected lump in my throat.

After Sarah had said goodbye, I quickly dialled

Cassie, glancing at my watch. The phone rang so long I was afraid it was going to go over to voicemail, but just as I was about to give up, my sister answered, sounding out of breath.

"Hi, Am! I'm about to go into class, make it quick."

"You're back at school already? How are you feeling?"

"I'm fine. Never better."

I chewed my bottom lip. Cassie's recovery had been surprisingly fast, and it worried me that her body might have changed irrevocably after the werewolf attack. "Are you sure? Not feeling..." I hesitated, wondering how to ask the question delicately, "... angry? Craving meat, perhaps?"

Cassie snorted. "If you're wondering whether I'm turning into a werewolf, the answer is no."

"You're sure? You know it's a full moon tonight?"

"Is it?" Cassie sounded dismissive. "I hope it doesn't interfere with my plans. I have a date with Pavi tonight."

"Sarah offered to come over too, if you need help. She... uh... She has handcuffs, in case things go wrong."

Cassie laughed. "Oh, I'm sure there will be handcuffs involved, but we won't need Sarah to be there."

I felt my cheeks heat. "Alright then, 1 don't need details. If you're not worried..."

"I'm not worried."

"Okay." I paused. How could she have healed so fast? It wasn't natural. "You're sure you're not –"

"Bye, Ambrose," Cassie laughed, and ended the call.

I glanced at my watch. Time to head back. I wouldn't want to keep my cranky mentor waiting.

※※※

"You're late." Nadiya was sitting in the shade on the doorstep outside her house, sipping a glass of red wine. A cool breeze wafted through the narrow alley, rustling the leaves of potted plants and chasing the afternoon heat away.

"Sorry, I had to make a few phone calls. I'm ready now."

"I doubt it," Nadiya huffed as she stood up and ushered me into the house. She put her glass down and went into the living room, where she lifted the handwoven carpet to reveal a trapdoor cut into the wooden floor. She pulled it open and I peered at a set of steel stairs disappearing into the darkness.

"You first," I joked. After all, what did I really know about this woman? Sarah's warning still lingered in my thoughts. There could be anything down there. Knowing my luck, 'weapons training' could be code for an hour in an iron maiden or a turn on the rack.

Nadiya smiled mockingly as she descended the stairs. A light flickered on. "Are you coming? I don't have all day."

I went down and suppressed a relieved sigh. It wasn't a torture chamber – it looked more like a martial arts dojo. A padded red mat covered a cold stone floor and a single exposed globe hanging from the ceiling cast a warm yellow light around the room. More impressively, every kind of weapon imaginable was hanging around the walls – everything from curved steel swords to pikes to beautifully embossed shields. There was even one of those weighted nets that Roman gladiators had used in the arena. Apparently Nadiya had a thing for ancient weaponry.

I glanced back at her. Tights and a sleeveless

117

vest accentuated her lean body, highlighting toned muscles. Her fingers played with a razor-sharp fang dangling from a piece of string around her neck as she watched me. I didn't doubt for a second that she could use everything here if she needed to.

"Choose your weapon," she said.

I inspected the assortment of handheld weapons on display. The swords all had nicks in the blades, as if they'd seen much use. I considered the flail and the morning-star, then decided I'd probably do myself more damage than anything, before stopping before a variety of evil-looking knives. I didn't feel comfortable picking any of it up.

"What are you going to use?" I asked.

Surprise flickered across Nadiya's face, and for the first time I saw a hint of approval in her eyes. "Very good, Ambrose."

She picked the staff up I'd seen her use last night, and it suddenly dawned on me that it hadn't been a walking aid at all. She pressed a button and a doubled-edge knife flicked into view, turning the staff into a spear. "This is a modified *rogatina*," she explained. "My ancestors used it for bear hunting. And to kill invaders with."

"Is it sharp?" I asked, looking dubiously at the pointy end.

"Of course," Nadiya replied, shrugging, as if training with sharpened weapons was the most natural thing in the world.

I turned back to the wall of weapons, considering my options. If I picked something short, like a sword or a mace, she'd be poking holes into me with that spear long before I could get close to her. And while she might feel comfortable slicing me open during training, I certainly wasn't going to risk anything with a sharp blade. I picked up a sturdy-looking quarterstaff, hefting it in my hands to feel its weight.

When I turned back to her, Nadiya was grinning. "At least you're not stupid," she said.

A backwards compliment, but I'd take it.

Nadiya lunged at me with her spear. Instinctively, I lifted the staff up to block her attack. She retaliated with blow after blow, coming at me faster with each strike. I yelled out as the butt-end of her spear hit the side of my arm, sending a spasm of pain down to my fingers. I dropped my staff and Nadiya glared at me.

"Pick it up," she growled. "Again."

I bent down and scooped up the weapon. Nadiya attacked immediately, swiping my feet out from under me. I landed on the mat with a thump.

"On your feet. Again."

I gritted my teeth and rose, lifting the quarterstaff just in time to ward off a blow to the head. Lightning fast, Nadiya spun on her feet and used the momentum to whack her spear against my side. I grunted and parried a thrust aimed at my stomach. Stars flashed before my eyes as she hit me underneath the chin. I staggered back, using my staff as a crutch to prevent losing my balance.

"You need to be faster, Ambrose. Stop reacting and fight me!"

Easy for her to say.

I shook my head, clearing my vision. I gripped my staff and charged at her. She sidestepped and slapped me across the back. I cried out again and spun around, anger heating my blood. I lunged at her, but she parried easily. I dodged another swipe meant to push me off my feet again and roared when she landed a hit on my side. I was going to be covered in bruises tomorrow.

Despite her limp, Nadiya gave no quarter and didn't slow for an instant. I dodged and deflected hit after hit, barely launching an attack of my own. She drew no blood – due to her skill more than my own – but she chased me around the room until I was out of breath and my sweat-soaked shirt was clinging to my back.

I had no idea how long we sparred, but it felt like hours. Time was a foreign concept in that basement, measured only by the increasing ache in my muscles and the occasional water break Nadiya allowed. Eventually, my strength faltered, and I blocked just a second too slow. I felt a sharp pain stinging my arm. A thin sliver of blood welled up from a cut across my forearm.

"That's enough," Nadiya said immediately, backing off. I swear the woman wasn't even breathing louder than normal.

I wiped at the blood. The cut was barely a scratch, not even deep enough to warrant a plaster. A newfound respect for Nadiya suffused me as I wiped the sweat from my brow.

"I could take a cold beer right about now."

Nadiya grunted as she took my quarterstaff and returned it to its place on the wall, along with her *rogatina*. "I guess you deserve one. You didn't do too bad for your first day," she admitted grudgingly.

I couldn't keep a goofy grin from spreading across my face. I was pretty pleased with myself, all things considered.

"Go get some rest," Nadiya said as we trudged back up the stairs. "I won't go so easy on you tomorrow."

My smile slipped. Did she think that was easy? Hell, if I ever made it out of Dubrovnik alive, I was going to enter the London Triathlon. I bet I would walk away with a gold medal.

✳✳✳

I had never in my life slept as soundly as I did that night. I startled awake the next morning, dawn's early light spilling in through my roof window. Nadiya was standing beside my bed.

I groaned. "Walls?"

"Walls."

Ten laps later I sat down on the bench by the pier again, resting my aching legs. I tore the plastic off the waterproof casing I'd bought and placed my mobile phone inside it. I'd been lucky so far. During my swim from Lokrum Island the other night I had fortunately only submerged the phone to a depth that it could handle, but you never know what might happen. I seemed to have developed the habit of getting wet over the last few months.

I was still admiring the new casing when my phone buzzed. A text from Cassie came through.

-- *No excessive hair growth last night and my canines are just as cute as always. Told you there was nothing to worry about.* --

I chuckled. That was a weight off my mind, at least.

-- *Damn. What am I going to do with this dog collar I got for you now?* --

-- *Keep it. Perfect excuse to get a pet.* --

I smiled. My sister was going to be just fine.

⁂

Nadiya was already armed and waiting for me by the time I descended the basement stairs. She barely gave me a chance to pick up my quarterstaff before she came at me with her *rogatina* as if I were

121

trying to kill her family and steal her land. Panting from the exertion, I did my best to deflect her, but almost every swipe penetrated my defences until my arms and chest stung from little nicks and cuts. My shirt was so shredded I could probably have posed for the cover of a romance novel if I'd had the abs to go with it.

I was so going to send Amari a bill for a new set of clothes after all of this.

"Stop defending and start fighting me!" Nadiya growled as I dodged another thrust. The woman circled me, looking for my weaknesses.

I wasn't going to defeat her. Not like this. She had years of experience on me, and even with a prosthetic leg she was much more nimble, much quicker and lighter on her feet than I was. Perhaps after a few weeks of her gruelling training I might keep up with her, but we didn't have that kind of time.

If I couldn't beat her physically, then I needed to outsmart her.

Instead of fighting to keep her away from me, I studied her movements, grunting every time she walloped me with the side of her spear. She favoured her left leg, shifting her balance slightly every time she swiped the *rogatina* at me. And she lifted her right shoulder just before she was about to thrust. The more I watched, the more I noticed little tells like this, until I finally pieced together the pattern in her attacks. She was too good to be obvious, but now that I knew what to look for, I could clearly see the same sequence of movements following on each other.

I waited until I saw her shift her weight and then, instead of ducking out of her reach, I moved forward into an attack.

It caught her completely off guard.

The butt of my staff hit her squarely in the

chest, sending her sprawling backwards. She reeled and I grabbed her by the hand, stopping her from falling over. As soon as she had regained her balance, she dropped my hand. Her lips thinned as her eyes narrowed. She launched into a flurry of attacks I was hard pressed to block. It felt like she really was trying to kill me.

I wouldn't be surprised if she did kill me just to prove a point.

I blocked a thrust and, as her right shoulder shifted, I ducked and slammed my staff into her side. She winced, but kept coming. I parried and whacked her on the arm, spun, and swiped her feet out from underneath her. She landed on her hands, slamming her palms on the mat and whooping. Jumping to her feet, she grinned at me.

"Finally!" she said, her eyes flashing in triumph. "Show me what you've got."

Our weapons clashed as we each gave as good as we got. Time congealed, until it was as if we were fighting in slow motion, although wind whipped past my face every time I dodged. My eyes stung as I tried not to blink, watching for every one of her tells, a never-ending motion of action and reaction.

Eventually, I saw a trickle of sweat running down the side of Nadiya's brow. She was getting tired, but I was exhausted. With one final push, I evaded her attack and slammed my staff against her spear, sending the weapon flying. Its tip thrust into the wall and it stuck, the shaft quivering as we both stared at in surprise.

Finally, Nadiya turned to me. "You're ready," she said, her tone filled with grim satisfaction. "Tonight, we go looking for the chimaera."

✳✳✳

"How do you know it's in there?" I asked. I was lying on my stomach in the dust, peering at a small cave in the hillside outside Dubrovnik's sprawling modern town. The sun was dipping towards the horizon. We had trekked here on foot, because Nadiya was afraid that the creature, with its three sets of heads, would have heard us if we'd used anything as noisy as a car or public transport.

"The local news reported dogs and livestock going missing near here the last two days. I knew about the cave. It seemed the logical conclusion."

I shrugged. It made sense if the chimaera had been looking for another hideout, after we'd chased it out of the cave at the beach. But I had assumed it was trying to find its way back to Greece. Why would it linger here?

"Come on," Nadiya said, pushing herself up. "We've wasted enough time. Let's go while we still have the advantage of the light." She hefted her *rogatina* in her hands.

"You forgot this," I said, picking up the net we had brought from where she had left it lying in the dust. Although the Greek hero, Bellerophon, had defeated his chimaera by dropping a ball of lead into the fire-breathing mouth of the lion's head, killing it through asphyxiation, I merely wanted to capture the legendary monster's offspring. Nadiya had grudgingly agreed to my plan by suggesting we use her gladiator's net. Once we had disabled the creature, I could summon Amari to take care of the rest.

Nadiya took the net from me, a wry smile playing across her lips.

Quietly, we crept up towards the cave. The stench struck me first when we reached the entrance. I gagged as the acrid smell of rotting meat and excrement wafted on the night air. Nadiya shot me a stern look. This was no time to be delicate. My stomach roiled as we sneaked into the cave.

Something crunched under my foot and I recoiled as I saw bones littering the cave floor. Even though the chimaera hadn't been here long, it must have decimated the local sheep population. I hoped it was sheep. My eyes darted across the small cave, looking for the monster, but all I could see was the mangled remains of something it had devoured for dinner, and a patch of compacted dirt towards the back where it must have rested its bulk.

Of the chimaera itself, there was no sign.

Nadiya turned to me, her eyes wide with alarm. "Where is it?" she whispered urgently. Her hand fluttered to her neck, clutching at the fang I knew dangled there concealed beneath her shirt. Her face paled. "The town!" she shrieked, her voice shrill with panic.

The Word was on my lips before I could think it through. White flashed and the next thing I knew I stood in the square next to the Rector's Palace in Dubrovnik. Instinct had led me here, and luck had served me well. The chimaera was prowling along the pillared entrance.

"What's the plan, sensei?" I said, turning to Nadiya. She was nowhere in sight. I'd left her behind!

"Shit," I breathed, gripping my staff tighter. It was up to me alone to stop this monster. And Nadiya still had the net.

The thing's keen ears had heard me swear. The lion's head turned towards me as the snake tail lashed from side to side. It sniffed the air. The creature must have recognised my scent, because its entire posture changed, puffing its chest out to look bigger than it already was.

It watched me for a moment, unmoving except

for the tail. I tightened my grip on the staff. It was all encouragement the monster needed. The goat's head bleated, and the chimaera stormed towards me.

Faced with danger, the human mind has three primitive responses: fight, flight, or freeze. My body chose the latter.

My legs turned to stone as the creature barrelled towards me. I braced myself for the impact, lifting the staff just in time to ward off the lion's fangs as the beast bit onto the weapon, nearly pushing me off my feet as I slid along the smooth limestone tiles of the square. The chimaera's black lips parted, and I saw a red haze forming inside its maw. I surrendered the staff and rolled sideways as a gust of fire burst from the lion's mouth, narrowly missing me.

The creature lurched forward, two halves of my scorched staff dropping uselessly to the floor.

The goat bleated, and I jumped out of reach as the chimaera's snake-head tail darted at me, its single fang dripping with venom. Why did it only have one fang? The lion growled ominously, its leg muscles bunching as it prepared to leap at me again.

It was three against one. I was completely outnumbered. I turned and ran.

I shot through the stone archway leading towards the harbour, pulling the tables and chairs of one of the outdoor restaurants over, hoping it would hamper the monster. They clattered as the creature stampeded through them. I sprinted straight into the sea and didn't stop to look back until the water had reached my chest.

The chimaera stood at the end of the pier, glaring at me. It roared and pawed at the ground, but it didn't come in after me. Again, saved by water. I should have drowned my fear ages ago.

Sudden laughter rippled through the air and all three of the chimaera's heads swivelled to the side. I followed the thing's gaze to see the couple from yesterday walking along the path against the outer walls, clutching on to each other and swerving unsteadily like they'd had too much to drink. They were oblivious to the danger a few feet away from them.

Adrenaline spurted through my veins. A flash of white and I was next to the chimaera on the dock. The goat's head bleated and, finally realising the creature had a pattern just like Nadiya did, I ducked beneath the snapping snake-tail and slapped my hand against the chimaera's flank. The lion roared as the light blinded me again.

The first thing I saw was the ground below, far below, as I teetered on a ledge on top of one of the wall's defensive towers. My arms windmilled as I tried to regain my balance, and I planted my feet firmly on the stone ridge.

The chimaera was not so lucky. It hung in the air for a moment, almost cartoonishly, just long enough for the snake's head to strike and latch onto my arm, its fang piercing painfully into my skin. I cried out in agony as horror rippled through me like a tsunami, threatening to drown me. Then gravity claimed it and the chimaera plummeted to the ground. The snake's head ripped out of my arm, leaving its fang behind.

I nearly toppled off the tower behind it, but I steadied myself and jumped from the ledge and onto the rooftop floor of the tower. I looked down to see the chimaera sprawled out on the rocks below, narrowly missing the decline that would have sent it tumbling into a busy street.

Amari was going to be furious that I had killed the creature.

I gasped as the chimaera stirred. Slowly, it

pushed itself to its feet. The tail dangled limply as it shook its other heads. It whimpered before limping down the slope. It had survived the fall, but it was injured.

I had to follow it. I had to catch it somehow, before it could hurt anyone.

I shook my head. The world suddenly seemed a little shaky. I placed a hand on a parapet to help steady me, but it didn't help. My vision blurred. My arm throbbed where the snake had bitten me. My legs gave in, and I slumped to the ground.

Nadiya. I needed to warn Nadiya. The chimaera would return to its lair now to lick its wounds and recover. It would find her there. She needed to be warned.

I tried to crawl, but my entire body was shaking and my head was pounding like Hephaestus at his anvil. I turned onto my back, gazing up at the sky. The stars twinkled shyly before they slowly faded into blackness.

※※※

"Ambrose." My name was a lullaby, a sing-song word filled with nonsense. The voice was sweet, almost familiar, a caress. "Ambrose."

Moss green eyes filled my vision. Sarah smiled down at me, her scent a citrusy longing that ached in my chest. Freckles were spattered like constellations across her cheeks. Her eyes faded into endless sapphire pools, scarlet hair cascading like a fiery waterfall, tickling across my face. Caitlynn? Laughter bubbled.

"Ambrose." The voice was filled with yearning now, with a need so desperately ravenous it threatened to consume me. Blue turned to grey, her touch cold as frost. Hatred stabbed icicles down my spine. Don't let her touch me! I struggled, but she held me fast.

"Ambrose!" she said, more urgently this time. The face sharpened into hard angles, a strong cheekbone, a bold nose, dark brown eyes.

I blinked.

"You're alright, Ambrose. You're alright." Nadiya held me fast until I quieted down, slumping back into bed. I swallowed. It tasted like something had crawled into my mouth and died. Where was I?

"You're in my house," Nadiya said. "You're safe." I hadn't realised I'd spoken the question aloud.

Nadiya. The chimaera! I had to stop it!

I tried to struggle upright again, but she pressed me down onto my back again. She sat down in a chair beside my bed. I blinked again, the room slowly coming into focus. A bedside lamp cast a warm glow around Nadiya's loft room. How did I get here?

"Just take it easy. You had me worried for a while, but you're stronger than you look. You'll pull through."

"What..." I swallowed, trying to work some moisture back into my mouth. "What happened?" Nadiya handed me a cup of cold water. I gulped it down like someone who'd been lost in the desert for three days.

"I'm guessing the chimaera's snake head bit you. You were lucky I found you when I did. The poison had run through your bloodstream by then. Nasty stuff. If I'd been a few minutes later..." She pursed her lips into a thin line.

I gave a dusty laugh. "Told you I was lucky."

She grunted. "So you did."

I slowly pushed myself into an upright position. My left arm was bandaged and felt a little numb, and bruises covered my aching body, but that was hardly the chimaera's fault. My stomach grumbled loudly. I was suddenly starving.

Nadiya reached over to the nightstand and handed me a bowl of something brown and steaming. My mouth watered as the smell hit my nostrils.

"It's goulash," Nadiya said as I tucked in, smacking my lips in pleasure. "My mother's recipe. Good for curing almost anything, including chimaera poisoning."

I chuckled and watched a smile flicker across my hostess' lips. "How did you find me?" I asked between mouthfuls. It was the tastiest stew I had ever eaten in my life. Simple and hardy, not like the fancy stuff my mother served.

"You disappeared on me. Again." Nadiya didn't hide the hint of exasperation in her voice. "I knew you'd get yourself in trouble without me, so I hastened back to town. I was about halfway back when I heard something crashing through the bushes. I hid just in time, and I saw the creature limping back towards the cave. Whatever you'd done, you'd injured it badly. My first instinct was to follow it back to its lair and make an end to it while it was down, but then I realised if it was in that kind of state, you must be worse off."

I nodded, still slurping my stew. It was a fair assumption. I was just surprised that she'd decided I was more important than the chimaera.

"Luckily, the creature had left a trail that was easy to follow," Nadiya continued. "I found the place where it had fallen off the tower, but there was no sign of you. Then I realised you were probably still on the tower. And so you were, white as a winter's morning and looking like Marzanna had already come for you. Luckily —" She paused, frowning. "There's that word again. I'm beginning to think there might be something to it, as you say." She cleared her throat. "Luckily, you were close to the Apothecary Museum, and I happen to know a bit of herb lore. I broke in, got the supplies I needed, and managed to get them down your throat before it was too late."

I gulped. "You broke into the museum? I'm grateful, but I wouldn't want you to get into trouble."

Nadiya waved my concerns away. "Don't worry. The curator is a friend of mine. In fact, Sergei helped me to haul you down from the tower and back to my house."

"Thank you," I said, suddenly feeling all warm and grateful and awkward. "I owe you my life."

Before it could get too sentimental, Nadiya stood up and took the bowl from me. "You would have done the same for me," she said. "I'll leave you to your rest. Call me when you feel a bit better."

"And the chimaera?"

"We have time. It will be resting too, now."

"Alright," I said, yawning. "Hey, Nadiya… What's that fang you have around your neck?" I nearly cracked my jaw as I yawned again.

Nadiya didn't answer, and there was something in the way she was looking at me… My eyelids felt like Atlas himself wouldn't be able to hold them up and my head seemed wrapped in cotton wool. Had she put something in the goulash to make me sleep? I wanted to ask, but my tongue wouldn't cooperate, and my bed was so warm, and then the world slowly faded into darkness again.

⌘⌘⌘

I came to with a start. The room was pitch black; not even starlight came in through the slanted window. I stumbled out of bed, flexing my bandaged arm. It throbbed a little, but it wasn't too bad. I had a sharp taste in my mouth. Had Nadiya really drugged my food? Why would she do that?

I blundered around in the dark, pulling some clothes on and slipping my feet into my lucky trainers. I dug around my bag until I found Amari's whistle and put it around my neck, just in case.

"Nadiya!" I called, stumbling downstairs. No response. The apartment was empty.

A sense of foreboding washed over me. Had she gone to confront the chimaera without me? I could think of no other reason why she would have drugged me. But why go without me? And how long had she been gone?

I hefted the trapdoor open and descended into the training room. I flicked the light on. Sure enough, her *rogatina* was gone, and the gladiator's net was hanging in its place on the wall.

It could only mean one thing: she was going to kill it.

I looked at the assortment of weapons, all pointy, all deadly. What I really wanted was a fire extinguisher. Not having one to hand, I grabbed the net instead. It would have to do.

"Come on, don't let me down now," I murmured, my heart racing in anticipation. I said the Word, pumping my fist into the air as a white light whisked me off.

The full moon illuminated the hillside just outside the chimaera's lair. There was no sign of Nadiya, but she could be in the cave already. I scrunched up my nose at the smell wafting from inside. I hesitated as a rumbling noise broke the still evening air. It sounded like boulders cascading down a mountainside.

Carefully, I entered the cave. It was dark inside, the light from the moon just enough to cast eerie shadows against the rocks. Could I risk turning on my mobile phone's light? The rumbling was louder in here. I waited for my eyes to adjust to the gloom.

Slowly, I started discerning shapes from the shadows. I could just make out the chimaera's bulk at the back of the cave, the source of the rumbling. It was asleep, the lion's head resting on its two front paws, the goat's head laying to one side on its back, snoring like someone suffering from sinusitis. The snake-headed tail was curled up, its crimson tongue occasionally darting out, tasting the air.

It looked so peaceful. Without the threat of a horrific death looming over me, I could almost appreciate the creature's odd beauty. There was a certain strange symmetry to its form, in the raw power of the lion and the silky softness of the goat's coat. I wasn't too fond of the snake, but hey, no one's perfect. As I watched the chimaera breathe deeply in passive slumber, I realised it wasn't a monster at all. In fact, the only reason I had ever seen it attack was because it had been provoked first – at the beach cave, earlier today in town, even back in Rome.

Was it possible that Amari was right? That this creature actually needed protection from us?

What had happened to the tooth the snake had left in my arm?

My head snapped back to the shadows as gravel crunched. I squinted and recognised Nadiya by the shape of the *rogatina* strapped to her back. She was kneeling with one knee on the ground, an old-fashioned rifle in her hands, the kind you'd see John Wayne protecting the Wild West with. Her eyes were trained down the gun's sightline, aimed straight at the sleeping beast.

"Don't do it," I whispered hoarsely.

Nadiya jumped at the sound of my voice. The

chimaera growled as it lumbered to its feet, all three heads fully awake. Nadiya swore, shooting me a look that promised I'd be next, before quickly aiming at the creature and pulling the trigger. The bullet hit the chimaera's tough hide with a loud thud and fell uselessly to the ground. Fire erupted from the lion's throat and I threw my body against Nadiya, shoving her to the ground as heat sizzled past us.

"You idiot!" Nadiya yelled, pushing me off her. "Do you want to get us killed?"

"It doesn't have to be this way!" I shouted back, and then scrambled out of the way as the creature swiped the gun out of Nadiya's hand with its massive claw. She ducked and rolled out of its way and when she came to her feet, her knife-edged spear was in her hands. With a wordless battle cry, she charged at the chimaera.

"Nadiya, no!" I shouted, but she either didn't hear me or chose not to. The goat's head bleated and the snake-head tail lashed out, but Nadia batted it away with her *rogatina*, before lunging for the centre of the chimaera's torso. The creature dodged her thrust clumsily, and she sliced a long bloody gash across its chest. It roared, fire blazing again, as it shied away from her.

I grabbed her arm as she lifted her spear again, but she shook me off and seized the net I still carried. She tossed it over the chimaera and stood back, watching with a satisfied smirk as it struggled in the entanglement. It opened its mouth to let its fiery breath loose, but all the fight seemed to have gone out of it, even its fire was depleted. Finally, it slumped to the ground, whimpering.

Nadiya yelled in triumph, darting forward. With one well-aimed swipe, she sliced the snake head off the chimaera's tail. The creature howled in agony. I watched, horrified, as blood spurted from the stump.

"Enough!" I shouted, wresting the *rogatina* from Nadiya's grip. "You've won. Let me call Amari so she can take it off our hands."

"You don't get it, do you, Ambrose?" Nadiya said, glaring at me. "This monster doesn't deserve to live. It needs to be exterminated. You may not be man enough to do it, but I am!"

She tried to grab her knife-edged spear from me, but I held fast. I planted my feet firmly, blocking the chimaera with my body. She screeched in frustration, a sound more banshee than human, and swooped towards the floor. She lifted the rifle up and pointed it at me.

"You're not serious," I said, laughing in disbelief.

"Step away from that monster."

"The chimaera's not a monster, but I'm beginning to think you are." Nadiya's face turned a dangerous shade of red. "Is that the snake's fang around your neck? Is that why it was in town earlier? Looking for you?"

In answer, Nadiya cocked the gun. "Last chance, Ambrose."

I stared at her. A sneer was carved deep into her square jaw. She wasn't going to give up.

And neither was I.

I dived for the chimaera, slapping my hand against its flank for the third time in so many days as I said the Word. A bullet whistled past my head just as the blinding light carried us away.

Nadiya's frustrated scream still rang in my ears as the chimaera and I landed on the pebbled beach at Lokrum Island. The creature growled as it tried to get up, still entangled in the net.

"Easy now," I said, putting the rogatina down and lifting my arms in what I hoped was a comforting gesture. "I'm not here to hurt you. I want to help."

The chimaera settled, watching me warily. Slowly, trying not to startle it, I took my shirt off. Then I carefully lifted a corner of the net and wrapped the mutilated tail with my shirt, trying to stanch the bleeding. The goat's head bleated pitifully.

Still keeping a close eye on the chimaera, I removed the rest of net. The creature stayed unmoving, watching me in return. I tossed the net to one side and lifted my palm up, inching it towards the lion's head, ready to pull it back instantly if it showed any sign of aggression. It sniffed at my fingers and I nearly ran for it, but it seemed docile, so I placed my hand on its mane, stroking it softly.

"You've had a rough time, haven't you, Stavros?" I asked, giving it the first Greek name that popped into my head. "You just want to go back home, don't you?"

The chimaera leaned into me, placing his lion's head against my chest and almost pushing me over with his weight. I steadied myself and kept stroking his mane, smiling in surprise as he started purring softly.

We stayed like this for a few minutes, and then I extricated myself and walked to the water's edge, watching the false dawn glowing on the horizon. If I let the chimaera go, there was every chance that Nadiya could find him again, or that he might hurt someone, whether on purpose or in self-defence. The Repository really was the best place for him. Amari would make sure he was safe and comfortable there.

I pulled the silver whistle out from around my neck and blew on it. As always, no sound could be heard, but I knew Amari would come. I waited for the now-familiar flash of white light, but nothing happened. She was probably asleep right now. I'd give her another few minutes.

Stavros gave a low moan, and I walked closer again. He was licking his chest where Nadiya had sliced him with her spear. The fur was matted with blood.

"I'm sorry she hurt you. *We…*" I corrected. I was just as much to blame for his injuries. The goat bleated, and I rubbed my hand along his silky neck. "I'm going to take you someplace safe. They'll take good care of you there."

Where was Amari? I blew the whistle again and waited a few minutes, but still no response. Was she really that sound a sleeper? I pulled my mobile phone out of my pocket and dialled my father's number. He answered almost immediately.

"Ambrose?" his voice sounded tinny. Reception wasn't very good inside the mountain.

"I'm trying to get hold of Amari," I said without preamble. "I have something for her to come and pick up."

"You have the chimaera? Well done, boy!" Father sounded more excited than I'd expected. And surprisingly alert for this time of the morning, especially since he was an hour behind me. "Send me your location and I'll send someone to come pick it up."

"Okay…" I hesitated. "Is everything alright there?"

"It's fine. We'll talk later." The call ended abruptly.

Strange. Still, maybe Amari was preoccupied with something else. I quickly texted him my coordinates.

That done, I sat down next to the chimaera again, leaning my back against his body for some warmth. My shirt was soaked through, but it looked like the tail had stopped bleeding, at least.

I wondered what must be going through the creature's mind, or minds, now that one of his heads was gone. The loss must be indescribable.

An hour or so later, just as the real dawn was painting the sky a rosy pink, the sound of helicopter blades sliced through the air. Stavros lifted his head warily, the hackles on his back rising as the aircraft drew closer. Wind whipped as the unmarked heavy-lift helicopter, large enough to carry cargo, landed on the shingles of the little beach.

"It'll be alright," I said as a small growl rumbled through the chimaera's chest. We both climbed stiffly to our feet, and I retrieved the *rogatina* as four men jumped from the helicopter, armed with assault rifles and grim expressions. I placed a soothing hand on Stavros' mane again as the leader of the group walked up to us.

"Are you Ambrose Davids?" He had the bearing and the buzz-cut of a military man, although there was no insignia on his black bomber jacket. He eyed the spear I carried with professional curiosity.

"Who's asking?"

"Your father sent us. We're here to pick up an asset."

An asset? I didn't like the sound of that.

"Put your guns down," I said. "You're scaring him, and believe me, you don't want this creature feeling threatened."

The man hesitated, but then lowered his gun and signalled for the rest of the men to do so too.

"We have a cage in the back of the helicopter for the asset. I am authorised to use force to get it inside."

"That won't be necessary," I said, feeling a muscle tighten in my jaw. I turned towards the chimaera again. His teeth were bared in a snarl. I

138

deliberately placed myself between him and the man with the gun, filling the creature's field of vision. "Trust me," I said gently. "It may not look like it, but these men are here to help you."

Stavros' lion eyes were golden and very bright, and slowly the snarl faded. He lowered his head, and I placed my hand on the back of his neck again. I turned back to the man. "Lead on."

Slowly, I escorted the limping chimaera towards the helicopter. He growled when we passed underneath the whirling blades and up the loading ramp and snarled when he saw the cage, but either because he trusted me or because he was just too tired to care anymore, he let me coax him inside. The man shut the gate and slammed a lock on it.

Those golden eyes were filled with sadness as they stared at me through the bars. The goat was silent, and the dead tail hung limply. I swallowed back a lump in my throat. I couldn't help but feel I had betrayed him, even though I knew it was for the best.

"Get this man a jacket," the leader said, and I gratefully accepted one from one of his comrades. "Let's head out. This way, Ambrose."

"No thanks, I'll stay here." I sat down by the cage, my hand touching one of the chimaera's paws.

"Are you sure? We have a long flight ahead of us."

"I'm sure," I said. I'd persuaded Stavros to get into this cage. The least I could do was stay with him until we arrived at the Repository.

As the helicopter lifted into the air, I looked out the window at the cobalt waters of the Adriatic Sea, sparkling in the rising sun. The orange tile roofs and stone buildings of Dubrovnik lay like a jewel below me, beautiful and austere.

My fingers tightened around the rogatina. I had come here looking for a monster and, instead, had learned that it wasn't as simple as that. The chimaera wasn't evil, and neither was Nadiya. A thin grey line straddled the border between the realms of right and wrong. It was all just a matter of perspective.

I looked at Stavros again. He was sprawled out in the space the cage afforded him, fast asleep. It had been an exhausting night for all of us. I followed his example and rested my chin against my chest, closing my eyes as the helicopter carried us to safety.

※※※

Father was waiting for us when the helicopter landed on a helipad set high in the mountains. The heavy oak doors of the Repository stood wide open, welcoming us. An icy wind blasted in as the helicopter's loading ramp lowered and the men started pushing the cage out. I shot Stavros a reassuring look, before climbing out to greet my father.

"Magnificent!" Father exclaimed as he shook my hand. "How did you capture it?"

"I'll tell you later. Stavros is badly hurt. He needs medical attention."

Father frowned as he inspected the chimaera through the cage bars. "You named it?" he asked, distractedly. "Jupiter's beard! What happened to its tail? Never mind. Bring him in, boys. Holding cell fifteen. It's going to need a salve for that wound on its chest, but the healing properties of this place are remarkable. It'll be right as rain in no time. Except the tail, of course. I doubt that's going to grow back."

I put my hand through the bars, ignoring the hiss of surprise escaping Father's lips, and rubbed the chimaera's mane. "They're going to take good care of you here, Stavros. Don't worry. I'll come visit you whenever I can."

The chimaera's chest rumbled, but he was too weak to do much more. I watched with a lump in my throat as they pushed the cage out of view.

"Come on, my boy," Father said, putting an arm around my shoulder. "Let's go get you a cup of coffee. You look dreadful. That thing must have put up quite a fight."

Instead of taking me to the kitchen, Father led me down a long corridor and ushered me through the heavy oak door that led into Amari's study. I looked around the familiar room. It felt different. The fire wasn't blazing in the hearth and the enormous mahogany desk, usually so neat and meticulously arranged, was littered with pieces of paper, all scrawled in Father's tight handwriting. A coffee machine stood on a table in one corner, filling the room with its heavenly aroma. Father walked over to it and poured us each a steaming cup of the bitter brew.

I leaned the *rogatina* against a bookshelf and accepted the drink.

"That's an interesting weapon you have there."

"Not mine, although I know first-hand how sharp it is. And so does Stavros."

"So, the tail…?"

"Probably being harvested as we speak," I said, my voice almost as acidic as the coffee. I should have made the connection between Nadiya and her friend Sergei earlier. "There's an apothecary in Dubrovnik that I suspect might be peddling creature parts under the guise of 'traditional remedies'. Nadiya, Amari's contact in the city, is his supplier."

141

"Interesting…" Father said, sipping on his coffee, not as alarmed by this news as I'd thought he'd be.

I glanced around the room again. I couldn't shake the feeling that something wasn't right. I noticed that the picture of Diana, the stern blonde Keeper from about a century ago, was no longer hanging on the wall behind Amari's desk.

"Father, where's Amari?"

"About that…" He put his cup down on the mahogany desk, pulled the chair out, and sat down in it. His lips twitched, but he kept his face neutral. "Amari isn't here anymore."

The news hit me like a blow to the stomach.

Of course, it all made sense now. The changes to her study, the lack of response when I'd summoned her, the goons who came to collect us by helicopter. I looked at Father, relaxing back in her chair and kicking his feet up onto her desk, dreading the words I knew he was about to say.

They still came as a shock when he uttered them, and it felt like my entire world had suddenly been turned upside down when he confirmed my suspicions.

"You're looking at the new Keeper of Exotic Animals now."

PART 7.5

KEEPER'S BANE

Amari, the Keeper of Exotic Animals, felt a little overwhelmed.

For the first time since she had accepted her post, the shouts and grunts of many people echoed through the mountain-carved tunnels of the Repository. Bellowing cries mingled with the sounds of hooves clopping on the stone floor, leaves rustled in non-existent breezes, and somewhere a five-headed elephant trumpeted loudly.

At the sound, the little griffon in Amari's arms squirmed nervously, pressing himself tightly against her body. "There, there, Caerus, don't be afraid. You'll be with your family soon," Amari said, stroking the crest of blue feathers sticking up from his leonine head. The cub settled down, purring softly and Amari wished she could calm her own anxiety so easily.

"Miss Kerubo." One of the men who had been assisting with the transportation of creatures from the Colosseum walked up to her, wiping a slimy substance from his hands onto his already grimy pants. "All the creatures are in the holding cells. The rest is up to you now."

"Thank you, Councilmember Ravel. I appreciate the Council's help tonight."

The man's grin split his dark face in two. She suppressed a wince as he slapped her enthusiastically on the shoulder. "There is hope yet, *n'est-ce pas?* So many in one night! Imagine what is still out there!"

Amari nodded. "Indeed."

She couldn't help but wonder how many of these blood moon markets were still being held. Diana, the Keeper whose portrait hung in Amari's study, had made it her life's work to put an end to the illegal sale of mythical creatures. She had hunted the sellers down until the practice had died out, or so the Council had thought. Judging by the amount of people who had attended the event in Rome earlier tonight, they had been sorely mistaken.

"You will come celebrate with us?"

Amari stiffened. No one from the Council had ever invited her to join in any celebrations. She couldn't think of anything more awkward than partying with people who signed her pay cheque. Before she could tactfully decline, a booming voice interrupted her.

"This is no time to celebrate! It's a disgrace! Much worse than I expected!"

Councilmember Ravel shot her a look of commiseration before retreating to join the rest of the members of the Elder Council waiting for him. Amari would normally escort them towards the West Gate from where they would use a Word to travel back to their respective destinations, but tonight they would have to find the way themselves. She had more urgent things to attend to.

Sighing, Amari turned towards the centaur striding towards her. "It's only temporary, Commander Equustos." The Keeper stood her ground as the horse-man halted in front of her, the human half of his armoured torso towering head, shoulders and chest above her. His nostrils flared as he glared down at her.

Amari was not so easily intimidated. "Each of these creatures will get their own tailor-made enclosure, unless they'd be better off in an existing

147

one," she said. She glanced towards the five-headed airavata, looking even larger than it truly was in the confined space. "Their stay in the holding cells will be as short as I can possibly make it."

Commander Equustos folded his arms across his bronze Roman breastplate. "I don't like the sound of this word – enclosure." His heavy Italian accent twisted his speech with scorn. "How do I know it is any better than this – this prison! – you're currently confining them in?"

A nervous mew sounded from the griffon cub in her arms, and Amari gently stroked his head again. "Come," she said to the centaur. "I'll show you."

Commander Equustos snorted, but she heard his hooves clop on the polished stone floor as she led him out of the tunnel and towards the Repository's main hold.

"I hope the stairs won't be a problem," she said as she held the heavy iron door open. The centaur passed through, pausing on the landing as he looked out at the pens below them. His frown deepened. "They're much bigger than they look from here," Amari quickly reassured him. She hurried down the steep steel stairs as the centaur awkwardly clomped down after her.

"This way," she said, leading him past the enclosures until she found the door she was looking for. A quick Word opened the lock, and she ushered the centaur in, pulling the door shut behind her again.

An icy wind tugged at her curls as she stood on the edge of a narrow ledge running along the side of a craggy mountain. A great plain stretched out far below them, with fluffy white clouds casting enormous shadows across the verdant grasslands.

Caerus chirped excitedly and squirmed in her

arms. "Go on," Amari said, lifting him up. His little wings fluttered as he leaped into the air, bobbing clumsily up and down like a blundering bumblebee.

An eagle's cry ripped through the air, and suddenly a flash of white streaked towards them. Commander Equustos reared up onto his hind legs, his hand on the pommel of the sword strapped to his side, as an enormous white griffon landed in front of them, its lion's tail whipping from side to side and the blue feathers on its crest spread intimidatingly.

"It's alright, Apollo," Amari said calmly. "He's with me. And look who we brought."

The mighty griffon's stance relaxed as the centaur stood down, and he squawked happily as Caerus fluttered towards him. He nuzzled the cub affectionately, a proud father finally reunited with his stolen son. Amari blinked back tears as she saw the little griffon tuck himself under one of Apollo's wings.

The older griffon nodded majestically at Amari, silently thanking her. Then it lifted its enormous wings and propelled itself into the air. The little cub flapped eagerly by its side as they returned to their nest.

The Keeper turned towards the centaur. "Well, Commander," she said, sweeping her arms out to encompass the vast expanse stretching out below them. "Will this do?"

Commander Equustos rubbed a hand across his clean-shaven chin as he surveyed the scenery. "Where are we?"

"Inside the Repository. Each enclosure is a fold in reality designed specifically to suit its inhabitants. Griffons are creatures of both land and sky, and they need crosswinds for flying, a mountainous lair, and extensive hunting grounds.

As you can see, their enclosure provides them with everything they could ever want, and they're safe here from anyone that might want to harm them."

The centaur nodded. "A fold... Yes, the Green Grove is a similar construct."

"I expected as much," Amari said. "Ambrose wouldn't tell me the exact location of the Grove, but I assumed it would be the same if it were hidden somewhere in Rome."

Commander Equustos coughed. "Yes, well. The Grove's whereabouts are best kept hidden. I am glad to know that I can trust Ambrose Davids to keep a secret." He looked across his shoulder to the steel gate embedded in the mountainside. "What happens when the creatures leave their enclosures?"

Amari blinked. "Why would they leave?"

The centaur frowned. "Do you not value your own freedom, Keeper? Do you never leave the confinement of this mountain?"

"Of course," Amari shrugged. "My duties sometimes require me to travel outside the Repository. But I'm not in any danger from the outside world. No one is going to misuse me for their own gain outside the Repository."

Commander Equustos lifted an eyebrow. "No one?"

Amari grimaced. "Well, I can take care of myself if they try."

"And you think we can't?" the centaur rumbled, his tail swishing irritably.

"Frankly, no," Amari said, folding her arms across her chest. "The world outside has changed so rapidly in the last few years that most mythical creatures haven't adapted to survive in this modern age. I commend the Army of the Green Grove for persevering in Rome, Commander, but think about it... Can you imagine a unicorn going unmolested in that great city's streets? She would be hunted mercilessly, her head displayed as a trophy on someone's wall and her horn ground into a powder that may or may not improve someone's love life. They'd use her blood to cure hangovers! Her skin would be a rug on someone's floor!"

Heat flushed through Amari's body, and she took a deep breath to calm her suddenly soaring blood pressure. "In here," she continued, her words clipped, "she's safe from anyone who'd want to harm her. I see to that."

The centaur's gaze was contemplative as he considered her response. Then, he said: "I've seen enough. You can send me back to Rome now."

Amari opened the enclosure gate and the centaur stepped through, his face unreadable as she locked the door behind them again. "Where would you like me to drop you off?"

"You will not catch me that easily, Keeper," Commander Equustos replied gruffly. "Return me to the Colosseum. I can make my way from there."

"As you wish." She was about to say the Word that would whisk the centaur away when he interrupted her.

"One more thing. I believe your heart is true, Keeper, and I am satisfied with these... enclosures, for now. But they are no replacement for true freedom. I will send a representative to ensure the suitability of the accommodation provided to the creatures currently inside the holding cells, while I discuss the terms of their rehabilitation with the Council."

A flicker of annoyance ran through Amari. Why did the centaur not see that the Repository was the best way to protect mythical creatures? They simply wouldn't survive outside these fortress walls. She tried to keep the irritation from her voice. "If you insist."

"I do. And Keeper…"

Amari paused again.

Commander Equustos offered her a sad smile. "Keeping us locked away is not the only answer, and we are not as helpless as you think. At some point, the world will have to learn that lesson."

Amari shook her head slightly. The Green Grove must be completely isolated from the real world if the centaur could believe that. The Word floated across her lips, summoning a searing white light. When her vision returned, she was alone.

⋇ ⋇ ⋇

Fireflies twinkled like little enchanted stars in the grove. Beyond the trees, a brook murmured quietly, just out of sight. Amari kicked off her shoes, her toes curling in the soft, dewy grass, and inhaled deeply, savouring the sweet perfume of night-blooming lilies, their white petals lifted towards the full moon as if in adoration.

A sense of peace washed over Amari as Una trotted into the clearing. The pure white unicorn was almost luminous in the darkness, her single silver horn glimmering like a forgotten treasure. She whinnied as she came closer, dipping her head in welcome. Amari rubbed her hands down Una's velvety coat, breathing the mythical creature's scent in – a mixture of apples, fresh grass, and something indefinable that Amari liked to think of as pure magic.

The Keeper's fingers brushed over the small scars left behind when an intruder had stolen the unicorn's blood a few months ago and her brows furrowed. She'd made her peace with the culprit since then, but it still rankled that something like that had happened on her watch. Una was the world's last unicorn, but she was also Amari's friend. She clenched her fist. It would never happen again, not while she was the Keeper.

"You know everything I do is to keep you safe, don't you?" Amari whispered fiercely.

Una neighed softly and Amari thought she detected a hint of sadness in the sound. After all these years on her own, the unicorn must be just as lonely as she herself was.

It was suddenly all Amari could do to hold back tears. If only she could trust the rest of the world not to harm Una. If only they could leave the mountain fortress behind and return some magic to the world.

But she'd been in the company of myths long enough to know when something couldn't be believed.

A tear trickled down Amari's cheek. Una nudged her gently, and Amari threw her arms around the unicorn's neck. She stood like this for a few minutes, breathing deeply. Her fingers tangled in Una's silky mane as she listened to the unicorn's steady heartbeat.

Then she pulled away and wiped the tears from her cheeks.

"Thank you, Una," she said. "I always feel better after seeing you." It was true. It renewed her sense of purpose.

The unicorn snorted, giving Amari another affectionate nudge, and then she turned and disappeared back into the shadows of the trees. The grove felt empty without her.

Amari slipped her shoes back on and locked the enclosure gate behind her. Tomorrow, she would start housing her newest residents. They were victims of mankind's greed and selfishness, just like Una's kind had been. Amari owed them some peace and happiness.

No matter what the centaur might think, this was their home now.

✕✕✕

After the morning rounds, Amari made her way to the holding cells, armed with a knapsack full of treats and a notebook and pen. The battle at the Colosseum had been nothing but chaos, and afterwards she'd been too busy with the logistics of moving the new acquisitions into the Repository to take a tally of the creatures. Her priorities now were to find out what exactly was in the holding cells, get them fed and reassured that they were safe, and then figure out how best to house them.

A cacophonous trumpeting greeted her when she stopped in front of the first cell. "I remember you," Amari said, taking a quick step backwards as the five-headed elephant slammed into the gate, five sets of sharp tusks thrusting through the bars. The gate rattled, but held fast, as Amari knew it would. She'd sealed it with a Word – no amount of physical force would budge it.

"There now, boy," Amari said in a soothing voice. "Quiet now, hush." The lights dangling from the ceiling flickered and Amari drew in a breath as an ominous rumbling rolled down the corridor. She remembered the airavata summoning lightning in the Colosseum and the hairs on her arms lifted as the air crackled with electricity.

Slowly, she reached into her satchel and pulled out a small bushel of bananas. The airavata's many eyes lit up and all five of its pure white trunks reached for the fruit. Amari let the creature have it, smiling as the hairy snouts tickled her hands and arms.

When the last banana had been claimed, Amari extended her hand towards one of the trunks, but the airavata quickly retreated, pressing itself into a corner of the cell, one of its heads watching her as the rest set about devouring the fruit. Amari clicked her tongue in frustration. It was going to take some time to win the creature's trust.

She pulled out her notebook and added the creature to the top of a list. She tapped her pen against her cheek as she watched one tusk fending off the others trying to get at the last banana. Five heads, but one stomach. How much food would this creature need? She had a feeling elephants, even the non-mythical variety, ate a generous amount – more than she could sustainably keep up with if she had to feed it by hand. She made a note to research elephant eating habits and to check her inventory. It would probably be a good idea to build the airavata's enclosure first, even if just to keep costs down. And besides, her largest holding cell was really much too small for this creature.

She moved on to the next cell, where a voluptuous young woman clutched onto the barred door, watching Amari with anxious eyes. Her long red hair hung in greasy strands and her waxen skin had a greyish tinge to it. Behind her, Amari could see three more women looking just as haggard, one of them nursing a badly burnt arm. That one glared at her with undisguised hatred, and Amari grimaced. That must be the nymph that had attacked Ambrose.

The redhead was clearly a naiad, a river nymph, while the wounded one and her wispy friend with the hazel eyes were dryads, or wood nymphs. The fourth one had a stocky build and a sturdiness that could only belong to an oread, a mountain nymph.

Amari quickly jotted the tally down in her notebook.

"What's going to happen to us?" the naiad by the doorway asked, her bottom lip trembling.

Amari wondered what had broken the nymph's spirit. She hadn't even attempted to seduce the Keeper. Amari tried not to take that personally, although she did wonder if she should do something about her hair... She shook her head, returning her attention to the nymphs. It was just a sign of how these women had been mistreated.

Amari tucked her notebook and pen into her satchel and unlocked the door. Immediately, a shaft of wood shot towards her. The Keeper sidestepped it just as vines lunged for her feet and a stalagmite sprouted from the ceiling, plunging down towards her. Amari lifted a hand, not even bothering to say the Words aloud. The rock fissure crumbled to dust, raining pebbles around her, and the vines dried up and withered to dust.

"Enough!" Amari said as the nymphs cried out, their movements suddenly frozen as an invisible force gripped them. "I'd ask you not to damage the ceiling further," Amari said with a pointed look at the oread. "You know how much weight we have on top of us right now."

The mountain nymph's cheeks coloured, and she dropped her gaze to the floor.

"You wanted to know what's going to happen to you?" Amari turned towards the naiad. "I'm going to take you for tea. But only if you behave yourselves." The nymph's eyes widened. "I will release you and you can walk with me, or –" She stared at the wood nymphs. "I will put you to sleep, and you will wake up somewhere else. Either way, you'll be safe. I know you have no reason to trust me, but I'm asking you to give me a chance. Can you do that?"

The nymphs glanced at each other until they each finally nodded. Amari stood aside as they filed out of the gate, watching warily for any sign that they might attack again. The last nymph to exit the cell was the dryad with the scorched arm.

"I'm sorry about that," Amari said, eyeing the tender skin. "You were attacking my friend and I had to react fast. As soon as you're settled, I'll bring a salve that will help it heal."

"Where are you taking us?" the nymph responded, her dark eyes clouded with distrust. Amari noticed patches of hardened skin on her neck and arms, almost like bits of tree bark, as if the woman were armouring herself for protection.

"You'll see," Amari replied, before a flash of blinding light deposited all five of them in front of an enclosure door in the main cave. "This way," Amari beckoned, opening the door and ushering them inside.

The nymphs hesitated, clearly reluctant to enter another cell. A warm gust wafted through the door, bringing with it the scent of grass fresh after the rain, of honeysuckle and spruce, cedar, and pine. The dryads visibly perked up, their shoulders lifting and theirs backs straightening. Laughter drifted through the door as a bee buzzed past. The scorched dryad was the first to pass through the door, the others following closely on her heels.

Amari also stepped through and into the woods, her gaze immediately drawn towards another, much larger, group of women sitting by the banks of a burbling river running past the trees. Each woman held a porcelain cup in her hands, sitting around a makeshift table formed from twisted roots and vines and groaning under the weight of baked goods. The scent of honey and fruity tea filled the air.

The women cried out when they saw the newcomers, dropping their cups and running towards Amari and her group, welcoming them with excited squeals.

"Oh, you poor dears!"

"Come, have some tea. You'll feel so much better."

"Here, have a slice of cake. I baked it myself!"

The Keeper extricated herself from the group and took a few steps back, smiling as the nymphs herded the wide-eyed newcomers towards the festivities.

The naiad was the first to overcome her fear. With a little shriek, she jumped into the stream, water splashing all over the dryads. The oread dug her toes into the ground as a rumble shook underfoot, and suddenly a hill erupted on the other side of the river, pushing into the sky. The mountain nymph stretched her arms out and rolled her shoulders, as if stepping out of a small space, her lined face smoothing out into relief.

Raucous laughter flared and Amari saw a bottle of ouzo being passed around, the nymphs lavishly flavouring their tea with the strong spirits. The Keeper smiled and shook her head when they beckoned her to come join them. "Not today, ladies," she said. "Have fun."

She waved her goodbyes, stopped to pick a score of bright red apples from a nearby tree, and then stepped out of the enclosure and returned to the holding cells.

The airavata trumpeted loudly when it saw her and five trunks darted past the bars of its pen, sniffling at her arms, and trying to get into her satchel. Amari laughed as she pulled the apples out and fed them to the creature. Perhaps it wouldn't take that long to gain its trust, after all. She ran a hand up along one of its trunks, surprised at how hard the bristly hairs on its skin were, before pulling the inquisitive appendage out of her satchel and saying goodbye to the pale-skinned elephant.

Amari walked past the nymphs' empty cell to the next one, and a spike of panic shot through her heart. She dropped her satchel and sprinted towards the kitchen, wrenching open the larder and grabbing a jar of habanero chillies. Her breath came in ragged gasps by the time she slid to a halt in front of the cell again, her hands shaking as she struggled to unscrew the lid. Finally, the top popped off and she tossed the peppers into the cell.

She slumped against the cell door in relief as the congress of blue salamanders fell upon the chillies, their yellow stripes slowly turning a bright orange as the hot habaneros blazed inside them. When a little fire sparked in a corner of the cell, Amari breathed more freely and made a note to have more peppers delivered, even hotter if possible. She'd have to move the salamanders into an enclosure where they could bond with a new blaze before it was too late.

Homesickness gripped at Amari's heart when she saw the next cell's occupant. She recognised it immediately as a yale, a creature that had featured in many of the stories her grandmother had told her as a child. It looked like a black antelope, but with a tawny red mane and white tribal-like markings painted across its chest and back. Two curved tusks jutted out between its white lips and obsidian horns on its head glinted in the fluorescent light.

"We're both a long way from home, aren't we?" she said, stepping closer. Immediately the yale retreated and both its horns swivelled so that the pointy ends aimed at her like two sharpened spears. It bleated a warning, and Amari froze. "Okay, not friends yet, are we?"

Slowly, she reached into her satchel and pulled out a carrot. The yale shot her a disgusted look and she dropped the offending vegetable back into her pack. "Right... Not your thing." She tapped a finger against her cheek, digging deep through her memories for the fables from her youth.

"How about this?" She pulled a slab of meat from her bag, unwrapped the surrounding plastic, and dangled it in front of the door. The yale sniffed the air, suddenly much more interested. Amari tossed the meat into the cell and watched as the creature inched closer and nibbled at the slab's edges.

"Okay, one carnivorous antelope – check." Amari noted the creature down on her list. She would have to read up about it, since it didn't look entirely happy with its lunch. Perhaps she could use it as an excuse to go visit her *gogo* again...

She moved on to the next pen. It was empty. No, wait, something moved in the shadows at the back of the cell. Amari swore under her breath and clenched her eyes shut, gulping down breaths as her heartbeat drummed against her ribcage. Summoning her courage, she opened her eyes again.

A forked tongue flickered, and then the sinuous body of a snake moved into the light. Its body was as thick as Amari's thigh and, uncoiled, she guessed it must be almost twice her length. Its black scales shimmered with an iridescent purple sheen.

Amari's hands were clammy with sweat. "Lamia," she breathed, and averted her eyes as she felt the weight of the snake's purple-orbed scrutiny. She licked her lips, then reached into her satchel and pulled out another hunk of meat. "Here," she said, tossing it into the cell. The snake darted, lightning fast, and swallowed the meat in one gulp. Nauseated, Amari hurried on to the next cell.

An opalescent glow surrounded a beautiful white bird perched on one foot in the middle of the cell. It was as tall as a stork, with a short beak and long, spindly legs. Its ice-blue eyes fell on Amari and her shoulders loosened, the tension fading like mist before the morning sun. For a second, the Keeper wondered if she could make a nest for it in her study, before she caught herself and frowned at the idea.

"What are you, then?" she asked. She hadn't seen that telltale spark of sentience in its eyes, but it never hurt to ask. Mythical creatures were full of surprises.

The bird merely ruffled its feathers, sending firefly sparks floating in the air, then closed its eyes and seemed to fall asleep.

Amari dug into her satchel again, placing the last apple and a Tupperware box full of dead crickets just inside the cell. She'd find out later what the bird's tastes were.

She made a note of the last two acquisitions in her notebook and checked to make sure that the rest of the holding cells were empty. Apart from the nymphs, there were four new creatures within her care, as well as a bevy of blue salamanders she could easily relocate to another section of the existing fire salamander enclosure.

A good haul. The best she'd had in years.

Perhaps she could designate one of her Procurement Specialists to focus on sniffing out these blood moon markets, if the practice had taken root again despite Diana's best efforts. Better that the creatures should come to her here in the Repository than be sold off at auction to the highest bidder.

Amari walked towards the kitchen as she

contemplated this idea. It would have to be someone who could go deep undercover. Someone who had the right contacts and who could find leads to the sellers and then convincingly pose as a buyer. Giddiness washed over her at the thought of the influx of new residents this might bring to the Repository.

She grabbed a microwave meal from the fridge, heated it up and sat down at the kitchen table, a sixteen-seater remnant of a very different era in the Repository's history. She pulled her notebook out as she attacked her dinner – polenta and braised beef tonight – although Amari was too excited to pay much attention to the food. It was time to plan each new creature's enclosure.

She opened her notebook and went over the list one more time. As she wondered again what type of bird that last acquisition was, it suddenly occurred to her that there were no kitsunes in any of the holding cells.

Riku had sworn to her that the only reason he had infiltrated the Repository was because his mate was being held captive by Marco, the unscrupulous ex-Councilmember turned black market dealer. The little kitsune had pleaded with her to let him join Ambrose on his mission in Rome, but she had always refused, fearing that the two-tailed fox would either be recaptured, or inadvertently jeopardise Ambrose's assignment.

Now that she thought about it, she hadn't seen Riku in a few days. The kitsune was a shapeshifter, and wily enough not to be deterred by any of the enclosures' restraints. Certainly, nothing she had tried so far had kept him either inside his own compound or out of the others he wasn't supposed to get into.

As she finished her meal and did the washing up, she mulled that thought over. Just because she hadn't seen a two-tailed fox in the pens didn't mean there wasn't a kitsune hiding there in plain sight. The very idea triggered a headache in her right temple.

Wearily, she returned to the main cave. Inside Riku's enclosure, the setting sun painted the meadow in shades of orange and pink. A rabbit scurried past Amari and ducked into one of the burrows that dotted the grassy hillside, while a lark sang a warning somewhere out of sight.

"Riku!" Amari called, knowing already that the two-tailed fox wouldn't answer. The gentle breeze brought nothing but the scent of honeysuckle on the air.

She called again, but after a few minutes had passed with no response, Amari exited the enclosure. There was no point going in search of the kitsune. If Riku didn't want to be found, nothing short of a Word would uncover him. She didn't have to resort to that just yet.

The Keeper returned to her study and flopped down into the wingback chair in front of the fire. She pulled her mobile phone out and quickly texted Ambrose. It was a long shot, but perhaps Riku had taken matters into his own hands and had joined Ambrose without her consent.

Ambrose's response was quick.

-- *Sorry, no.* --

Amari clicked her tongue. This was what happened when you gave creatures too much free rein. Who knew what the kitsune was up to this time?

Since he'd arrived at the Repository, and they'd moved past the fact that he'd stolen creature parts and that she'd nearly killed him for it, Amari had grown rather fond of the crafty kitsune. He'd caused no end of good-natured mischief that had kept her on her toes, but he had a sense of honour that she found intriguing, and he was one of the few friends she had inside these mountain walls.

If only she knew what he was up to! If only there were a way that she could track him… Some Word perhaps…

Amari surged to her feet and walked over to the bookshelf, searching for something that could give her some ideas. Her eyes roved across the spines until she noticed a book from Diana's exotic collection, covered in blue silk and with embossed gold letters on its spine. Her heart fluttered when she read the title: Brahma's Creation: A Bestiary.

She pulled the book out, admiring the gilded flowers and intricate scrollwork embroidered on the cover. Carefully, Amari flicked through the pages. It was not the original – fortunately, since she'd never had the time or opportunity to study Sanskrit – but it was sufficient for her purposes.

She returned to her place by the fire with the book in her hands. It didn't take long to find the section she was looking for. There were no illustrations, but she recognised the airavata from its description immediately. The five-headed elephant was a named entity, revered in Hindu mythology as the mount of the sky god Indra. She wondered if the creature in her holding cell had ever borne anyone important.

Engrossed, she delved into the literature, until her eyes started drooping and the book slipped from her hands. The Keeper's breath came slow and steady as the fire in her study smouldered, ever-burning.

Amari glared at the mess surrounding her, her nose wrinkled in disgust. The putrid stench of rotten meat hung cloyingly in the air. She lifted a half-gnawed bone as long as her arm from the ground and grimaced as a viscous, gooey slime stuck to her hand.

"This is unacceptable, Ody," she said, turning to the creature hulking behind her. She lifted the bone as high as she could, making sure the cyclops couldn't miss it. "Who do you think is going to clean up this mess? Me?"

The giant covered his face with both hands, shoulders slumping. He moaned something unintelligible, a muffled rumble so low Amari barely heard it. He lifted his fingers and peeked out at her with his single bloodshot eye.

Her mobile vibrated and Amari tossed the bone back onto the pile. She wiped her hand on her pants and then pulled the phone out to look at the display. She frowned. A proximity alert.

She turned back to the cyclops. "This place had better sparkle when I come to visit you again, Odysseus," she warned, wagging a finger at him. "It's a breeding ground for germs and disease. You'll catch your death like this. You clean it up, you hear me?"

The cyclops nodded his head vehemently, stooping to grab a pile of bones with one of its calloused hands. Amari nearly gagged as a cluster of flies flew up from what looked like the remnants of one of last week's meals.

Shaking her head, Amari left the enclosure and hastened to the East Gate. She thrust the enormous doors open just as a large helicopter touched down on the helipad. As the rotors slowed down, a side panel slid open and a well-groomed man stepped out, followed by a centaur Amari didn't recall seeing at the battle of the

Colosseum.

The unknown horse-man did not have the military bearing Commander Equustos had presented, and looked more like someone from the ancient Roman patrician class. A stylised goatee framed his chubby cheeks, while a white toga enveloped his stocky upper body and a red mantle draped across his shoulders. A pair of leather saddlebags hung across his glossy brown back.

Amari stepped forward to greet them. "Mister Chairman," she said, shaking the man's manicured hand. His palms were unpleasantly warm in her own. His nose wrinkled and she realised too late that her hands were still sticky from the cyclops' mess.

"Miss Kerubo," the Chairman said, pulling a white handkerchief from his pocket. "May I introduce Senator Flavius Regulus of the Green Grove."

The centaur inclined his head haughtily. "Keeper."

"Senator Regulus is here on behalf of the Army of the Green Grove to oversee the containment of your latest acquisitions," the Chairman said as he wiped his hands. He turned towards the centaur. "I trust you will find everything in order, Senator."

"We shall see," the senator replied in a nasal voice that immediately grated on Amari's nerves. "From what the Commander has told me, I have my reservations." A hint of an Italian accent flavoured the centaur's impeccable English.

"Well, let's put your mind at ease immediately," Amari said, careful to keep the irritation she felt from her voice. The sooner this bureaucrat was satisfied, the sooner she could get on with her work. She turned back towards the gates, but paused as the Chairman cleared his throat.

"Miss Kerubo, a moment, if you would."

She turned to face her visitors again, a sudden sense of foreboding settling in her stomach.

"Commander Equustos and I have agreed upon a prolonged stay for Senator Regulus. He will remain a guest in the Repository until his fears have been addressed."

The centaur harrumphed, glancing across his shoulder towards the saddlebags. "I am prepared to stay as long as it takes."

"The guest accommodations were designed for humans," Amari replied brusquely. "I'm not sure you would find a long stay comfortable. Unless you would allow me to prepare an enclosure for you, too?"

The Chairman's lips quirked into a smile, but Senator Regulus' tail whipped sideways agitatedly. "Certainly not! I can bear a little discomfort if my duty demands it. Show me to my *rooms*, Keeper." He spat her title as if it had left a sour taste in his mouth.

Amari bristled, and the Chairman stepped between them as if expecting a confrontation. "Senator, please," he said in a conciliatory tone. "I can assure you, Miss Kerubo is only concerned about your welfare." He shot her a warning glance. "We all have the same aim. Let's try to remain civil, at least."

The centaur's mouth pursed into a thin line, and he planted his hooves stubbornly, as if to prove that he would not be budged. Amari wondered suddenly if centaurs necessarily had to be half horse or if there could be a bit of mule in there, too.

She pursed her lips. If she wanted him out of her hair sooner rather than later, she needed to make him her ally. If that meant she had to butter him up a bit, then so be it.

"Forgive me, Senator Regulus," she said. "I was out of line."

The centaur's stance relaxed a little, and he unclenched his jaw. "Apology accepted," he finally said, although his tail was still swishing back and forth irritably.

"Wonderful." The Chairman glanced at his Rolex. He signalled to the helicopter pilot and the rotators slowly started up again. "I'm afraid time waits for no man, and I have to be off," he shouted over the increasing noise of the moving blades. "Miss Kerubo, please keep me abreast of the situation. Senator, I look forward to reading your reports."

Amari's brows furrowed as her unwelcome visitor shook the Chairman's hand. She didn't like the idea of the centaur writing reports to the Council. Since when have they wanted an outsider's opinion?

She watched the Chairman climb into the helicopter, its blades slicing through the chilly mountain air like the wail of a banshee, before the chopper lifted off and disappeared into the distance.

The Keeper couldn't help but feel as if the Chairman was abandoning her.

A few feet away, the centaur snorted impatiently. Amari squared her shoulders. She was used to managing the entire Repository on her own. She could handle one officious centaur.

"Let's get you settled first, Senator, and then I will answer any questions you may have."

The centaur nodded, and she ushered him through the South Gate. He hesitated for a few seconds before crossing the threshold, and a bead of sweat formed at his temple as Amari closed the great gates behind them. He was subdued as she led him through the mountain, his hooves clip-clopping loudly on the stone floor.

"Commander Equustos mentioned holding cells," the senator said, breaking the awkward silence. "He painted a very unflattering picture of the situation here in the Repository."

"The holding cells are not ideal," Amari admitted. "But they're only temporary, a place to keep the new acquisitions for a day or two only while I build specialised enclosures for them. Commander Equustos seemed satisfied with the enclosure I showed him."

"He said it would suffice. For now. Tell me, Keeper –"

"Please call me Amari," she interrupted him. "If we're going to be working together for a prolonged period, there's no need to be so formal."

The centaur nodded. "Very well. Then you may also call me Flavius."

"Thank you." Amari smiled to herself. She'd win him over yet. She inclined her head towards a passage leading off to the side. "You'll find the kitchens this way. Please help yourself to anything you need. I'm afraid I don't keep regular mealtimes."

A pinched expression crossed Flavius' face and Amari felt a flush of annoyance heat her cheeks. Had he thought she'd be waiting on him hand and foot? That this was a five-star hotel, the Keeper standing ready at his beck and call to bring him hors d'oeuvres whenever he felt peckish? What did a centaur even eat?

"These holding cells…" Flavius said, his nasally voice wrenching Amari's thoughts back to the present. "How many creatures captured during the blood moon market are currently in there?"

"Four individuals, as well as a clutch of blue

salamanders." She couldn't help a hint of excitement from entering her voice. "The airavata's enclosure is my highest priority. I've read the literature and I believe it would be most comfortable in a tropical forest with lots of exotic fruit to feast on, perhaps leading out onto grasslands. Plenty of space to roam —"

"Yes, well." Flavius cleared his throat. "We'll see about that. As a matter of interest... What kind of enclosure would you create for one of my kind?"

Amari directed the centaur down the corridor leading to the guest rooms as she considered her answer. "Something similar to what the nymphs have," she mused. "A temperate forest filled with broad-leaved trees, deer, and all manner of woodland creatures. Birds. Maybe a stream running past for fishing." Her heartbeat quickened as her imagination sparked. "There would be rock to build with, ore for crafting. Plains to gallop across and hold athletic tournaments. And at night, a sky so dark and stars so bright it would seem as if the old gods were close enough to touch." The Keeper smiled at the centaur's astonished face. Perhaps she could persuade him, after all.

Flavius shook his head, as if wakening from a dream. "Yes, well," he harrumphed, folding his arms across his chest. "You paint a pretty picture, but we shall see if it lives up to expectations."

Amari stopped in front of the first door. "After you," she said, opening it before following Flavius into the room. An enormous four-poster bed stood up against the wall, with a sitting area to the side and a desk in one corner. Luxurious by human standards, but cramped by equine.

"It's... adequate," Flavius said, manoeuvring past the bed towards the sitting area. He reached sideways towards the saddlebags strapped across his back and bumped against the coffee table, knocking a Greek urn over. It cracked as it landed on the stone floor.

"I'm sorry," he stuttered. He took a step backwards, accidentally kicking the bed with one of his hooves and somehow entangling it in a curtain. He yanked his leg and the curtain, as well as the attached beam, crashed to the floor. The centaur's tail flicked nervously as Amari stepped in to untangle the material from his leg. She helped him haul the beam up and replace it in its position again.

"May I?" she asked, and Flavius nodded, a hint of red tinging his puffy cheeks. The centaur's flanks quivered as her fingers brushed against his brown coat, quickly untying the saddlebags and placing them on the bed. The senator's discomfort was almost palpable as she swooped down and picked up the cracked urn.

"Don't worry about it," she said, putting it on top of the dresser where it would be out of the way. "It's a reproduction."

She eyed him as he floundered around the room, inspecting the furnishings and peering into the ensuite bathroom. Heaven knows what he was going to do in there. "Are you sure you'll be comfortable here? My offer still stands."

"Quite sure," Flavius replied quickly. "Besides, my comfort is hardly relevant. I'm here to see to the needs of the creatures imprisoned here."

"Come on then," Amari said, suddenly impatient. Imprisoned indeed! "Let me show you the holding cells."

※※※

Amari had never seen anyone's face turn that

particular shade of puce before. Flavius pulled himself up to his full height, his hands folded across his chest, and glared down his nose at her.

"I feared the worst, Keeper, but I was not prepared for this!" His left front leg stomped irritably on the ground. "Not only have you deprived these creatures of their freedom, but you're confining them to cells I wouldn't deem fit for the worst of human reprobates. I demand you set them free at once."

"Come now, Flavius, you know I can't do that." Amari absentmindedly patted away a rogue elephant trunk snuffling at her. "As I've said, the holding cells are only temporary. We'll have them out of here within a week or so, as soon as I've completed their individual enclosures."

"A larger prison, but a prison nonetheless," the centaur snorted derisively.

Amari sighed. "Would you like to see one for yourself? Perhaps then you'll believe me when I say that this is not a prison. It's a haven."

Flavius theatrically whipped his red cloak about his shoulders and pulled his face into a pinched expression. "I doubt that. But it is my duty to report on the state of all the creatures in your custody. Lead the way."

The Keeper wondered if she was doing the right thing as she led him towards the iron gate that separated the administrative wing from the main cave. Did she really want the centaur to be poking his nose into everything? But she had nothing to hide, nothing she was ashamed of. Best to let him discover the truth of her words for himself.

She opened the gate and paused on the balcony overlooking the Repository. Flavius' mouth drew into a thin line as he looked out over the cave, and Amari hurried down the steel stairs before he could say anything. A quick glance across the pens reminded her she needed to check in with the cyclops again to make sure he had cleaned up his lair. If he hadn't, then perhaps his enclosure wouldn't be the best one for Flavius to visit.

Instead, she opened the door of an enclosure that she was particularly proud of. A warm salty breeze wafted past her as she ushered Flavius through the door and onto a spit of sandy beach flanked by a craggy mountain. Seagulls soared overhead and the sun was so bright she had to shade her eyes while they adapted to the light. Before them, a cobalt sea stretched out towards the horizon, white breakers reaching for their feet.

Flavius edged backwards as his hooves sunk into the wet sand. "What is this inhospitable place you've brought me to?" he asked, his behind pressed up against the rock wall.

"It's very hospitable to the creatures I designed it for," Amari said. She gave a low whistle, scanning the waves. "There!" She pointed as sunlight flashed on magenta scales.

The next minute, a pod of capricorns breached the water, the air suddenly filled with their bleating. A smile spread across the Keeper's face as she watched the creatures leap gracefully through the air, the white coats of their goat halves shining in the sun, their elegant fishy tails curving sinuously, golden fins flapping as they propelled themselves forward, the curl of their horns as they plunged back into the ocean. Her heart lifted at the sight.

She tore her gaze away from the pod to look at the centaur. His nose was wrinkled, and his lips turned down in a scowl, as if something particularly unpleasant was assailing his nostrils.

"It's not ideal, is it?" he asked, the wind almost

whipping his nasally words away.

"What do you mean?"

Flavius gestured at the frolicking capricorns receding behind the waves. "It's hardly the habitat I would have imagined for a herd of goats."

Amari lifted an eyebrow. "You did notice their fishy tails, didn't you?"

"Of course, but that's only one half of the story," he said dismissively. "What do they eat and where do they sleep? They are essentially land-based animals. All this water can't possibly be amenable to them."

Amari stared at Flavius, at a loss for words. They may look somewhat like goats, but she'd personally tended to the fungal infection in their gills when they had first arrived at the Repository, and she knew for a fact that they had a particular fondness for a certain kind of kelp that grew along the north of Scotland's coast. Although she'd seen them come ashore to nibble on the grass and wildflowers clinging to the craggy cliffs, they much preferred being underwater.

"I've seen enough," the centaur said. "I'm ready to write up my first report. I assume you have a computer available for sending emails?"

"Perhaps I should explain the reason for the habitat that was chosen —"

Flavius held up a hand, cutting her short. "I will provide my own impressions and suggestions to the Green Grove. No need for further clarification."

A muscle jumped in Amari's cheek as she clenched her jaw. "Very well," she said, opening the door in the mountainside again. She led the centaur through and secured it behind them.

"Follow me," she said curtly.

She led Flavius back up the steel stairs again and to a sparsely decorated room just outside the

West Gate. Functional shelving lined one wall, and a small desk with a laptop on it stood against another wall.

"Wi-Fi is patchy inside the repository, but there is a cellular tower a little lower down the mountain," Amari said. "We get just enough signal for an adequate connection in here. It's also about the only place where the laptop will work." She shrugged as Flavius cast her an inquisitive look. "Magic and technology don't gel well."

"We have had very little success with technology inside the Green Grove," Flavius agreed as Amari booted up the laptop and showed him how to turn the modem on. "I'd much rather use more reliable means of communication, but this will do under the circumstances."

He opened his Gmail and started typing slowly, using only his index fingers to prod at the keyboard. Amari glimpsed the words 'regrettable state of neglect' and 'inadequate amenities' before he shot her a pointed look and she stomped out of the room, her blood pressure skyrocketing.

She stood in the corridor, taking deep breaths as she tried to calm her racing heart. Her hands clenched into fists. Who knew what irreparable damage this officious centaur would cause with his misguided reports? It took all her self-control not to scream.

There was only one thing that would calm her down right now. With purposeful strides, she returned to the main cave. It was only once she stood in Una's grove, her hands tangling in the unicorn's silky mane, that her jaw finally relaxed.

✳✳✳

"Keeper."

Amari's shoulders tensed, but she kept her eyes

175

firmly closed. Now was not the time to lose focus. In her mind's eye, she pictured a lush jungle forest. Rainbow birds flapped lazily through the cloying, humid air to the soundtrack of a million buzzing insects. Reeds rustled as a tiger strutted past, its tail lashing as smaller creatures scuttled away.

"Amari. I need to speak with you."

The Keeper clenched her fists. "Not now, Flavius," she said between gritted teeth. A river meandered languidly through the forest, burbling past ancient trees drooping with sweet fruit until it reached the mudflats. Nearby, tall grasses swayed in a warm breeze.

Amari gasped as something prodded her shoulder. The image slipped from her mind as her eyes shot open.

The centaur stood in front of her, one hoof tapping irritably against the stone floor as he folded his arms across his chest. His lips were pursed into a thin line.

"Can't this wait, Flavius?" Amari asked, pulling her hands behind her back as she resisted the urge to push him back. "I was about to create the airavata's enclosure."

"That's exactly why it can't wait," the centaur replied haughtily. "You haven't submitted your proposed design for my approval yet."

A vein in Amari's temple started to throb. "Submitted my proposed design. For your approval." Her teeth ground together as she clenched her jaw. At this rate, she feared she might wear them down to the gums.

Flavius nodded. "In triplicate," he said, oblivious of her ire. "Appropriate records need to be kept."

The Keeper glared at the centaur, but he didn't so much as flinch. In fact, one corner of his mouth lifted into a self-satisfied smirk as he studied her in return. He knew full well he had the advantage.

"Are you proposing I delay the creation of the airavata's enclosure until you've filed *paperwork*?" Amari growled. "In triplicate? I thought we had agreed that its comfort was the highest priority and that it should be moved from the holding cell as soon as possible."

"Oh, I want to get it out of there as much as you do, Keeper," Flavius said, waving a hand dismissively. "But if you refuse to set it free, then the correct procedures need to be followed. I can't allow you to create an unsuitable enclosure."

"Can't *allow*?"

The centaur harrumphed. "The agreement between the Council and the Green Grove is quite clear, Keeper. The comfort and safety of the creatures detained during the blood moon event are to be determined to *my* satisfaction. If you prefer, I can file a report that you were unwilling to cooperate. I'm sure an alternative arrangement can be made."

Amari's eyes narrowed. So that's how things were going to be? For a moment, Amari stood transfixed by the temptation to set the centaur to sleep and deposit him in an enclosure with one of her less amicable residents. Her fingers twitched behind her back.

But she couldn't risk letting this pompous ass separate her from the creatures already in her care. She would play by his rules until she could break them.

"Fine," she said finally, her nails digging grooves into the palms of her hands. "As long as you take full responsibility for the delay."

Flavius shrugged. "Can't be helped. I'll be expecting your report before the end of the day."

He turned on his heels and trotted off, leaving the Keeper to fume by herself.

Amari slammed the heavy oak door of her office behind her and stomped towards her desk. She flung herself into her chair, hands trembling as she took deep, calming breaths. The nerve of that arrogant bureaucrat! After she had spent the entire day writing up a detailed proposal, he had given it a cursory glance before brusquely dismissing her, saying he would 'review her request and provide her with recommendations in due course'!

As if he knew how to do her job better than she did.

She pulled her phone out and typed a furious text message to the Chairman. Her relationship with him had always been strictly professional, but she was just too annoyed to be bothered with diplomatically worded letters right now. She pressed Send and tossed the phone onto her desk.

Amari stared at the mobile for a few minutes, her elbows resting on the desk and her hands clenching and unclenching in front of her, until she finally huffed and pushed herself to her feet. She walked over to one of the bookshelves. If Flavius wanted paperwork, she'd give him paperwork.

Her fingers hovered across their spines as she perused the books, careful not to touch the ancient tomes, some of which were hundreds of years old. She still didn't know what the species of the bird in the last cell was. If she was to write up a proposal for its enclosure, she'd first have to have some kind of idea of what to do with it.

Her eyes lit upon a thick book bound in red leather entitled *Fire and Ash: Creatures of Hot, Humid and Hellish Landscapes*, which reminded her that the case of Carolina Reapers she had ordered from America for the salamanders was due to arrive the next day. They didn't need a new enclosure. Perhaps she could bypass the admin and get them moved without Flavius' interference...

She spotted the book she was looking for, a silk-clad handwritten edition of *An A – Z Compendium of Birds of Various Paradises*. As she pulled it from the shelf, a small book bound in brown leather came along and fell to the floor.

Amari set the compendium aside and stooped to pick the little book up. She recognised the initials stamped onto the front cover immediately – DH. Her breath hitched in her throat as she realised she held another one of Diana's diaries in her hands, one she'd never seen before! Who knew what forgotten knowledge lay hidden within its pages? Excitement tingled down her spine as she cracked the cover open.

Her eagerness ebbed as she scanned the first page, and then the second and the third. Lists of supplies, their prices, and the dates they had been ordered and delivered filled the pages, all written in Diana's archaic, but neat, hand. Amari's eye caught on a particularly large entry for chillies from India. That must have been when the fire salamanders had arrived at the Repository.

Amari flipped through the next few pages, disappointed at the continuing list of purchases. The information could be valuable – it gave her insight into how Diana had run the Repository – but it was hardly the thrilling discovery she had hoped for.

Her mobile pinged loudly and she nearly dropped the diary as her heart lurched into her throat.

She tucked the little book back into its place on the shelf. She'd scrutinise it at a less pressing time.

A blue light flashed on her phone. The Chairman had responded. Amari swiped to unlock the screen and stared at the message, her mouth suddenly filled with a bitter taste.

-- *Humour him.* --

The Keeper sighed. She'd get no help from the Council. At least not at this stage.

She retrieved the compendium and sat down behind her desk. She had work to do. If Flavius was going to second-guess her ideas, she had better make sure they were flawless.

✕✕✕

Amari eyed the pond suspiciously. It was deceptively still, but she knew what lurked in those waters, and while most of the Repository's residents could be dangerous, none of them meant her any harm.

Except the one living in this enclosure.

Amari inched closer, extracting the water sampler from the pocket of her jeans. A few months ago, the water had been green and covered in a layer of scum, a reflection of its resident's state of mind, but now it was clear and glinting darkly in the moonlight.

She dipped the gauge quickly into the pond, then retreated as she waited for the reading.

"Something amiss, Keeper?"

Amari's eyes whipped towards the sound of the icy voice. The asrai stepped out from behind the waterfall, her pale hair bobbing around her shoulders, a lacy Victorian dress clinging to her shapely body. The nymph's grey eyes were as cold as an early morning mist as she stared at Amari, as if looking for a sign of weakness.

"You tell me," Amari said, planting her feet firmly as she folded her arms across her chest.

A brief smile flickered across the asrai's lips. "I have no fresh complaints."

"Only old ones?"

"You know what I want."

"If you're lonely, I'm sure the other nymphs would welcome you —"

The asrai snorted. "Those empty-headed gossips. I have no stomach for that. No, Keeper, I don't want a different prison. I want my freedom."

"You know I can't give you that."

"But there is someone else here who might," the asrai said, running a hand through her short hair, as if to remind the Keeper of her previous failure.

Amari frowned. Riku might be able to carry messages between enclosures, but she doubted he and the asrai were on sociable terms after what he'd done to her. Besides, she still hadn't seen or heard anything from the wily kitsune since the blood moon market. She was getting worried about him.

"What makes you think that?" she asked.

"The centaur told me so himself," the asrai replied. "He said the Green Grove would be most interested in my story." Her lips pulled into a smirk. "I can make life very difficult for you if I want to."

Amari's teeth ground together. How had Flavius entered the enclosure? Did he know the Word of Opening too? He must do… There was no other way to unlock these doors.

And how dare he talk to her charges behind her back!

She inhaled sharply and let out a long, calming breath, acutely aware of the asrai's scrutiny. It wouldn't do to let the nymph know just how upset she was.

Then she sighed. "Of everyone in my care, you are the only one who isn't content." She looked at the water sampler and nodded to herself, relieved when it showed acceptable parameters. She returned her attention to the asrai. "You won't even tell me your name. I think you're making your own life difficult."

The phone in her pocket vibrated and she pulled it out, checking the display. Ambrose was summoning her. Did he have a new acquisition for her so soon? She put the phone away again and looked up to see the asrai studying, a crease between her brows.

"I have to go," Amari said. "Whatever Flavius has told you, just remember this: the Repository is your sanctuary. Your life is forfeit outside these walls. Think on that."

She deliberately turned her back on the asrai, the hairs on her nape rising as she felt the weight of the nymph's gaze upon her as she headed for the door. She slipped out of the enclosure, carefully sealing it with a Word, before she said another that illuminated the world around her in a blazing white.

※※※

Amari stepped onto scraggy green grass beside a vast grey lake. An overcast sky threatened a storm above.

"What is it, Ambrose?" she asked. "I'm quite busy —" Her jaw dropped, and her eyes widened as she looked up at an enormous dragon looming over her. The creature's blue scales glistened in the wan light, its face drawn into a look of irritable resignation. "Keeper, may I introduce Kentigern Mor, Chief of Chieftains," Ambrose intoned formally. "Great Mor, Amari Kerubo will assist your transition to the Repository."

Amari stared at Ambrose. Had she heard correctly? She couldn't see any restraints on the dragon, and it did not seem to be under any kind of duress. Could it be coming willingly, of its own accord? She wanted to punch a fist into the air, but she contained herself, barely, and nodded respectfully at the dragon. "I would be honoured, great chieftain."

"Ambrose has promised me solitude, Keeper," the dragon rumbled, its voice like thunder rolling across the hills. "Can you deliver?"

"Of course," Amari said immediately. Was that really all it wanted? She'd be willing to do so much more to have this creature safely ensconced inside the Repository. "I will build you an enclosure that will rival this lake for splendour, and you can decide who may come and go as you see fit."

The dragon swept its head from side to side, its eyes roaming across its domain. "Can you replicate this castle?" it asked, a note of wistfulness in the question.

"Easily," Amari said, looking at the ruin sprawled along the banks of the lake. She recognised the castle. She'd seen pictures of it many times, back when she'd had time to pore over travel brochures, when she'd thought she'd be free to explore the world. Before she'd found her calling. Her eyes widened. If this was Urquhart Castle, then it meant the lake was Loch Ness. Could it be? Was this…?

She stared at the dragon again, trying to keep her composure. "Ruined or…?"

"As it is now," Kentigern Mor replied. "It's rather poetic in its current state, don't you think? I never liked the humans who lived here, anyway."

Amari bit her bottom lip. It was all she could

do not to dance with excitement. "It will be as you wish, great dragon."

"Then let us proceed," the creature said. "But first..." It turned towards Ambrose and rumbled: "A tear for you, Ambrose, as agreed."

Amari blinked, suddenly sober again. What was this? Had Ambrose acquired the dragon in exchange for a tear? He knew very well what her stance on creature relics was. She watched as he collected a droplet in a little glass vial, and then she held her hand out at him. "I'll have that."

Ambrose sighed. "I need it –"

"Haven't we discussed this before, Ambrose? No parts out in the world, even if freely given. It's just too dangerous."

"I agree, but –"

"What would you do with it, anyway?" she asked, quirking an eyebrow at him.

Ambrose hesitated for a moment, before shrugging. "Never mind," he said, handing the bottle over.

Amari frowned as she pocketed the vial. "We'll discuss this later," she promised. Then she turned towards the dragon. "Ready?"

"Ready," Kentigern Mor replied without hesitation.

Amari said the Word, and a bright light whisked them away.

※※※

When the light faded, Amari stood beside Kentigern Mor in an empty corner of the Repository's main cavern. The dragon glanced around with an inscrutable look upon its face, but Amari could sense its unease in the way its sinuous body hunched in on itself.

"I am concerned about this cave you have

brought me to, Keeper," it rumbled. "I was expecting open air and a lake, as you had promised." It eyed the nearest enclosure and the scales on the back of its neck shifted slightly, as if they were hackles trying to stand on end. "Are these cages?" it growled ominously.

"Not cages," Amari said quickly. "I promise you haven't been deceived. If you give me a moment, all will become clear. I will give you everything you asked for."

Kentigern Mor's eyes narrowed, but he nodded curtly.

Amari closed her eyes and took a deep breath. "Any other special requests?" she asked. Better to get it perfect from the start.

"Fish," the dragon said. "Lots of tasty fish."

A smile broke across her lips. "As you wish, great dragon."

She formed a picture in her mind of the loch she had seen only a few moments ago. Murky blue water stretched out towards the hills, lapping on the shore beside a ruined castle sprawled across the lake's banks. Silvery fish darted through the water, flashing past a pebbled beach where a red deer hunched over for a drink while a white-tailed eagle soared against grey skies overhead. Underbrush rustled as a pine marten hunted, and red squirrels chattered in the trees. Somewhere, a family of wild boars grunted. The scent of wild thistles carried on the breeze as a gaggle of geese landed noisily on the lake's choppy water.

Pain exploded in Amari's forehead, and she gasped as she released the Word and all its power of creation. A wind rushed past her, threatening to pull her off her feet. Her eyes shot open as she lurched unsteadily, grabbing at something to hold on to. She drew in a breath as she felt cool scales beneath her fingers.

She looked up at the dragon looming over her.

It looked across the landscape she had created, its chest rising as it inhaled deeply. The scent of primrose and pine wafted past, mixed with the sharp tang of fish and fowl. The dragon's head turned towards Amari.

"Perfect," Kentigern Mor sighed.

Then its sinuous body surged towards the lake. It leaped from the shore, scattering the geese in all directions, and dived into the cold water. Amari darted backwards, narrowly missing the splash that sent water splattering in every direction.

The Keeper allowed a smile to spread across her face.

She was tempted to stay in the enclosure for a while to see if Kentigern Mor would return to shore, but a soft drizzle started falling from the sky. She pulled her scarf over her head and hurried towards the ruined castle, where she'd placed the doorway leading to the Repository.

A gust of warm air met her as she stepped into the cavern. She nearly walked straight into Flavius, who was waiting just outside the door, his tail swishing angrily back and forth.

"What's this?" the centaur demanded, his nasal voice setting her teeth on edge. "I thought it was quite clear that I am to approve all new enclosures first."

Amari pulled the scarf from her head and folded her arms across her chest. "All new enclosures for creatures acquired during the blood moon market. This was not one of them."

"That's a technicality," Flavius said, his nostrils flaring.

"But an important one," Amari replied, trying not to sound smug. "Besides, its resident was in a hurry to get settled. Delaying would not have been a good idea."

Flavius frowned. "Who's in there?" He tried to push past her, but Amari stood her ground, blocking his way.

"Someone who asked to be left alone. I wouldn't advise going in there. Not unless you value your life."

The centaur scoffed. "You're bluffing."

Amari lifted an eyebrow. "Do I look like I'm joking? I am the Keeper of Exotic Animals. It is my job to protect the creatures in my care. What makes you think I wouldn't do anything in my power to ensure their safety?"

Flavius glared at her, his chubby cheeks red with anger. "I will not be denied, *Keeper*. Mark my words, or there will be consequences."

"Mark mine, *Senator*," Amari shot back, anger lacing her voice. "If I find out you've entered an enclosure without my express permission again, we will have a diplomatic incident on our hands."

Flavius looked taken aback, as if he hadn't expected her to oppose him. Then he pulled himself up to his full height, tossing his red cloak imperiously across one shoulder, and said loftily: "This isn't over yet." He turned on his heels and stormed off.

Amari's shoulders slumped as she stared after him. It had felt good standing up to the bureaucrat, but she had the feeling she was going to regret it later.

Moodily, she thrust her hands into her pockets and was startled to find the little glass vial she had taken from Ambrose in one of them. She pulled it out, inspecting the droplet shimmering inside.

What had Ambrose wanted with this? He knew how she felt about creature parts being out in the world. Dragon tears were particularly potent and highly sought-after. People believed they brought power and wealth. If Kentigern Mor was truly the Loch Ness Monster, his tears would be worth millions.

Amari unstoppered the bottle and let the tear fall to the floor. She rubbed at it with her shoe, until it had faded into the stone.

She would have to talk to Ambrose about this at some point. Surely, he couldn't be strapped for cash already. The Council had compensated him generously for his two previous acquisitions. She pulled out her mobile phone and patiently navigated to the Council's intranet. Her eyes widened as she looked up the fee for dragons.

Well. If he had financial difficulties, his worries were over now.

She made her way to the computer room near the West Gate and logged onto the intranet again. It took her a few minutes to fill in the payment request before she sent it off for approval. There. Ambrose had no reason to covet dragon tears anymore.

Rising to her feet, Amari pulled the water sampler from her pocket and looked at the reading from the asrai's pond again. The water was fine, but perhaps she could do something that would make the nymph's life more bearable for her. Amari couldn't give her the freedom she craved, but she could expand her enclosure – perhaps extend her pond into a series of terraced lakes and waterfalls, maybe even with a forest to explore.

Her head filled with possibilities, Amari returned to the Repository.

✳✳✳

The yale bleated excitedly as Amari shoved a six-pack of eggs into its enclosure. She watched, fascinated, as one of its horns swivelled until it pointed sideways, allowing the creature to pierce a hole into an egg. It slurped the insides out noisily and then licked its lips in satisfaction.

Amari nodded, making a note in her notebook. The manuscript she'd found the previous night had specified basilisk eggs, but even if she'd had any, she wouldn't have fed them to the yale. Chicken eggs would suffice.

Something soft and wet suddenly touched her hand and she looked down at the yale, startled to see its head poking out between the bars of the cell door. It was sniffing her hand, looking at her with wide, friendly eyes.

Hesitantly, she brought her hand closer and slowly stroked the yale's tawny mane. It was surprisingly soft, although tangled with knots, and she wondered if the creature would let her brush it. The yale bleated happily. Amari ran her hand down the side of its neck, patting it gently. The creature gave a short bark, almost like a cough, before stepping out of reach and resuming its attack on another egg.

Amari nodded. As much as she wanted to befriend it, it was best to remember that the yale wasn't a pet. She was on good terms with most of the residents, but they were all still untamed creatures, only suffering her touch if they chose to.

She hoisted her satchel over one shoulder again and continued on her morning rounds, making sure all the creatures in the holding cells were still alright. The lamia was curled up in a corner, fast asleep and clearly still digesting the previous day's meal. Amari pursed her lips as she hurried past to check in on the white bird. It was sleeping too, its head tucked underneath one wing, the talons on one foot twitching occasionally. Amari still hadn't identified it, and it worried her that she couldn't let it out to stretch its wings for a bit. It must be incredibly bored inside its barren cell.

Satisfied that her newest acquisitions were all still holding out reasonably well, Amari made her way to the main cave. She paused on the landing, letting her eyes roam over the enclosures. Rain drizzled down on Kentigern Mor's grey lake and there was no sign of the great dragon. Amari couldn't make out individual nymphs from her vantage point, but it looked like the dryads and the naiads were holding a competition of some sorts, and in her separate enclosure, the asrai was floating peacefully in one of her new lakes.

"Uh oh," Amari said as her gaze wandered over the cyclops' enclosure.

She hurried down the steps and entered the paddock, quickly making her way to the giant's lair. The cyclops sat in the dirt, cradling his left foot. Bones littered the ground again, but Amari didn't have the heart to berate him when she saw the tears brimming in his single eye.

Amari winced as blood welled up from the deep gash in his foot.

"Amri," the cyclops moaned, his lower lip trembling. "Me hurt."

Amari's heart clenched in sympathy. She crouched down beside him, gently pushing his hands away as she inspected the injury. The magic of the Repository would heal it in a day or two, but she needed to clean it to prevent an infection. She dug into her satchel and pulled out a bottle of disinfectant spray.

"Hold still, Ody. This is going to sting a little." Amari squirted some of the spray onto the cyclops' foot. The creature howled in pain, trying to wrench his foot away, but Amari held on resolutely. "This wouldn't have happened if you'd just kept your cave clean like I asked you to."

A tear spilled from Odysseus' eye, and Amari

immediately regretted her harsh tone.

"There now," she said, wiping the blood away with a tissue. Unfortunately, she didn't know any Words of Healing, but she whispered the one she used to close doors with as she ran a finger along the gash. The flesh tightened a little, leaving a thin red cut behind. Amari nodded to herself, satisfied. The magic of the Repository would do the rest.

The cyclops suddenly growled, and Amari nearly dropped his foot, startled. The giant was aggressive by nature, and strong enough to rip boulders apart. Mix that with pain and there was no telling what he would do.

She shot him a wary look, but his eye wasn't on her. He was glaring at something behind her.

She turned to see Flavius standing at the entrance of the lair, his face a thundercloud. "What's this?" the centaur demanded, storming closer.

Irritation welled up like the blood from the gash had earlier. "What does it look like? I'm tending to an injured creature."

Flavius let out an exasperated breath. "I can see that, Keeper. Why is the cyclops injured?"

"He sliced his foot open on a sharp bone. It's painful, but not too serious. It should be good as new in a day or two."

"That is beside the point," Flavius snapped. "You assured me that the Repository's residents were completely safe. It seems you were lying, Keeper."

Amari gently lowered the cyclops' foot, patting his leg reassuringly as she stood up to face the centaur. She wished he wasn't quite as tall. It would be much easier to reason with him if he weren't looking down on her the whole time.

"The creatures are safe from people who'd want to abuse them in the Repository, but they are not enclosed in bubble wrap. They live normal lives here, and that can be just as dangerous as anywhere else. I take care of them whenever something happens, but you can't expect them never to get hurt."

"I can and I do." A smug smile slipped across the centaur's face. "An important technicality, you might call it. I'll be filing a report about this." He turned on his heels and trotted away, and was out of sight before Amari realised she hadn't told him off for entering the enclosure without her permission.

The Keeper clenched her fists. She wanted to run after him to give him a piece of her mind, but she knew it would be no use. She'd long since lost any hope she might have harboured of collaborating peacefully with the Green Grove's representative. The centaur wanted to find fault, and so he would. There was nothing she could do about that.

Behind her, the cyclops whimpered again. She turned around and helped him to his feet, giving him a little support as he hobbled towards the slab of rock he slept on. She helped him lay down, and then stayed with him until his one eye drooped into sleep, her hand enveloped in one of his large palms.

⋇⋇⋇

Amari took a sip of rooibos, inhaling the familiar fragrance of the red tea. It reminded her of home and always calmed her down when she was feeling overwhelmed. Her eyes strayed towards her phone and, before she could stop herself, the Chairman's message flashed before her eyes again.

-- We CANNOT show the centaurs any weakness. The Council has plans for the Green Grove that must not be compromised. I have always trusted your competence in the past. Do not make me regret it. --

The Keeper sighed as she relaxed into the leatherback chair next to the fire. She stared into the flames, wishing their heat could warm her aching heart. Had Flavius been right? Had she let Ody down? She had known the bones in the cyclops' lair were dangerous, but all she'd done was berate him. She should have done more. She should have made sure he couldn't get hurt.

She took another sip of tea, closing her eyes and just savouring the aroma.

What was done, was done. She would do better in future. She would prove that damn centaur wrong.

Amari placed the empty cup down and reached for Diana's diary. Perhaps she could glean something more from the lists of inventories. If nothing else, it might take her mind off things and help her fall asleep.

She opened the diary and skimmed past the first few pages until she found the place she had last stopped at. She started reading, not paying particular attention to the details, just letting the words and the numbers scroll through her mind, until she felt the vice around her heart loosen and her eyelids started drooping.

"Last page," she promised herself as she suppressed a yawn. Lately, sleep had not come easily to her, and she lay awake long into the early hours most nights, tossing and turning and worrying over the creatures in the holding cells.

She turned the yellowing page and blinked, confused. It was covered in peculiar symbols.

Amari peered at the cyphers, and then gasped

as she recognised one of them. She shot to her feet, all thoughts of sleep forgotten, and raced towards the shelf where she kept the rest of Diana's diaries. Her fingers travelled across the spines until she found the one she was looking for. She pulled it out and flipped through its pages. There! She returned to the fireplace and picked up the other book, comparing the symbols.

She was right. It was the Word for Travel! And there! She recognised the Word for Opening as well. That would mean...

Amari slumped back into the chair, stunned. She stared at the list of Symbols, the capitalisation clear in her mind's eye now. There were at least fifty of them, all noted down in neat rows in Diana's archaic hand.

Amari was only familiar with less than a dozen of them.

Hands shaking, the Keeper moved the books to her desk in the middle of the room. She pulled out a piece of paper and a pen and then retrieved the rest of Diana's diaries from the shelf.

She had some research to do.

✕✕✕

Amari glanced across her shoulder to see if Flavius was skulking anywhere nearby. With no sign of the centaur, she ducked into an enclosure, clutching onto her hidden cargo. Heat blasted at her like she'd stepped into a furnace, and she wiped at a bead of sweat that immediately formed on her forehead. The back of her shirt already felt damp with perspiration.

The smell hit her next. Her nose wrinkled as the stench of sulphur assailed it. She opened her mouth a little so she could breathe through it, her parched lips sticking together unpleasantly.

A rumble sounded and the solidified magma beneath her feet trembled. She looked up just in time to see one of the nearby volcanoes blast a cloud of searing gas into the sky.

Good. That meant a new fire was just about to be born. Her timing was perfect.

As quickly as she could, Amari clambered up the slopes of the volcano. She wanted to be out of there before lava came bubbling out of the crater. Her foot slipped on scree and she stumbled to her knees, one hand still clutched to her side, the other stopping her from falling flat on her face.

Wincing, Amari pushed herself erect again. She looked at her hand. It was scraped and burnt red, but not blistered. She'd be okay. She continued her climb.

Her breath was ragged by the time she reached the rim, her hair plastered stickily to her face. Carefully, she peered into the volcano. Red lava bubbled inside. She'd better hurry.

She pulled the blue salamander out from underneath her clothes. She'd only brought the one, fitting snugly into the palm of her uninjured hand, to see if the creatures would adapt to the enclosure built for their fiery cousins before she tried to move all of them here. And she was pretty sure Flavius wouldn't notice if one of them went missing from the cells. Gently, she put the little lizard down on the edge of the volcano.

The salamander's orange stripes flared to life and yellow spots she hadn't noticed before lit up, turning the lizard into a light show as psychedelic as police sirens on a bad night in Hillbrow. The creature's head darted left and right as it looked at its new surroundings, alternately lifting its feet off the hot soil. It stepped up to the edge of the volcano's rim, its tongue darting out to taste the sulphurous air.

And then the salamander leaped into the air.

Amari's eyes widened. Swearing, she turned and dashed down the side of the volcano, slipping and sliding down the loose gravel. Somehow, she kept her balance. She stumbled down and reached the bottom just as the volcano gave an almighty roar. The ground lurched and she nearly fell, but managed to stay on her feet.

The Keeper spun around to see blue lava shooting into the sky. A relieved laugh burst from her chapped lips. She was pretty sure that meant the salamander had bonded with the new fire. Now all she had to do was check in again to see how the colony of existing fire salamanders reacted to the new resident. Hopefully, they wouldn't have trouble getting along.

Clutching her injured hand to her chest, Amari gratefully exited the enclosure. She could do with a cold shower and a glass of water right now.

She stopped dead in her tracks when she saw Flavius stumbling through the door leading to Kentigern Mor's paddock.

"Flavius!" she almost growled. "I told you to stay out of that enclosure."

The centaur's tail swished nervously as he looked at her, avoiding eye contact. "Yes," he mumbled. "Indeed." He ducked his head and, apparently forgetting all about his dignity, turned away and galloped out of sight.

Fuming, Amari stalked through the open door and stepped out into the ruined castle. Rain pelted down as she made her way to the lake's shore, where the blue dragon was angrily rolling through the waves. Amari hesitated. Perhaps it would be better to wait until he had calmed down?

"Keeper!" his voice boomed across the noise of the falling rain.

Amari sighed, and hurried down to the water's

edge.

Kentigern Mor reared up out of the water, his enormous body looming over her. Amari swallowed as the dragon's head lowered down to her, his razor-sharp teeth snapping so close to her she could smell the odour of fresh fish on his breath. She didn't take a step back, but she wanted to.

"You promised me solitude," the dragon snarled. "I didn't agree to come here so officious little pencil-pushers can badger me with questions and scare the fish away!"

"I'm sorry, great Mor. I warned him not to disturb you, but I should have done more. I've failed you."

The dragon glared at her with unblinking, reptilian eyes until it felt like he was staring straight into her soul. Amari stood her ground, although the hair on the back of her neck was on end. She started as laughter bubbled forth from the dragon's belly, a rumble like waves crashing to the shore.

"He won't come again," Kentigern Mor chortled, lowering himself back into the water, and Amari let out a relieved breath as the dragon released her from his scrutiny. She lifted an enquiring eyebrow. "He didn't receive the welcome he'd expected. Or the answers he wanted. Who is he, anyway?"

Amari scowled. "Someone who has been making my life very difficult." She quickly explained the situation to the dragon, feeling some of her anxiety fade as Kentigern Mor listened attentively, growling at all the right places. "And now it's been nearly a week and still none of the creatures have been moved out of the holding cells, while the centaurs blame me for that, too."

The dragon snarled. "Let him come see me

again, Keeper. One gulp and your troubles will be solved, and my hunger appeased for a while."

Amari stifled a laugh. "I appreciate the sentiment, but I'm not sure that will solve the problem. The Green Grove would send someone else, and I'd have to explain what had happened to Flavius."

Kentigern Mor grunted. "Explanations are for the weak, and you are not weak, Keeper."

Amari stared up at him, surprised. The dragon nodded graciously, and a warm feeling settled somewhere in her chest.

"But I see your point," the dragon continued. "However, if he sets foot in my territory again, you will have to convey my condolences to his superiors in Rome."

This time, Amari did smile. "I'll give him the warning, great dragon."

"Please, call me by my name, Keeper. I am Kentigern to my friends."

Amari's heart leaped. "And I am Amari to mine, Kentigern." She wiped the rain from her face and looked out across the lake. "Are you satisfied with your accommodations?"

"I am, Amari," the dragon replied. "The fish are plentiful and juicy, and I've even sampled one of the highland cows who came foolishly close to the water. Very tender." The dragon smacked his lips appreciatively. "But I have a boon to ask."

"Of course. If it's in my power, I'll do what I can."

Kentigern Mor looked up at the clouds. "I've had centuries of grey skies. I would see the sun a little more often, if possible."

Amari nodded. "It is possible." She closed her eyes and concentrated, the Word caressing her lips as the rain stopped and a ray of sunlight fell across her face. She opened her eyes again to see the clouds retreating, leaving a pale blue sky in their wake.

The dragon sighed as the sun glinted on his blue scales. "Thank you."

"You're very welcome," Amari said, smiling at the dragon's obvious pleasure. "I must go now, but I'll come check in on you occasionally to make sure everything is alright. How frequent would you prefer my visits to be?"

"You can come as often as you like, Amari. I would appreciate your company. Farewell for now." The dragon sunk back into the water and Amari watched his sinuous form undulate through the ripples until he was out of sight.

She stood on the banks of the lake for a while, enjoying the sunshine on her face. She'd made an ally today, but better yet, she'd made a friend. That was worth more to her than all the fish in this lake, and something Flavius could never take away from her. Knowing she had Kentigern Mor's support somehow made her feel ready to tackle the Green Grove again.

The centaurs might have the Chairman's ear right now, but she was the Keeper, and she would do whatever was needed to keep her creatures safe.

❋❋❋

She found Flavius tapping furiously on the laptop in the little computer room. He huffed when he saw her and pulled the screen down so she couldn't see what he'd written. Judging by the ferocity with which he'd been attacking the keyboard, Amari was fairly certain the Green Grove would not be getting a favourable report on her newest resident.

"I come bearing a message from the great dragon." Annoyance flashed across the centaur's face, but she noticed him looking over her shoulder, as if afraid the dragon might be close by. "He warns you not to come into his enclosure again."

Flavius snorted. "That overgrown lizard. I wouldn't waste any more time on him. Let him have his precious solitude. I have more important matters to convey to the Green Grove."

Amari lifted an eyebrow. "Such as?"

Flavius smiled smugly. "Such as creatures being held here against their will. The one I spoke to told me she had been assaulted and kidnapped before being imprisoned here."

"If you're referring to the asrai, I'm afraid you're out of luck. The Council will not agree to her liberty, no matter what the Green Grove says. She's dangerous and has been linked to multiple murders. She's lucky to have the Repository as a sanctuary."

"Be that as it may," Flavius continued haughtily, adjusting the red cloak across his shoulders. "The Green Grove was assured that this was a facility where creatures come to escape the dangers of the outside world. When Commander Equustos learns someone is being held against her will, I am certain the terms of our agreement will be altered."

Amari's hand balled into a fist, and she winced as pain shot through her burned palm. "Flavius, what are you doing? Why are you trying to find fault everywhere?"

The centaur looked genuinely confused. "I am not trying to. I'm merely completing my assignment. It's unfortunate that there are so many flaws to find."

"If you're looking for flaws, look towards your own bureaucracy. While you're filing reports in triplicate, the airavata is still stuck in a holding cell much too small for it."

Flavius shrugged. "I expect a reply from the Green Grove any day now. I will inform you of their recommendations in due course."

"I don't need a bunch of paper-pushers to tell me how to do my job! And I thought I warned you not to go into any more enclosures without my express permission."

"And I don't need your permission to do mine!"

The centaur's tail flicked irritably as Amari glared at him. She folded her arms across her chest, refusing to budge, and the centaur planted himself stubbornly in front of her.

Finally, Amari took a deep breath. "I think it's time we need to admit to ourselves that this isn't working and that what we're doing here is not in the best interests of the creatures of the Repository."

Flavius shifted his weight, but he didn't interrupt her.

"You have an assignment to complete, and I respect that," she continued reluctantly. "I'll allow you access into all the enclosures, but –" She held up a finger when he started saying something. "Only if you promise to bring any concerns you may have to me first so that we can sort them out together. Does that sound reasonable?"

The centaur considered her words before nodding. "I can agree to that."

"And in exchange, you will let me house the creatures in the holding cells the way I see fit."

Flavius shook his head. "That I cannot agree to, unfortunately. My orders were explicit: the Green Grove were to determine what is best for those creatures. I cannot let you confine them –" He coughed when Amari's brow wrinkled. "I mean, house them, without approval from the

Grove."

The Keeper sighed. "Fine. But promise me you'll try to speed the process up a bit. I don't want to keep the airavata, or any of the others, in there any longer than they absolutely need to be."

"Agreed." Flavius' frown faded as his lips quirked into a begrudging smile. "The dragon, at least, seemed quite content with his new home."

Amari laughed. "Thank goodness. I wouldn't want him upset with me."

"Yes, well…" Flavius said, pulling on his goatee. "I will abide by his wishes and not disturb him again."

"Very wise," Amari said, her lips twitching in a smile. She glanced at the laptop again. "I'll leave you to your correspondence. I'm glad we've had this talk."

The centaur nodded, turning back to the computer. "Indeed. I will follow up on the airavata enclosure as soon as I am done with my current report."

"Thank you," Amari said. She lingered a moment, curious to see if he was going to change what he'd written so far, but when Flavius looked pointedly at her, she inclined her head graciously and stepped out of the room.

Even though they still didn't quite see eye to eye yet, Amari's shoulders felt lighter as she walked down the hall. Hopefully, the two of them could work together now rather than bumping heads over everything. And who knows, perhaps he would convince the Green Grove of the urgency to move the airavata and she could ease the poor creature's discomfort soon.

※ ※ ※

Two days later, Amari still didn't have approval

from the Green Grove to move the creatures. She stood in front of the holding cells, absently scratching at her nearly healed palm, watching the white bird peck listlessly at the stone floor. She opened the silk-clad copy of the compendium she had found previously and carefully paged through it, comparing descriptions with the elegant creature before her.

As she looked at an illustration that covered two sheets, she felt her breath quicken. It depicted a graceful white bird sitting on the edge of a bed, staring intently at a man lying limply beneath the covers. Amari's eyes widened as she read the flowery handwritten caption at the bottom of the image: "Caladrius, healer of all manner of illnesses."

She tucked the compendium under her arm and walked closer to the barred door. The bird froze and peered at her with one of its grey eyes. Amari held her sore palm out at it. The bird tilted its head, its unblinking eyes enquiring. A warmth fell across her, like she was being wrapped in an invisible blanket. The bird let out a mournful cry that echoed through the cell, tugging at Amari's heartstrings. Then the heat faded and the bird flapped its wings once, before it resumed pecking at the floor again.

Amari stepped away from the cell, looking disappointedly at her still-tender hand. Nothing had changed.

"Illness, not injury," she muttered underneath her breath as she flexed her fingers, wincing slightly.

Still, a bird that could cure sickness was a remarkable find! Could it cure cancer? No. She shook her head. If anyone ever learned of the creature's abilities, there would be no end to the things they would do to exploit it. She shuddered at the thought of it, confined to a cage somewhere in a lab, anonymous scientists in white coats prodding and picking at it with blue latex-covered fingers, jabbing with needles and plucking at its feathers.

No.

Science would find a different cure one day. This one was too precious to risk.

She dipped into her satchel and pulled out a Tupperware box, tossing its contents into the cell. The caladrius darted towards the chopped pieces of mango, gulping them down eagerly. Amari made a note in her diary. Apparently, the bird had a sweet tooth.

Her phone beeped and she pulled it out and glanced at the display. Ambrose was summoning her. So soon again after the dragon? She'd been right: she'd known he'd make an excellent Procurement Specialist from the moment she first saw him. There was just something about Ambrose... He didn't have that mercenary drive that most of her other Specialists had, but he was smart and resourceful and seemed to genuinely care about the creatures he brought to her. He would have made an excellent assistant to the Keeper.

She tucked the compendium into her satchel and stepped into the shard of light her Word had summoned.

A soft breeze caressed her curls as Amari emerged into a secluded part of a public garden. Leafy plane trees swayed in the wind and, sitting on a bench underneath one, was Ambrose. Amari glanced around, but there was no sign of a new acquisition. Her stomach tightened into a knot. This probably wasn't good news, then.

Ambrose smiled and waved her over. She joined him on the bench.

"Since you don't have anything new for me, I hope this is just a social call," Amari said, trying to push her unease away.

Ambrose ran a hand through his mop of sandy-blond hair. "It's not. I'm sorry, Amari." He hesitated for a moment, his one hand still nervously stroking across his head. He dropped his arm, expelling a loud breath. His eyes were intent as he said: "Thank you for your most recent payment, but I won't be working for the Council any longer."

Amari pursed her lips. "I'm sorry to hear that. May I ask why?"

Ambrose sighed. "It's just... I don't know. I'm just ready for a normal life again, you know? I'm ready to go back to the office and forget about everything that's out there." His face was so plaintive, Amari nearly felt sorry for him.

She placed a hand on his arm. "Can you ever forget what you've seen?"

A look of anguish crossed Ambrose's face. "I want to try."

Amari's brows furrowed together as she considered him, the bitter taste of disappointment tingling on her tongue. She hadn't realised he felt this way. She thought she'd found a kindred spirit in him.

But perhaps she'd been wrong.

She pulled away from him. "Why did you ask for the dragon's tear?"

Ambrose blinked. "What?"

"The day you delivered Kentigern Mor. Why did he give you one of his tears?"

"Oh, that..." Ambrose had the good grace to blush, at least. "It was stupid. I was on a quest. I should have known better."

Amari stood up. "Yes, you should have." The breeze suddenly turned chilly and she pulled the scarf wrapped around her neck tightly into place. "I don't know if you can leave this world behind once you're in it, Ambrose, but I'll respect your decision to try. I hope you find the normal life you're looking for again."

He held out his hand and his silver whistle dangled between his fingers. "You probably want this —"

"Keep it," Amari said, hitching her satchel across her shoulder again. "You never know."

She still felt the weight of Ambrose's gaze on her as the white light swept her away. She opened her eyes to the familiar sights of her study – the fire crackling in the hearth, the plush Persian under her feet, the windowless walls lined with shelves. Did the room suddenly feel smaller?

A knock on the door startled her.

"Amari," Flavius' voice called through the heavy oak door. "Can we discuss the dryad enclosure? I don't believe there's enough room for the mountain nymph in there..."

The Keeper's shoulders tensed. She didn't think she'd seen the last of Ambrose yet. But, just for a moment, she envied him his freedom.

✖✖✖

"I still think the forest is too cramped for that many nymphs," Flavius whined as they stepped out of the dryad enclosure. "The oread on her own should have twice as much space to roam —"

"They're sociable creatures," Amari interrupted him. "Trust me, the nymphs are more than happy with their current arrangement."

"Why is the asrai not in there too, then?"

"She prefers not to be."

"You said yourself she has... dangerous tendencies. Don't you think she'd benefit from the company of a group of well-adjusted peers?"

"I think she'd murder a group of well-adjusted peers."

Before Flavius could object, Amari opened the door to the salamander compound. She stepped into the furnace, sweat dampening her forehead, and immediately regretted bringing the centaur along.

Dead fire salamander bodies littered the ground.

"Oh, shit," Amari swore as the blue salamander she had re-homed a few days ago strode into view. When she'd left it here, it had been small enough to fit into her palm. Now its head would reach Amari's hip, and the creature was easily as long as she was tall.

She watched in horror as it pounced on a wriggling fire salamander, shaking the smaller lizard until its spine snapped and the yellow markings on its black body dulled to grey.

"What is the meaning of this?" Flavius shouted, panic tinging his words.

"Not now, Flavius."

Out of the corner of her eye, Amari saw the centaur retreating until his back legs pressed up against the enclosure door. He wasn't going to be any help.

Fortunately, the Keeper didn't need any help.

She balled her hand into a fist and the blue salamander froze in place, its victim's body still clenched between its jaws, dripping yellow blood that did nothing to improve the sulphurous stench already permeating the air. Amari walked towards the overgrown lizard, grimacing as she stepped over the carcasses scattered across the solidified magma underfoot. Her eyes caught movement and she gasped with relief as a handful of fire salamanders skittered away. At least some had survived.

"What am I going to do with you now?" Amari said as she reached the blue salamander. Putting it back in the holding cell with the rest of its congress was out of the question – it might eat them too. She'd have to keep it separate. The salamander's unblinking eyes stared back at her.

Amari turned to Flavius. His face was pale with shock, but now that she'd handled the threat, he had regained some of his composure. He stomped at the ground, trying to shake salamander blood off his hooves.

"I need to make this one its own enclosure."

"Absolutely not!" Flavius spluttered. "Not without the Grove's approval."

"It can't stay here."

"Then release it."

Amari lifted an eyebrow. "Look around, Flavius. You really want me to set it loose in the countryside?"

Flavius considered for a moment, and then shuddered. "Return it to the holding cells until I've conferred with the Green Grove." He paused, his eyebrows knitting together, as if just realising something. "What is it doing here, anyway?"

Amari coughed, embarrassed. She could admit her blunder or she could have Flavius think the creature had somehow made its way here on its own. Either way, this would not end well. "I take full responsibility. I wanted to see if I could move the blue salamanders to an existing enclosure. Obviously, that was a mistake."

"A mistake." Flavius' face had once again turned that shade of puce she was learning to loathe. "A costly mistake indeed, Keeper." He turned on his heels and strode out of the enclosure, his tail whipping angrily.

Amari clicked her tongue, before turning back

to the salamander. "Now see what you've done?" She gingerly touched the lizard's flank, flinching at the heat emanating from its blue scales. She whispered the Word and watched its eyes glaze over with sleep before she released her hold over the creature. The enormous salamander slumped to the ground, the corpse of the fire lizard it had been holding in its mouth flopping limply to the floor.

Amari eyed the surrounding carnage. How could she have been so wrong? She should have done more research. If only she'd read more, if she'd been more meticulous, she would have known this would happen. Her only comfort was that she'd arrived in time to prevent all the fire salamanders from being slaughtered. She hoped there were enough of them left for the congress to recover.

She'd have to come back later and take care of the bodies.

If Flavius didn't get her fired first.

She shook her head. She'd have to deal with that later.

Ignoring the uncomfortable warmth, she gripped the blue salamander's leg and said the Word. Radiance flared, and when she could see again, she stood in front of the holding cells.

Grunting, she dragged the heavy body towards the nearest empty cell.

"Bloody centaur couldn't stay to help," she muttered under her breath as she struggled with the comatose creature. Down the corridor, the airavata trumpeted loudly, and the caladrius flapped its wings, likely alarmed at yet another monstrously large reptile moving in next to it.

Her back and arms ached by the time she'd deposited the blue salamander in the cell and firmly locked the door behind her. She'd make a quick trip to the kitchen to fetch the biggest chillies she could find before returning to the enclosure to clean up the carnage.

And then she'd have to report the incident to the Council, hoping they'd be more understanding than Flavius had been.

✖✖✖

Much later that night, Amari finally sat down at her desk. Her back and arms ached from dragging fire salamander corpses around all afternoon. She'd had no good way of disposing of the bodies, so she'd dumped them into the boiling lava pit of one of the few volcanoes still active within the enclosure. Judging by how many of the fire mountains had gone dormant, she'd lost a significant amount of the congress.

It was a disaster.

Sighing, she reached into her drawer and pulled out Diana's diary, the yellowing pages falling open to the list of Symbols. She'd matched up the Words she already knew with their written counterparts, but despite her best efforts, the Keeper had made no progress in deciphering any of the unknown characters.

She jumped as her phone shattered the silence.

"What now?" she muttered irritably, glancing at the display. Her heart nearly stopped. The Chairman was calling her. He never called her.

"Miss Kerubo." His voice sounded cold on the other end. "I trust this is a good time to talk?"

Amari's mouth was suddenly as dry as the Kalahari desert. "Yes, sir," she managed, reaching for her teacup and finding it empty. "If this is about the salamanders, I can explain…"

"Senator Regulus' report was most disconcerting, I'll admit, but I assume the centaur was exaggerating, as usual." There was an expectant pause, but Amari kept quiet, too ashamed to admit that Flavius had had reason to complain this time. The Chairman cleared his throat. "Be that as it may, this only serves to highlight something I think should have been rectified a long time ago."

Amari felt heat rise to her cheeks. The empty teacup rattled as she put it down again, her hands shaking. "If my work is not up to standard –"

"I've had no reason to question your judgement in the past, Miss Kerubo." Amari swallowed, waiting for the inevitable dismissal. "But I fear this many new acquisitions at once may be too much to handle, even for someone as capable as you. I will send your new assistant tomorrow. Please show him the ropes. In due time, I'm sure he'll make your life much easier."

"Of course, Mister Chairman," Amari said, not sure if she should feel relieved or affronted, but glad that she hadn't been fired, at least. Most Keepers before her had had assistants. In fact, she'd been selected as an assistant for her predecessor. It was only his untimely death a few days before her recruitment that had prematurely elevated her to the position of Keeper.

Perhaps this was not an unwelcome development after all. "Thank you. I will do better in the future."

The Chairman grunted. "Do not let Senator Regulus undermine your authority, Miss Kerubo. Our arrangement with the Green Grove is a courtesy, nothing else. You are still the Keeper of Exotic Animals."

Was she imagining the way the phrase 'for now' lingered unspoken in the air? Amari shook her head. The creatures in the Repository were her responsibility. She would let no one take that away from her. The Chairman must know how important her position was to her, that she would do anything to ensure their safety.

"I understand, sir," she said, her resolve turning to steel. "I'll remember that."

※※※

Amari couldn't believe her eyes. "This place is… spotless," she breathed. She scrutinised the cyclops' den, peering into dark corners and behind boulders, but not a single discarded bone was to be found. She even wiped her finger along the walls of the cave, and they came away grime-free. Not even her mother would have been able to find fault. "This is amazing, Ody!"

The cyclops' face broke into a toothy grin, and he launched into a gleeful little caper. Clearly, his injured foot had fully healed. Of course, Flavius wasn't around to witness this astounding recovery.

Amari's phone beeped and she glanced at the proximity alert. It was coming from the East Gate.

She patted the cyclops' arm and gave him an encouraging smile. "I hope you keep it like this, Ody. I'll bring you something special for lunch as a reward." The one-eyed creature's grin broadened, and Amari waved goodbye as she exited the enclosure.

She hurried over to the East Gate and thrust the heavy wooden doors open just as a small helicopter landed on the helipad. The door opened and a man stepped out, carrying an old-fashioned brown suitcase in one hand. Amari blinked, surprised, before she realised it was not Ambrose walking towards her, but his father. He held his hand out in greeting and she shook it as the helicopter took off again.

"Mr Davids," Amari said. "You're my new

apprentice?"

"Please call me James," Ambrose's father said, shaking her hand vigorously. "I'm so excited to be here! Ambrose was quite tight-lipped about this place, and the Chairman even more so, but –" He looked up at the Repository gates, practically bouncing on his feet. "To finally be here, at the heart of everything! I can hardly believe it!"

Amari felt a twinge of apprehension run down her spine. James Davids was almost a minor celebrity in the mythological world. A disgraced scholar, he'd spent years trying to prove the existence of mythical creatures, publishing many papers that had made him a laughingstock in a world where the creatures she dealt with daily were nothing but fables to his peers. She'd even read a few of his articles. They had been meticulously researched, but she knew first-hand that the history books can't always be trusted, and some of his conjectures had been wildly off the mark. He'd disappeared for a few years, but Ambrose had rescued him during the blood moon market, where he'd been working – voluntarily, at first, and then under duress – for a man who had been dealing illegally in mythical creatures.

With some effort, she freed her hand from his grasp. "What do you know about what we do here?"

James' pale blue eyes turned back to her. "I have some experience working with mythical creatures, but of course, nothing like you have," he babbled excitedly. "I mean, I've seen my fair share of strange things, but this… This!" His gaze swept towards the entrance again.

"Let's –"

"What you must have hidden behind these walls! I can only imagine. Are there unicorns? What am I saying? Of course there are! Entire

213

herds of them, probably. How do you keep them contained?"

"James –"

"How do you house them inside the mountain? I mean, all the literature indicates that they prefer forest groves and that they only allow a maiden's touch. I don't mean to be forward, and I certainly don't mean to pry into your personal life, but –"

"James!"

The sheer excitement on James' face was so comical that Amari couldn't help but smile. "Why don't you come inside and I'll show you?"

He grinned and gripped his suitcase. He took a deep breath. "I'm ready."

Amari pulled the great doors closed behind him and then led him down the rock-hewn tunnel towards the guest quarters. She could almost feel excitement exuding from the man. His eyes swept everywhere, as if he expected something fantastic to jump from the shadows any minute now. She half expected Riku, or even Reese, to oblige, but they reached the guest wing without incident.

Traditionally, the apprentice's rooms were next to the Keeper's but, since Flavius had joined her, Amari had come to value her privacy. A few months ago, she would have chosen company over solitude any day, but the centaur had changed all that. She showed James to a room just down the corridor from Flavius.

The scholar hardly glanced at his lavish suite, carelessly tossing his suitcase onto the four-poster bed. He paused for a second, his hand patting at his breast pocket, as if making sure something underneath his jacket was still in place, before turning back to Amari.

"I'm ready. Show me everything."

Amari laughed. "Want to start with the

kitchen? It's nearly lunchtime…"

James waved a hand dismissively. "That can wait." He hesitated. "Unless it's part of my duties to prepare meals…"

"Only for yourself. I don't expect you to wait on me. As far as I'm concerned, you're here to help me take care of the creatures." She looked at his beaming face. "That's not as glamorous as you may think."

"I'm not afraid to get my hands dirty," he replied. "Just tell me what you need and I'll be happy to do it."

Amari sniffed. She was pretty sure he wouldn't be as enthusiastic a week from now, after the glamour had worn off and he was hip-deep in basilisk bile. But she'd let him have this moment.

"Come on then," she said. He followed her eagerly out of the room and down the hall. "This corridor leads to the kitchen," she said, pointing down a junction. "And that one over there goes to the holding cells. That's where I need your help most now, and I'll take you there soon, but I think you're most eager to see the Repository itself."

James nodded eagerly, his footsteps echoing hers along the corridor. They reached the iron door and she opened it for him, waving him through. James gasped as he stepped onto the platform and his eyes widened as he surveyed the main cave and all the enclosures within it.

"Amazing," he breathed. "I hadn't known what to expect, but this…" His gaze flitted from one enclosure to the next. "They're even free to roam between habitats! All of them, or only the rational ones?"

"What?" Amari asked, blinking. Had a creature escaped? She followed the direction of James' gaze and saw Flavius exiting Una's enclosure. Amari sighed. "No, that one isn't a resident. He's here on behalf of the Army of the Green Grove, supposedly ensuring we treat the creatures acquired during the blood moon market humanely, but generally just making life difficult for me."

"Oh," James said, wiping a palm across his stubbly cheek. "The Chairman briefly mentioned something about an audit, but I hadn't realised the centaurs were involved. Isn't it a little… awkward to have a non-human dictating procedure for you?"

Amari shrugged. "I wouldn't mind Flavius' suggestions if they made more sense. This morning he told me he'd recommended to the Council that the enclosure I'd built for the gargoyle be modernised. For some reason, he thinks Thierry would be more comfortable in a post-modern loft. Apparently, his Gothic cathedral is too intimidating, and I quote: 'some natural light would lift the gargoyle's mood'." She rolled her eyes, and James chuckled.

"Does he even know what sunlight does to a gargoyle?" James asked.

Amari threw her hands in the air. "Clearly not! And this is the person I must defer to when making decisions. But he's headed this way. Let me introduce you to him."

She led James down the stairs and intercepted the centaur before he could enter another enclosure.

"Senator Flavius Regulus, this is James Davids, my new assistant."

James extended his hand in greeting and, after a brief hesitation, the centaur gripped it in his own.

"Well met, Mr Davids," Flavius said. "I'm sure your presence is most welcome. Miss Kerubo is sorely in need of some assistance."

Amari bristled, but before she could respond,

James said: "The safekeeping of the Repository's residents is our mutual priority. I'll do my best to assist the Keeper in whatever way she deems best." He winked at her, and Amari suppressed a smile.

"Yes, well…" Flavius said, straightening the red toga hanging from his shoulders. "As to that. Amari, the unicorn. Are you sure the solitude is good for her? Equine creatures are by nature a herd species."

Amari scowled. "It's quite difficult to form a herd when there is only one surviving member of the species, Flavius," she replied, trying to keep the sarcasm from her voice.

"Of course, of course," the centaur agreed, nodding. "But what steps have you taken to rectify that?"

Amari lifted an eyebrow. How could she respond to a question like that?

To her surprise, James stepped in. "Are you suggesting interracial breeding?" he enquired, a sparkle of enthusiasm lighting up his eyes. "Because I've read a few studies regarding the resurrection of the extinct quagga, an animal which I'm sure you're familiar with. Scientists have postulated that intermingling of horse and zebra genes could, with selective breeding and enough time, recreate the same genome signature. If that's possible, we could certainly speculate about unicorns as well. Perhaps horse and rhino? Much of the commentary regarding classic literature proposed that unicorns were, in fact, rhinos in reality, so there must be some similar characteristics, the horn not the least among them. I mean, the breeding process might be a little awkward at first, especially for the female of the species, but if it's for a good cause…"

Flavius' eyes widened as James jabbered on. "Perhaps… perhaps we should give it more thought…" he stammered. "If you'll excuse me, I have some paperwork to file." He pushed past them and clomped hastily up the stairs.

When the iron door clanged behind him, Amari finally let herself laugh out loud. "Brilliant!" she said. "I should let you handle all of Flavius' suggestions from now on."

"Happy to," James said, grinning. Then the smile faded. "Is there really only one unicorn left in the world?"

Amari nodded, wiping tears of laughter from her eyes as she sobered up. "Her name is Una. Would you like to meet her?"

"Very much," James said, his hand straying to his breast pocket again for a moment, as if trying to touch his heart. Amari wondered if he had a health condition. Magical healing properties aside, the Repository really wasn't a place for the fainthearted.

"This way," she said. As they walked, she pointed out enclosures to him. "The cyclops is in that one. And over there is the minotaur's maze. The pens are unmarked, but you'll learn your way around soon enough. I'd advise spending some time on the platform at first to familiarise yourself with the layout."

When they reached Una's enclosure, Amari hesitated. Should she teach James the Word that would open the lock? As her assistant, it would certainly be more efficient if he could come and go without needing her to open gates for him. And yet… she hesitated.

Words of Power came with a measure of responsibility. Could she trust him with this knowledge?

She studied her new apprentice's eager face. She saw no guile there, just excitement. He was a scholar. He understood the power of knowledge.

"Listen carefully," she said, and then said the Word. The enclosure's door clicked open.

James' mouth formed a surprised oh. "What…?"

"Congratulations. You've just learned your first Word."

The scholar's brows wrinkled in confusion. "My first word?"

"We'll discuss this later. For now, remember. And keep it secret."

"Of course," James stammered. His lips formed the Word under his breath.

The familiar sense of serenity washed over her as she led James into the twilit grove. She breathed deeply, feeling her worries fade and the knot in her shoulders loosen. Maybe she should start sleeping in here…

"Astounding," James breathed beside her. "From the outside, it looks just like a pen in a zoo. How is this possible?" Fireflies danced around him as he spun in a circle, illuminating the wonder on his face.

"Magic," Amari said. James turned to her, astonished. "The Repository is one of the few pockets left in the world where magic still works. We think it's because of the high concentration of mythical creatures in this relatively small area."

A soft nicker behind her alerted her to Una's presence. "And this is what we're fighting to preserve."

James' gaze travelled past her and lit upon the unicorn. His hand trembled as he stretched out towards her. Una neighed softly and stepped deftly out of his reach.

James nodded to himself, pulling his hand back and tucking both arms behind his back. "Of course," he breathed. "Only a virgin's touch."

Una didn't retreat when Amari stepped closer,

and the Keeper ran her hand through the unicorn's silky mane, breathing in her scent. She hid her face in the unicorn's neck, frowning. She knew something the scholar didn't. Una didn't care about purity of body. The myths had it wrong.

The only touch the unicorn would allow was from someone pure of heart.

Amari squeezed her eyes shut. Now she had one more thing to worry about.

✕✕✕

She spent the rest of the afternoon introducing James to a few of the creatures she thought he could help her with without needing too much training. Her new assistant was as giddy as a schoolboy the entire time. He charmed the nymphs immediately, helped her deliver a roasted sheep to the cyclops den, and met the griffon family, although little Caerus hid behind his father's wings the entire time they were there.

When they finally reached the holding cells, James had that slightly startled look of someone who wasn't sure whether or not they were dreaming and was too afraid to blink in case they woke up.

"Please don't judge me by what you see here," Amari said, pressing her lips together as she stopped in front of the airavata's pen. "Under normal conditions, these creatures would have spent only two or three days in these cells. Unfortunately, the bureaucrats still haven't approved my plans for new enclosures."

She pulled a bunch of bananas from her satchel, and five trunks reached through the cell door, sniffing curiously. The five-headed elephant trumpeted in chorus as James stepped up to the door.

"Ah, I remember this one," he said, patting one trunk fondly.

Amari started. She'd forgotten about James' involvement in the events that had occurred in Rome. He'd obviously be familiar with these creatures - they'd been his responsibility before Ambrose had helped her free them from James' old employer, the ex-Councilmember turned smuggler.

"This cell isn't much larger than the one we kept it in at the Colosseum," James said. "I'm surprised it hasn't tried to break out yet."

"So am I," Amari replied, watching as the creature listlessly picked at the bananas. "I wish I could take him out for a walk or something. I'm afraid if he's cooped up here for much longer, both his physical and mental health will suffer. If he doesn't get his own enclosure soon, I may have to keep him sedated. Sleep might be less cruel than being confined to this small space."

She peered into the cell and clicked her tongue at the pile of untouched hay in the corner. "He's losing his appetite. That's not a good sign."

James studied the airavata, a frown creasing his forehead. "Have you tried feeding it jackfruit? The big guy loves it. Couldn't get enough of the stuff."

"I'll get some," Amari said immediately. She whipped out her mobile phone and added it to a shopping list. "I have suppliers who deliver once a fortnight. If there's something you think I need, tell me and I'll order it."

"Let me see…" James walked down the hallway, peering into each of the cells. "Chillies for the blue salamanders, along with insects and amphibians. Ah, the yale. You've been feeding it basilisk eggs, I assume?"

Amari's mouth fell open. Was James joking? She would never feed one mythical creature to another. And besides, Hector was the only one of his kind in the Repository, and he did not lay eggs. "You fed him basilisk eggs?" The mere thought made her feel ill.

"When we had some." James shrugged. "Normal eggs will also do. And he enjoys a bit of meat. Venison, if you can get it." He moved towards the next cell and quickly averted his eyes. "The lamia isn't picky. It'll eat anything." James hurried on and stopped in front of the caladrius' door. "The white bird likes fruit, the sweeter the better. I tried feeding it fish once – you know, because it resembles a stork – but it wasn't interested."

Amari felt a tinge of satisfaction knowing that James hadn't known what type of bird it was, either.

"It's a caladrius," she said.

James shot her an incredulous look. "The healer bird?" He whistled in amazement, and stepped towards the cell, looking at the bird as if for the first time. "It's a good thing I hadn't known. Marco would have sold it for millions!"

"And now that you do know?" Amari asked quietly.

"We must study it!" he exclaimed. "How can it heal something without becoming ill itself? And is it only illness or injury too? Can we use it against cancer? Can it solve someone's infertility problems? Regrow and amputated limb? The possibilities are endless!"

Amari cleared her throat. "Interact with it as much as you like, but no experiments, and no part of this bird, not even a single feather, is to leave the Repository."

James stared at her as if she had just told him the sun set in the east. "But... it could do so much good…"

"Not a single feather," Amari repeated, emphasising each word. "Are we clear?"

James swallowed, for once at a loss for words. He nodded.

"Come on then, I have something I think you'll find interesting."

James was subdued as he walked next to her down the corridor leading to her office, but when she pushed the heavy oak door open and he saw the shelves of books lining the walls, some of the sparkle returned to his eyes. His fingers twitched as he stepped towards her library.

"I know this must be particularly difficult for you, James, but please refrain from touching the books."

His face fell and a flash of remorse shot through Amari. She offered him the visitor's chair and he slumped into it. Before he could get too discouraged, Amari reached over and pulled *An A – Z Compendium of Birds of Various Paradises* from the shelf. James' smile returned as she offered him the silk-clad book. "You may want to start your research with this."

He took the book almost reverently. "I'll take good care of it."

Amari sat down in the chair across from him. "Now that you've seen what the job entails, are you still keen on being my assistant?" She thought she knew what the answer would be, and she wasn't sure whether or not she wanted him to accept.

"Are you kidding me?" he laughed. "I was made for this job."

Amari nodded, wondering if he meant the job as her assistant - which mainly involved cleaning up unusual messes and being covered in everything from slime to stardust – or the job of Keeper. She rather thought he meant the latter.

But the erstwhile scholar still had much to learn about the realities of the mythical world before he could think of taking over from her.

"Alright, then I am happy to have you here," she finally said, smiling as if she meant it. "Morning rounds start early. I suggest you set an alarm and get a good night's sleep. You're going to need it."

James immediately rose from the chair. "Thank you for the book," he said as he turned to leave. "I'll try not to let it keep me up all night." He grinned at her before closing the door behind him.

Amari fell back in her chair and swivelled it around to face Diana's portrait hanging on the wall. The image of the legendary Keeper stared back at her, a small frown perpetually creasing her brows.

"What am I doing, Diana?" Amari asked aloud. "Can I trust that man?"

The portrait, predictably, remained as stoic as ever.

Amari sighed, rubbing at a spot between her eyes where she could feel a headache brewing. Was she overthinking this? If she were honest with herself, she could probably use some help. First the incident with Ody's foot, and then losing most of the fire salamander colony... And who even knew where Riku was? She'd been stretched thin for so long, she hadn't even realised she wasn't coping anymore. And James had already proven himself useful at handling Flavius.

But Una didn't trust him.

Amari stifled a yawn. She should get some sleep. There was no use in worrying about anything right now. Only time would tell if James was true.

Until then, she'd just have to keep a close eye on him.

***

James was up early the next morning. Amari found him in the kitchen, eating a slice of toast with butter and jam. His eyes looked a little bleary. He must have found the book she gave him quite interesting.

"Morning," he greeted her as she made herself a cup of rooibos. "I hope you don't mind that I've helped myself to some breakfast."

Amari shook her head. "Of course not. This is your home now, too. Make yourself comfortable. The Council generously provides for all the Repository's residents, including you now."

"How are they funded?" James asked, accepting the cup of tea she handed him. "Judging by your stance on the caladrius' abilities yesterday, I assume the Council does not make a profit from the creatures."

"No, the creatures are strictly here for their protection and preservation," Amari said, sitting down at the table across from James, placing a bowl of yoghurt and some sliced mangoes down in front of her. "I'm not privy to any financial information, but I think they rely heavily on donations and private funding from Councilmembers."

"Interesting..." James said. "It's just that..." Amari lifted an eyebrow and he shrugged. "It feels like a lost opportunity to me."

"We are not commodities to be exploited for profit," Flavius said as he strode into the room. "The Keeper, at least, agrees with me on this."

Amari nodded as the centaur opened the fridge and took out a dozen eggs, half a loaf of bread, a pack of bacon, a handful of mushrooms, and a tin of baked beans. He might be Italian, but he ate like an Englishman with the appetite of a horse. The sharp scent of espresso filled the room as he turned the coffee machine on.

"Fair enough," James said, shrugging crumbs onto his plate. "I must admit, I think their abilities could do the world much good, but I'll abide by the Keeper's rules." He flashed Amari an easy smile.

Amari stood up as the sizzling sound of bacon filled the air. "If you'll excuse us, Flavius. I'm eager to take James on the morning rounds."

"Of course," Flavius said, cracking eggs into a bowl. "I have a few reports I need to send, but I'll catch up with you later. I'm keen to discuss the situation with the salamanders in more detail, Amari."

Amari pinched her lips together, but nodded before putting the dishes into the dishwasher and leading James out of the kitchen.

The rest of the day passed in a flurry of activity. She showed her new assistant where she kept the food and cleaning supplies, and how to place an order on the computer. Together, they cleaned out all the holding cells – Amari put each creature to sleep while she and James mopped the floors, wiped the walls, and refilled water and food bowls – before making their way down to the main cave.

Although the creatures in their enclosures were mostly self-sufficient, Amari liked to visit them as often as possible to make sure everything was still alright. She took James to the fire salamander pen and told him what had happened with the blue salamander. To her relief, he was just as astonished to hear about the blue salamander's unforeseen size and ferocity, and helped her take a survey of the remaining active volcanoes. Then she showed him how to make tea the way the nymphs loved it – dirty, with copious amounts of ouzo mixed in –

and spent the afternoon getting rid of some invasive weeds clogging up the dryads' wood. After that, she took James to see the cyclops again, just to make sure that the one-eyed monster still remembered him and didn't try to eat him. She left James there to clean out the lair that already had bones piling up in the corners again, while she fended off more ridiculous demands from Flavius, and enlarged the griffon enclosure to accommodate for the appetite of three growing cubs who would soon leave the nest in search of their own hunting grounds and territory.

By the time she met up with her assistant again, it was early evening and he looked exhausted as he leaned on the railing of the platform overlooking the main cave. He had dust smeared across his nose and a leaf stuck in his hair, but he smiled happily when he saw her.

"I can see why you're so committed to your job, Keeper. These creatures are amazing. I finally feel like my life has some purpose."

A warm glow spread through Amari's chest. Perhaps there was hope for him yet. "We'll talk again tomorrow morning, when today's aches have caught up with you," she laughed.

James grinned. "Want to join me for dinner? I make a mean pasta Pomodoro, and Flavius has promised to let us taste a bottle of wine from his own stock."

"I'll catch up with you soon. There's one more enclosure I need to visit today."

"I'll save you a serving," James said, winking, before he headed towards the kitchen.

Amari descended the steel steps and made her way to Riku's enclosure. Inside, crickets chirped, and a family of rabbits wiggled their noses at her while they chewed on clumps of meadow grass. Clearly, the kitsune hadn't been around in a while.

"Riku!" Amari called, watching the rabbits scampering for cover. Her voice echoed through the clearing, but there was no response.

Amari's shoulders slumped. Riku was gone.

She sat down on the soft grass. Amari knew she should feel furious. How dare he leave the Repository? How dare he not tell her where he was going?

Instead, she felt betrayed.

She had spared Riku's life when he'd deceived her, and since then had come to trust him. She'd thought the kitsune was her friend. And now he was gone.

Amari pushed herself to her feet again, wiping bits of grass from her jeans, and tried to ignore the ache settling in her heart as she walked out of Riku's empty enclosure.

✕✕✕

The days passed busier than ever. Instead of her responsibilities lessening with the addition of an assistant, Amari felt her troubles increasing exponentially.

The airavata was growing more listless by the day and had taken to sleeping more than Amari thought could be good for him, only perking up when she fed him some jackfruit. To make matters worse, the lamia had somehow contracted some sort of fungal scale infection and the Keeper spent hours rubbing a pungent ointment into the creature's iridescent body, carefully keeping an eye out for any signs of the enormous snake waking from its enchanted sleep. Then the yale, who had always bleated eagerly when Amari visited him with snacks, suddenly became aggressive again, ramming the gates with his horns until the Keeper feared he might give himself a concussion.

She winced as she flopped into the chair by her fireplace one evening, placing a hand across her bruised ribs. The minotaur was skittish at the best of times. What had possessed Flavius to sneak up on them while she was busy showing James how to comb nits out of the creature's mane? After pushing her over and nearly goring the nosy centaur, the beast had retreated deep into his labyrinth, bellowing like a demon possessed from the deep. It was going to take her months to win back his trust. And she needed to get him dipped before he was overrun by ticks and fleas.

And still, Flavius harangued her about every tiny thing he could find fault with in the Repository, while deftly evading her questions about the Green Grove's outstanding approval for new enclosures. Amari glared at the stack of papers on her desk – proposals she had written that the centaur had reviewed and returned scribbled with red ink.

She sighed. Just one cup of tea, she promised herself. Then she'd get started on those proposals again.

A knock on the door sounded. Amari rolled her eyes. All she wanted was five minutes of peace.

"Come in," she said, getting up out of the chair by the fire.

James entered, holding the compendium she had loaned him, one of his fingers marking his spot, as if he'd read something and, mid-thought, come looking for her. He was wearing a pair of reading glasses and had an ink smudge across his nose.

"Sorry to bother you," he said, his eyes immediately straying to the books behind Amari's back. "I was hoping you'd let me peruse your shelves. I found this fascinating entry on the Persian simurgh, a bird-like creature that can heal, much like our caladrius, and that got me thinking that if I could cross-reference what we know from the *Compendium* with some other citations, I might determine how we could make use of the bird's abilities. In an entirely humane and non-invasive way, of course." He adjusted his glasses, still looking over her shoulder. "Anything you might have on legendary birds – from Greece, Egypt, maybe even the Far East – would be useful."

Annoyance wrapped tightly around Amari's chest. "I'm afraid that's out of the question," she said, stepping in front of James to block his view of the books. "Some of those tomes are hundreds of years old and simply too delicate to be handled. Especially if you're going to handle them like *that*." James opened his mouth to object, but she quickly ushered him out of her office. "Besides, I think you'll find that the myths are unreliable. If you want to learn more about the caladrius, then spend some time with it."

"Yes, but –"

"Goodnight, James."

The scholar stared at her for a moment, then his shoulders slumped and he nodded. "Goodnight."

Amari closed the door before he could object further. She fell back into the wingback chair, pressing a hand across her forehead where the beginnings of a headache were brewing.

She hadn't lied – the books *were* delicate. And she'd thought James would know how to handle ancient manuscripts! She had half a mind to demand her book back before he manhandled it even further. He might be dog-earing a page at this very moment!

But that wasn't the real reason she wouldn't let him near her books.

All myths contained a grain of truth, and the

books in her collection were especially truthful. Amari couldn't shake the doubt Una had planted in her mind. She didn't trust James. Not yet. And certainly not with the knowledge he might discover in her library. He wasn't ready for it.

An icy fear stabbed through her, and she jumped up and hurried over to her desk, where Diana's diaries were still stacked in a pile. Her notes held the secrets of Words for anyone with the time and dedication to uncover them. Now that James knew the Word of Opening, a locked door would not deter him. And she had no guarantee that he would respect her wishes and stay away from her library when she wasn't looking.

Amari stuffed the diaries into her satchel – all but the last one she had discovered and which she was still trying to decipher – and rushed out of her study. Her footsteps echoed loudly as she hurried down the empty corridor towards the main cave. She glanced over her shoulder, sure James, or even Flavius, would confront her, but she met no one. She slipped through the iron door, down the steps and into one of the Repository's oldest enclosures.

Inside, it was pitch dark. Amari fumbled for her mobile and turned its torchlight on. Silhouettes of trees so enormous Amari wouldn't be able to touch her fingers if she wrapped her arms around their trunks came into view. A pair of eyes glinted down from the boughs towering above her.

"I'd like to speak to your grandfather," she called up. The eyes blinked and disappeared, and Amari heard the soft flap of wings fade between the trees.

Amari waited, glancing nervously around in the dark. A frog croaked by her foot and she nearly jumped ten feet into the air. She flashed her torch at it and the amphibian hopped off, leaving her alone with her heart racing, listening to the sounds of insects buzzing out of sight.

After what felt like ages, the soft flap of wings returned. She held one of her arms out and a winged monkey with a tuft of green fur across its chest landed on it. Amari grunted at the weight.

"You've grown heavy, Owain," she said. "One of these days, you'll be too big for me to hold you."

The creature smiled at her, its sapphire eyes twinkling in the light of her phone. "I'm entering the Trials two moons from now. Grandfather says I'm ready."

Amari chuckled. "Is that so? I wouldn't want to miss it. I'm sure you'll be the best in your clutch."

The little monkey's chest puffed up and he flapped his wings excitedly, ruffling Amari's hair.

"Grandfather says it's not a competition, but I'm sure I'll beat Cerys and Thomas. I've been practising."

The Keeper laughed. "You'll do just fine. Now, about your grandfather…"

"He's in his usual spot in the home tree, waiting for you. He's let a vine down. I'll lead the way."

The little monkey fluttered his wings and launched into the air. Amari hurried after him, afraid she might get lost in the dark. She stumbled through the underbrush while Owain flew effortlessly through the forest. At last, he landed in the branch of a tree so tall that the light of Amari's mobile couldn't reach its top. A vine as thick as her arm dangled down.

Amari grimaced as she turned her torch off and put her phone away. Her hands tightened around the coarse vine. She gritted her teeth. Climbing this tree was difficult when she could see what she was doing. In the dark? She wasn't sure if she could manage it, but there was no other way. There wasn't anyone else she could trust with Diana's diaries.

The vine lurched and she yelped as she was suddenly pulled off her feet and into the tree.

"Hold on, Amari," she heard Owain's voice from higher up.

Amari looked down as branches swept past her. She couldn't see anything below her. Probably for the best. Her grip tightened as she lurched upwards, her heart hammering against her ribcage.

Soon, the darkness faded until Amari could discern the outlines of branches around her. She looked up to see stars twinkling through the leaves.

And an enormous gorilla with sapphire eyes and a green tuft on its chest yanking the vine higher.

The gorilla held out its paw and helped Amari up onto a little platform at the tree's top. She exhaled in relief when she felt something solid underneath her feet again.

"That was terrifying," she admitted, her hands trembling as she placed them on the rough bark of the trunk. "But thank you, Owain. It would have been difficult to do this on my own."

"You're welcome," the gorilla replied. "Tug on the vine again when you're ready to come down." He swung downwards and out of sight, and Amari turned towards the lone rocking chair on the platform and the aged shapeshifter sitting in it.

Reese's silver coat gleamed palely in the wan light. He was looking up into the sky, but turned his head and smiled when he saw her, his sapphire eyes still as clear as ever. Even after more than a century, the Repository's healing powers ensured he stayed healthy.

"Keeper," he said warmly. "I was afraid the

height might prove too much for you."

Amari avoided looking over the edge of the platform. She wasn't afraid of heights, but she knew how tall this tree was. It was a long way down. "Don't you think it's time you moved a little closer to the ground?"

"I've always enjoyed being high, and my wings are still strong." He lifted his eyes towards the sky again. "And this is the best place to appreciate the new moon, don't you think?"

Amari peered between the leaves towards the sky, where the moon was only a faint outline against the blackness of space. No wonder it was so dark tonight. She sat down on the platform next to Reese's rocking chair. Now that her heart rate had slowed down a bit, she could appreciate the beauty of the night a bit more. She breathed the cool air in, letting the stillness of the forest wash over her. She felt the tension ease from her shoulders.

"It's peaceful here," she said.

Reese chuckled softly. "At my age, a little quiet doesn't go amiss."

"I'm sorry to disturb you."

"At my age, a little company doesn't go amiss, either."

"Sometimes company is overrated," Amari said.

"Is it the centaur that vexes you, Keeper, or the new assistant?"

Amari smiled. Of course, Reese would know exactly what was going on in the Repository. Just like Riku, it was impossible to keep him contained. She sometimes wondered if he knew even more than she did about what was going on inside the mountain.

"Both, but tonight I have a favour to ask." She patted her satchel. "I've brought you Diana's diaries."

"You fear the scholar's curiosity."

"No, I fear the scholar himself. Una wouldn't let him touch her."

The winged monkey's blue eyes widened for a second, and then he nodded. "Then the knowledge in those diaries is best kept from him."

"I'm glad you agree."

Reese stared up at the moon again. "Tell me, Keeper, do you know how Diana and I met?"

"You said you helped her discover her first Word."

The shapeshifter smiled. "Indeed. I assume you know which one?"

Amari nodded. "The one that reveals hidden things."

"Not extremely useful, under normal circumstances, but it has its moments."

Amari waited for Reese to continue, but when she looked at him again, the winged monkey had closed his eyes and was snoring softly. She climbed quietly to her feet and, leaving her satchel by the rocking chair, edged towards the vine dangling down the platform.

She didn't have to wait long for Owain to return, still in his gorilla form. Silently, the young shapeshifter helped her wrap the vine around her body until she felt secure enough to brave the journey down the tree again.

As the wind rushed past her, Amari couldn't shake the feeling that she had missed something in that conversation. She was sure Reese had been trying to tell her something, but what it was eluded her.

But if there was one thing she'd learned from shapeshifters over the years, it's that things weren't always what they seemed. The thought left a sour taste in her mouth.

"How are you doing, boy? You feeling alright?" Amari stroked one of the five-headed elephant's trunks as he stood listlessly in a corner of his too-small cell. A pile of uneaten fruit lay on the floor. Even his favourite jackfruit remained untouched. "I bet you're missing your home, aren't you? I bet you miss the trees, and the sun, and everything you can't have in this small room."

The airavata's ears drooped, and Amari's heart clenched at the sad expression on all his faces. And then anger flared again at Flavius and the Green Grove, for keeping this magnificent creature locked up, and at the Chairman, for not giving her the support she needed to make this right.

She frowned. Things couldn't go on like this.

Her thoughts warlike, Amari marched towards the main cave in search of Flavius, but instead found James standing outside the gate leading to the asrai's enclosure.

"You're not ready for that one yet," Amari said.

James' stance stiffened at her words, and he ran his hand through his hair in a way that reminded her immediately of Ambrose as he turned towards her.

"Is this the one my son brought in?"

"Yes, and of all the creatures in here, she's the one most likely to kill you."

"Fascinating," James said, not looking even a little bit afraid. "Ambrose said she'd been responsible for several drownings over the years, but I'd assumed they were all in self-defence. I didn't realise she's actively belligerent." He stared at the gate, and Amari could almost feel the curiosity exuding from him. "And now, is she content here in the Repository?"

Amari hesitated, but before she could answer,

Flavius trotted into view.

"Of course she's not content. She's being held here against her will!"

Amari sighed. "Good morning, Flavius," she said. "I hope you have an answer from the Green Grove for me?"

"Not yet," the centaur replied, his high-pitched voice setting Amari's teeth on edge. "The Grove is convening today to deliberate on whether the creatures in the holding cells need enclosures at all. By rights, they should be assigned guest rooms just like my own."

James scoffed and Amari lifted an eyebrow. "You want me to put the airavata in a guest room? The lamia?" The very idea was so absurd she was sure the centaur must be joking, but his face was as serious as ever.

Flavius nodded. "Or, ideally, you'd set them all free to return to their homes."

Red tinted the corners of Amari's vision. She couldn't be having this conversation. Again!

James' voice was dry when he said: "Forgive me for stating the obvious, but the reason these creatures are here is because they were captured and traded by unscrupulous poachers." There was no hint of irony in his tone, even though Amari knew he had played a pivotal role in those very events. "What would prevent such an occurrence from happening again? All things considered, it just makes sense for them to be here. The Repository keeps them safe and it keeps them fairly healthy. All that's left for us to do is to make them as comfortable as we can as soon as possible."

"The Green Grove would protect –"

"The Green Grove has no jurisdiction here," Amari cut him off. "The Elder Council has taken up the responsibility for their safekeeping, and since we have an agreement with the Grove, I will listen to their input, but I am rapidly running out of patience."

Flavius' tail whisked from side to side as he glared at Amari. She clenched her jaw, ready to argue some more, but before things could escalate further, James spoke up again.

"Senator, I've been meaning to ask your opinion. The minotaur has retreated deep into its labyrinth and it's overdue for a flea and tick dip. I'm worried that if I go in after it, I'd never come out. How would you suggest I find my way inside the maze?"

The centaur's chest puffed up. "Well, classically speaking, a rope woven from red thread would be most effective, but a trail of white pebbles would also work in a pinch." James started walking towards the minotaur enclosure and Flavius fell in beside him. "Breadcrumbs have proven to be ineffective in the past..."

James looked over his shoulder and winked at her, and Amari wiped a hand across her face wearily. Her new assistant was becoming indispensable for handling Flavius and his ridiculous ideas.

If only she could trust him.

The earlier reminder that James had worked for a man who had traded in creatures, and who had even had parts stolen from the Repository – and had Caerus abducted! – left her wary. Ambrose had told her that James had been an unwilling accomplice in the end, but there had been years before then when he had not been unwilling at all.

She worried about his intentions. She worried about them all the way up the stairs, and she worried about them as she stood in front of the door leading to his room.

Amari hesitated. It would be an incredible breach of privacy, but the safety of the creatures in her care was her first priority. She needed to know if she could trust him.

She said the Word and the door clicked open.

James' room was a shambles. The large four-poster bed was unmade, and clothes were strewn across the floor. A tower of books was stacked on the desk stand – only one of them hers, the one she had loaned him, she noted with some satisfaction – and a shelf that had once displayed a copy of an ancient Greek urn was now home to a collection of empty glass jars in various sizes, a watercolour painting of Tower Bridge in London, and a tacky gold frame containing a photo of Ambrose and his sister, Cassie, in their early teens.

She turned towards the desk in the corner, practically groaning under a mess of notebooks and loose pages, all covered in James' tight handwriting. She picked up a page. It contained an incredibly detailed description of the cyclops, from his physical appearance to his dietary preferences. James had been putting his time in the Repository to good use.

Amari carefully put the paper back in its place and surveyed the room. Nothing seemed suspicious.

She shrugged, feeling guilty at her unwarranted intrusion, and was about to leave when she recalled her conversation with Reese. The more she'd thought about it, the clearer it became that the aged shapeshifter had hinted at something being hidden from her. Could he have been referring to James?

It was worth a try.

She said the Word of Revelation and pursed her lips when the air above James' desk shimmered briefly. Carefully, Amari shuffled some papers away until she uncovered a small nest made of scraps of torn cloth nestled inside a fedora hat. Amari gasped as a tiny pink bird looked up at her with big, unblinking black eyes.

The phoenix! She'd forgotten all about it in the battle's aftermath at the Colosseum.

She leaned closer to peer at the little creature. A soft, contented purring noise emanated from its little throat as she rubbed one of her fingers along the back of its neck. The chick was still too young to take care of itself, and James was clearly hand-rearing the little bird. Normally, Amari wouldn't have condoned such close contact, but under the circumstances, it was probably the best way.

She suddenly understood why he'd touched his heart so often that first day. He must have had the phoenix tucked into his breast pocket. Why hadn't he told her?

Amari's phone beeped and she jumped guiltily. She needed to get out of James' room before he found her there. She quickly covered the nest up again. It would be interesting to see when he'd come clean, and why he'd been keeping the phoenix a secret from her.

Satisfied that the desk looked the same as before, Amari quickly ducked out of James' room. She hurried down the corridor, feeling both relief and guilt at snooping.

When she reached her study, she pulled her mobile out of her pocket. A summons! She said the Word and closed her eyes against the bright light.

When she opened them again, she stood at the edge of a cliff overlooking a fjord sparkling in the cold summer sunlight. A small town nestled far below her against the side of the mountain, the sloped roofs of red-shingled houses covered in green moss. Verdant farmland spread out towards the sea.

A muscular blond man with the rugged good looks of a Norse god stood a few feet away from her. Ivan Yarvik, one of her Procurement Specialists. He still had the silver whistle between his lips, and at his feet lay an unusually large black dog with three heads.

"What's this?" Amari asked, stepping closer to get a good look at the animal. The tongues of two of the heads were lolling out, two pairs of eyes rolled back in their heads. The third head was snoring loudly.

"Hellhound," Ivan said in his gravelly voice. Amari noticed fresh scratches along his arms and a smear of dried blood across his chiselled Viking cheek. He grunted as she lifted an eyebrow at him. "Not dead," he said. "Just knocked out. Bugger bit me. Twice."

"You should get a tetanus shot," Amari said as she knelt by the creature's side. She placed a hand on its warm fur and sighed in relief as she felt its chest rise. Ivan had a habit of taking things too far sometimes. He grunted noncommittally as she looked up at him from her crouching position. "Any others out there? A pack, perhaps?"

He shrugged. "Only found the one. Had been terrorising the local farmers, stealing their sheep, and frightening their children with its nightly howling."

"You're sure all three heads will wake up?" Amari asked.

"If they don't, you can dock it from my pay."

"Fair enough," Amari said. "Thank you, Ivan. Send me a list of the farmers and their losses. I'll make sure they're compensated."

Amari waited long enough for Ivan to nod before she whisked the comatose hellhound back to the Repository. She deposited the creature in an empty holding cell, closing the door firmly behind her.

The Keeper stood in the corridor, inspecting her latest acquisition. In the next cell over, the enormous blue salamander hissed spitefully, and she could hear the yale bleating further down, followed by an ear-splitting trumpeting that almost drowned out everything else. The rest of her charges were either welcoming the newest resident, or protesting loudly at the addition.

Her shoulders slumped. She should be happy. There hadn't been this kind of influx in years. If only she could give them all the homes they deserved.

She grunted. Patience. It would all work out soon enough.

Then she went looking for something that she could feed to an enormous three-headed dog.

※※※

Amari pulled at her scarf as she stood, arms folded across her chest, staring out of the boardroom window. Below her, the Grand Place bustled with tourists gaping at Brussels' majestic Gothic buildings, posing for selfies, and laughing as if they didn't have a care in the world. She wondered what they would say if they knew one of these buildings served as the headquarters of the Council for the Protection and Preservation of Cultural Creatures.

She heard the click of a door opening and turned to see the members of the Elder Council file into the room, silently taking their places at the long glass table in the centre of the room. Amari chewed on her bottom lip as an antagonistic atmosphere washed over her.

The Chairman, last to enter, closed the door

behind him before sitting down at the head of the table. He inclined his head and Amari took the seat at the other end, wincing as her chair scraped loudly across the hardwood floor.

"Let's get right down to business," Councilmember Finch said, pulling out a leather-bound ledger containing an alarming amount of paperwork. The grey-haired man cleared his throat as he adjusted the pair of spectacles resting on his bulbous nose.

Amari's gaze swept down the table, noting the grim expressions turned towards her. Even Councilmember Ravel, the man who had invited her to join in their celebrations only a few weeks ago, stared at her with hard eyes. She pulled at her scarf again. Maybe it was getting too warm for neckwear now.

"We are gathered here today to discuss some of the more concerning issues raised by Senator Flavius Regulus of the Green Grove," Councilmember Finch continued. "He notes here that he witnessed the massacre of an entire colony of fire salamanders, and that this event occurred because of the negligent actions of the Keeper of Exotic Animals. Miss Kerubo, can you explain to the Council how you could let such a catastrophe occur?"

Heat flushed across Amari's cheeks. "I believe the report I submitted explained the situation succinctly," she said.

"Indeed." Councilmember Finch held a piece of paper aloft, as if it were incriminating evidence. "I quote: *Due to the subsequent reduction in numbers of the fire salamander colony, it would appear that the two species are incompatible and should remain separated to prevent further loss of life.* Hardly an explanation of your actions, Keeper."

Amari pulled the scarf from her neck – was the

thing trying to strangle her? – and clutched it underneath the table. "With respect, Councilmember," she said, surprised at how steady her voice sounded. "There is no guidebook, no set of instructions, on how to take care of creatures that most people believe to be fictional. It is a continuous process of trial and error. What we know about fire salamanders is the result of years of careful observation. However, we don't have any reliable sources of information on blue salamanders, this being their first admission into the Repository." Amari's eyes met the Chairman's and he nodded in agreement. She felt her confidence return. "It was a reasonable assumption that the existing enclosure would be a suitable habitat for them too. Unfortunately, there was no predicting the test specimen's incredible growth or its brutal decimation of the resident fire salamanders."

"But surely you should have put measures in place for any unexpected events?"

Amari turned to the woman who had spoken up. She had the pinched expression of someone used to finding fault with everything. The Keeper knew from experience that Councilmember Silvetti was never easily satisfied.

"This is why I only moved *one* of the blue salamanders into the enclosure. It could have been much worse had I moved them all from their holding cell." The woman pursed her lips, as if looking for something else to say, and Amari quickly continued. "May I just add that although the losses were severe, it was not a complete massacre of the entire colony, as Senator Regulus so easily exaggerates. Enough fire salamanders survived that I'm confident the colony will recover fully, given some time."

"Let's move on to the next point then,"

Councilmember Finch said. "Senator Regulus also mentions the cyclops sustaining a devastating foot injury, and the newly acquired lamia suffering from a highly infectious disease he fears might spread through the entire Repository."

Amari's grip on her bundled scarf tightened. "Injuries and illness are not unheard of in the Repository, as this council should know by now. Senator Flavius is merely inflating minor events to make me, and by extension, the Council, look bad. What we should be discussing is the airavata and the fate of the rest of the creatures still stuck in the holding cells."

Councilmember Finch peered at her from over the top of his spectacles. "What of these creatures?"

"Why are they still in the holding cells?" Amari demanded. "It's been nearly a month since the new acquisitions have been confined to cells never meant to be in use for more than a day or two. The airavata barely has room to move. The caladrius can't stretch its wings out."

"A caladrius, you say?" the Chairman interrupted, leaning forward in his chair.

Amari nodded. "And a yale, and the rest of the blue salamanders. They can't live on chillies forever. They need proper fires to bond with or they will die, eventually. All the creatures need enclosures of their own as soon as possible. We can't afford to wait for the Green Grove's go-ahead much longer."

"Out of the question," Councilmember Silvetti said, tapping a fingernail the length of a harpy's claw on the table. "Our agreement with the Green Grove expressly states that no creatures will be housed without their sanction, and they have endorsed none of your suggestions to date." The woman's tone left no doubt in Amari's mind that the Council believed the fault was entirely hers. "In fact, one begins to wonder if your suggestions should carry any weight at all."

Amari's throat went dry as she stared at the unfriendly faces around her. Her glance wavered towards the decanter of water in the middle of the table, out of her reach. It felt like all the moisture in her body was suddenly congregating in her palms. "If my role as Keeper is under dispute –"

"It hasn't come to that," the Chairman interjected, and once again Amari felt the unspoken 'yet' lingering in the air. "Miss Kerubo, the Council would like to remain on amicable terms with the Green Grove. I trust you will do your best to keep both the creatures and the Grove content until we can agree on housing arrangements for the new acquisitions."

Amari nodded, swallowing relief down. "Of course."

"Good," the Chairman said. "Let us then move on to the matter of Mr Davids. The Council has had their doubts about his appointment as your assistant, given his history. How has he conducted himself since his arrival at the Repository?"

"He's been useful," Amari conceded, relieved that the focus was off her, for now. "He has a way with the creatures, and he's endlessly fascinated by them. He's studying them, as you'd have expected."

The Chairman nodded. "All in favour of Mr Davids continuing his research in the Repository – providing he makes the results known to this council alone – please raise your hands."

Unanimously, all the hands around the table lifted. Amari fiddled with her scarf. The thought of James scrutinising the creatures so intensely left her feeling slightly uncomfortable. But, judging by the nods of approval around her, she was in the minority.

Councilmember Finch cleared his throat. "With that settled, let's move on to the last point on the agenda." His expression soured as he said: "The matter of the missing kitsune."

Apprehension surged through Amari. Perhaps she shouldn't have reported her fears to the Council before she was certain he was actually gone. "He may still be in the Repository," she said.

"But you don't know for sure?" Sarcasm dripped off Councilmember Silvetti's words as she glared at Amari.

The Keeper steeled herself. "I don't know for sure," she admitted.

The silence that followed was as impenetrable as the smog hanging over Johannesburg on a winter's morning. Amari breathed deeply, forcing herself to meet the Councilmembers' gazes. Only sheer stubbornness stopped her from rising to her feet and shamefacedly fleeing from the boardroom.

"That is… disappointing," the Chairman said, breaking the silence.

"He may still be there," Amari quickly replied. "It's difficult to tell with shapeshifters. But if he isn't in the Repository, I have reason to believe he's gone in search of his mate, who was last seen in the possession of Marco Mazzoni."

"Who is now dead, I believe?"

Amari nodded. "But we recovered no kitsunes on the night of the blood moon market. Or if we did, they're disguised in another form. It's possible."

"But unlikely?" the Chairman asked.

"Unlikely," Amari conceded. "I don't see why they wouldn't have returned to Riku's enclosure if they were in the Repository. He was more than happy staying there before. And Riku has no reason to hide from me."

Councilmember Silvetti laughed scornfully. "Perhaps we should consider implanting tracking devices into the creatures, if our Keeper can't keep them inside their enclosures where they belong."

Amari shook her head. "I doubt that would work. Technology doesn't function well around mythology."

"Be that as it may," Councilmember Finch said. "What are you doing to retrieve the missing kitsune?"

"I will alert my team of Procurement Specialists. One of them is bound to come across him at some point."

"It's the least you can do," Councilmember Silvetti sneered.

Amari clenched her jaw. She'd like to see the woman survive a day in her shoes. She'd probably break a nail within the first hour. And lose that smirk sooner.

"Unless anyone has anything else to add...?" The Chairman looked around the room, but no one spoke up. "Then I think we can call an end to this meeting. Miss Kerubo, thank you for coming. I know how busy you are."

Amari nodded, her hands cramping a little as she wrapped the scarf around her neck again. She stood up from the table and watched as the Council adjourned. None of them looked at her as they filed out, and she realised she was digging halfmoon circles into the palms of her hands.

When had these meetings become about her? The Elder Council had always trusted her to take care of the creatures in the Repository as she saw fit. They'd never questioned her decisions like this before. Had Flavius changed their opinion of her so easily?

But what if Flavius was right? What if she wasn't doing a good enough job? Could she have handled the salamander incident differently? Could she have prevented Ody's injury from happening? The lamia's infection?

She knew she should have kept better track of Riku.

What-if's clunked around in her head as Amari showed herself out of the boardroom, and out of the building. She blinked as she stepped into the Grand Place, closing her eyes as she felt the sun on her skin, and breathed deeply, letting the tension ease from her shoulders. She walked through the jumble of people in the square, stopping to buy a waffle dipped in chocolate, and then went looking for a bench.

Her gaze roamed around the square while she ate. Children chased each other, their parents smiling indulgently as their smartphones recorded their antics. A young man bought a bunch of flowers for a blushing girl by his side. An older lady sat down to have her portrait painted by a street artist.

For a moment, Amari allowed herself to wonder what it would be like to be one of them, untroubled, her shoulders free of a mountain's weight.

But no, the Repository needed her. She licked her fingers, stood up, and stepped into a quiet alley.

※ ※ ※

Amari pulled her hands away just in time as the hellhound's jaws clamped around the sheep carcass and hauled it deeper into the cell. She slammed the door shut, the scent of fresh meat and blood almost overwhelming. She watched the animal tear into the dead sheep, noting with satisfaction that the bruises on two of its heads were nothing more than dim shadows. Judging by its appetite, and the snapping of bones on the other side of the barred gate, it was going to be alright.

Her phone beeped and she pulled it out quickly. She stared at the screen for a moment. It was from Ambrose.

She'd had no doubt that she'd hear from him again, but she hadn't expected it to be so soon.

White light blazed and she stumbled over something, feeling firm hands steady her. As her eyes adjusted, Amari's mouth fell open. She was in a tiny cubicle with a toilet in it. She grimaced as her shoes stuck to the floor.

"Ambrose! What's this? Are we inside a loo?" Her mouth drew into a thin line as an unpleasant smell wafted in from underneath the gap below the door.

"It's the only private space I could find at short notice," Ambrose apologised.

She wrinkled her nose as she studied the graffiti on the stall's walls. "You want to talk to me here, or can we take this someplace a little more civilised?"

"By all means," Ambrose said. "Let's get out of here."

She wasted no time saying the Word that whisked them back to her study.

✳✳✳

Much later that evening, long after she'd dropped Ambrose off in London again, Amari fell into the chair behind her desk, clicking her tongue irritably as her eye caught the growing pile of papers stacked to one side. She'd deal with Flavius' ridiculous suggestions in the morning. What worried her now was the news Ambrose had brought earlier.

He thought there was a werewolf loose in London, one that he'd encountered while in Rome. One that might have escaped from the Colosseum on the night of the blood moon market. It worried her. She remembered the chaos inside the Colosseum that night. Was it possible that something could have escaped in the confusion? And if one had broken out, how many others had slipped away unnoticed, too?

Surely James would know what had been up for sale that night? She glanced at her phone. It was well past midnight already. It could probably wait until a more reasonable hour.

She hid a yawn behind her hand. Yes, it could probably wait until morning.

She jumped as a loud banging suddenly shook her office door.

"Amari? Are you in there?" James sounded frantic.

Amari surged to her feet and flung the door open. James stumbled forward, his face as white as a yumboe's. A shiver of dread ran down Amari's spine.

"What's wrong?" she asked.

"It's Cassie." James said tersely. "She's in the ICU. I need to get to London."

Amari's eyes widened. "Of course," she said. "Where to?"

"St Thomas."

"Hold on."

Searingly bright light blazed and James gasped. When the world came back into view, the stark walls of the hospital loomed over them, lights from countless windows illuminating the surprise on her apprentice's face.

"I thought you had a helicopter," he said. She could see a hundred questions behind his eyes, but he clamped his lips together and started jogging toward the entrance.

Amari followed hastily in his footsteps.

⁂

The Keeper stifled a yawn behind her fist as they stepped back into her office. She glanced at the time on her phone. It was so close to dawn, she might as well not bother getting into bed now. She looked at James. His eyes were red from exhaustion and worry etched deep lines into his pale face.

"You can sleep in today. I'll take care of the morning rounds," Amari said, rubbing at her own tired eyes.

James shot her a wan smile. "Thank you, but I'm not sure I'll be able to sleep. My daughter's in hospital and my son is out hunting the thing that put her there."

"If you like, we can move Cassie into the Repository," Amari offered. "Its healing powers should have her back on her feet in no time."

James sighed. "I had thought about that, but I doubt the doctors would let her go in her current state. And besides, we'd have to deal with my ex-wife if we moved her. No, Cassie's in capable hands where she is at the moment. Maybe if things took a turn for the worse…"

"Let's hope it doesn't come to that. And you don't have to worry about Ambrose. He's resourceful. We'd better start planning an enclosure for the werewolf, because he'll be in a holding cell soon enough."

James' eyes narrowed. "He deserves a prison cell."

Amari shrugged. "We'll leave that for the Council to decide."

James yawned, and Amari ushered him towards the door. "Try to get some rest. There's nothing else we can do right now."

Her assistant nodded, swaying slightly on his feet. "Maybe you're right. And maybe later today you'll show me how you whisked us nearly a thousand miles away in the blink of an eye."

"Maybe…" Amari said, knowing full well that she would not.

James nodded, clearly sensing her reluctance, but not pushing the matter. "Good morning, then."

Amari watched him walk off, resisting the temptation to go in search of her own bed. But she knew if she closed her eyes now, she'd sleep for the better part of the day, and she simply had too much to do. She trudged wearily to the kitchen and sat down with a cup of rooibos, savouring the scent and the early-morning quiet.

Once she felt fortified enough to face the day, she loaded up a little cart with provisions and made her way to the holding cells. It was still early enough that most of the animals were asleep. All except one.

The hair on the back of Amari's neck stood on end as she peered into the last cell, and three sets of blood-red eyes returned her gaze. An ominous growl rumbled from a trio of throats as the hellhound stepped out of the shadows.

"Easy now," Amari said softly, holding up the enormous slab of mutton she had brought. "You want this?" Thick strands of slobber dripped from the creature's jaws in response as it stalked towards the gate.

"Hold!" Amari said, and the hellhound stopped, quirking one of its heads as it stared at her. "You can have it as long you don't take my hand off."

The hellhound stood poised as Amari inched the cell door open, keeping an eye on all three heads in case one of them decided to play dirty. One of its paws twitched and Amari's heart lurched into her throat.

"Stay!" she barked. The hound stilled and Amari stepped into the cell, her heart hammering in her chest.

The Keeper and the hellhound faced each other for an endless moment, and then Amari tossed the meat at the creature's feet. The hellhound was on it in seconds, all three of its heads tearing at the mutton, scattering globs of saliva that sizzled when they fell onto the stone floor.

Slowly, Amari backed out of the cell and locked the gate again. She watched the creature as it devoured its breakfast. Three heads were distinctive, a clear indication that this hellhound was a descendant of the legendary Cerberus. She'd have expected to find it roaming around Greece, not harassing farmers in Norway. She'd read about many fearsome wolves from Viking myths, but none ever mentioned three-headed dogs. Perhaps it was time she brushed up on her Norse mythology again.

A wave of weariness washed over her, and the thought of spending the day curled up by the fire with a good book suddenly looked enormously appealing. It was research, after all. She left the hellhound to its feast and returned to her study.

She stopped short when she entered the room to see James inspecting Diana's collection, his hands gently trailing along the spines as he perused the titles.

"I've asked you not to touch those books before," Amari said, heat suddenly surging through her.

James' hand snapped to his side as he flinched away from the bookcase. He cleared his throat guiltily. "I was trying to see if I could find anything about werewolves. Something that might help Ambrose catch the monster."

"If there were, I would have given it to him already."

James cleared his throat, a feint blush reddening his cheeks. "I'm sorry, I should have asked."

"Yes, you should have."

She stood aside, and James took her not-so-subtle hint and walked towards the doorway. He paused.

"Is there something else?" Amari asked, fatigue blunting her ability to curb her annoyance.

James took a deep breath. "I want to borrow the caladrius."

Amari frowned. "Borrow him? For what? You have unlimited access to him. You can study him as much as you like while he's still stuck in the holding cell."

James coughed nervously. "I'm afraid you misunderstand…"

Amari's eyes widened. "You want to take him out of the Repository? To Cassie?"

Her assistant nodded eagerly.

"I'm sorry, James, but it's out of the question." She held her hand up as his expression darkened. "The bird heals illnesses, not injuries. I've tested it myself. It wouldn't do any good."

"But can we at least try?"

"No," she snapped.

"Why not?" James snapped back. "You sit here, safe in your fortress, while my daughter is in ICU!"

Amari stared at the erstwhile scholar. His nostrils flared as he glared at her. With bags underneath his

255

bloodshot eyes and his hair standing up as if he'd been tugging on it again, he looked capable of almost anything.

She sighed. "You, of all people, should know why."

James' jaw clenched, hardening the lines on his face. "Not even for Cassie?"

"I would do anything to help Cassie, James, you must know that," Amari said, hoping he heard the sincerity in her voice. "But the caladrius can't help her. Nothing in here can."

The man's gaze flickered back to her bookshelves before dropping to the floor. He took a deep breath. "You're right. I'm sorry."

"It's alright," Amari said. "It's been a tough night. You should really try to get some sleep."

James nodded. He walked out of her office, his movements strangely stiff, and disappeared around the corner leading towards the guest quarters.

Amari chewed a corner of her bottom lip. Could she trust him not to go behind her back and take the caladrius, anyway? But without her help, he wouldn't be able to get to London. No, the bird was probably safe, but her books... At least Diana's diaries were hidden away with Reese, but she'd have to devise some other way to protect the rest of her library from him. And since she'd taught him the Word of Unlocking, it would have to be something a little more creative than just barring her study door.

A chill ran down her spine, and she wrapped her arms around herself. She'd faced monsters that were the stuff of nightmares without blinking, but the thought of so much knowledge in that man's hands...

The Keeper firmly closed the door to her study behind her. She had a sudden craving for some rooibos tea.

✳✳✳

Tired though she was, Amari kept herself busy the rest of the day. She finally cornered the minotaur and gave him his flea bath, she swept out the cyclops' lair, and dewormed the harpies. Around midday she went to visit Kentigern Mor and spent a few pleasant hours basking in the sun next to the lake, chatting to the great dragon about everything from the migratory patterns of Scottish kestrels to the vibrancy of the Grant clan's tartan kilts, until their talk dried up and her eyelids drooped and sleep claimed her.

When she woke up, the dragon was gone, and the sun lay low over the horizon. She brushed grass from her hair and returned to the Repository.

Raucous barking echoed through the corridor as soon as she stepped into the administrative wing. Amari hastened to the holding cells and found Flavius glaring at the three-headed hellhound.

"What's this?" the centaur asked, taking a prudent step backwards as the creature rammed against the bars of its cell door.

"Is that a trick question?" Amari asked wearily. *"Káne isychía!"* she commanded, and the barking suddenly stopped. The Keeper nodded to herself. "It's a hellhound."

"I can see it's a hellhound. What's it doing here?" The centaur's brows furrowed into a frown.

Amari inched closer to the cell door, watching the three-headed creature's movements. A low rumble came from deep within its belly, but she slowly stretched her hand out and, very carefully, rubbed behind the ears of the closest head. Her lips quirked into a smile as the hound's tail thumped against the floor.

"Why, Flavius, I thought you knew what the purpose of the Repository was," she said sweetly, grinning as the tongue of the second head started licking her hand, spreading thick slobber across her fingers.

The centaur's mouth drew into a thin line. "The Green Grove will need to be informed of this."

"Of course, feel free," Amari said, retrieving her tingling hand and wiping it on her pants. "But this creature was not a blood moon acquisition, and therefore does not fall under the Green Grove's jurisdiction. Tell me, how regular would you make the snowfall in its new enclosure?"

"Snowfall?" the centaur spluttered. "I thought the enclosures mimicked their natural habitat as close as possible! You should think of rocky fissures and olive groves, not snowfall!"

Amari nodded. "I agree." So, Flavius also thought the hellhound was more suited to a Mediterranean climate than the fjords of Norway. "Would you like to provide some input?"

"No, I would not!" Flavius said, stomping one of his front hooves. He pushed past her and clomped out of sight. Probably off to write a report. In triplicate.

Amari turned to the hellhound, who was sitting back on its haunches, its tongues lolling out as it watched her with its eerie red eyes.

"What were you doing so far north, boy?" she wondered aloud. The hellhound cocked one of its heads, its tail wagging in anticipation. Amari made a mental note to ask James if he had any ideas before moving on.

She checked in on each of the creatures still confined to the holding cells, her frustration increasing with each door she passed. At the last door, the airavata was fast asleep on a bed of straw, piles of uneaten fruit lying untouched in one corner. Amari's heart ached to see the creature so vulnerable. This was not right!

Her hands balled into fists, but then her shoulders slumped again. Flavius would file a report immediately if she dared to take matters into her own hands, and the Council had been clear enough on how important it was to keep the Green Grove happy. Amari knew Councilmember Silvetti wouldn't hesitate to get rid of her at the slightest provocation. And then who would look after her creatures? James? No, she couldn't let that happen.

The Keeper sighed. She cast one last regretful glance at the sleeping airavata and then returned to her study. She sat down next to the fireplace, pulled her phone out, and opened YouTube. She hadn't been to Greece yet, but she was sure to find some inspiration for the hellhound's enclosure online.

❋❋❋

It was well after midnight when the vibration of an incoming notification woke her up. Amari caught her mobile just before it could slip off her chest and fall into the flickering fire.

Blinking, she stared at the display. It took her a moment to realise what was going on, but when she did, she jumped to her feet. Finally!

"I'd hoped to hear from you tonight," she said as she stepped out of the beam of light. Standing beside a fountain in Trafalgar Square, Ambrose looked a little the worse for wear. A sleeve had been ripped off his tweed jacket, and his jeans were wet up to the knee.

Amari grimaced when she saw the bare-chested man lying in a puddle by Ambrose's feet. The man had an ugly wound in one of his shoulders and a lump forming on the side of his head. A tattooed snake crawled along one of his arms. Amari shuddered.

"Is that our werewolf?"

"Yeah," Ambrose replied, raking a hand through his hair. "Let's get him out of here before he wakes up."

Amari nodded, and the world turned white again as she swept them back to the Repository.

✳✳✳

"A werewolf, you say?" The Chairman's voice sounded incredulous over the phone. "I didn't think they were real. Just superstitious nonsense made popular by bad B-movies."

Amari laughed. "All superstitions are based on fact, sir."

"Of course, of course. And if there's one, there are more…?"

Amari played with the werewolf bracelet Ambrose had given her, testing the sharpness of the teeth with her finger. It didn't puncture her skin, but she could imagine a mouth full of these fangs doing some serious damage. "I would assume so. I haven't interrogated this one yet, but my Specialist said he used to be in the US Army. Went missing a year ago and was assumed dead."

"Interesting. Born a wolf, or turned somehow?"

"I don't know. But this poses the question: do we deliver him to the authorities and let them deal with him? James' daughter is in hospital after the werewolf tried to kill his son, and we can link at least two deaths to the creature."

The Chairman was quiet for a second, then: "No, keep him in the Repository. A normal court of law wouldn't know how to handle someone like him. He falls under the Council's domain now."

Amari nodded. "Agreed."

"I want you to find out what happened to him, Keeper. If he was fully human before, we need to know how he ended up like this. And if he was born that way, perhaps he can lead you to others of his kind."

"I'll find out," Amari said, grimacing. She'd already seen enough of this man to know she didn't want to spend more time than was absolutely necessary in his company. And if the military had trained him, he was unlikely to give up his secrets easily.

The Chairman cleared his throat on the other side of the line. "And Keeper, if he truly caused the deaths of two people, you needn't be in a hurry to make his life too comfortable."

"Understood."

Amari ended the call and sat back in her chair, still fiddling with the bracelet. Ambrose was adamant that Norton, the werewolf, had been at the Colosseum on the night of the blood moon market, and yet he hadn't been captured along with the rest of the creatures that were currently in the holding cells. The likelihood of more creatures escaping unnoticed seemed all too plausible now.

The thought sent a shiver of dread down Amari's spine. Who knew what could be out there still? Perhaps also harbouring a grudge, like Norton did.

A knock sounded on the study door.

"Come in, James," Amari said, tucking the bracelet into a desk drawer as her assistant walked in. There were dark circles under his eyes, and it looked like he might have had even less sleep than her. "How's Cassie doing?"

"She's still in a coma, but stable, at least. My ex-wife says the doctors are confident she'll make a full recovery."

"I'm glad to hear that. The offer is still open, if you want to move her to the Repository."

James shook his head. "I'd rather she stayed far away from all of this."

"Fair enough," Amari said, nodding. "Have you been to the holding cells yet?"

"No, I've been held up in the basilisk pen. How many times is that thing going to shed its skin this week?"

Amari laughed. "Hector is quite finicky. He always wants to look his best." She cleared her throat. "Your son brought the werewolf in last night."

James' face paled visibly, and his hands balled into fists. She hoped he had the sense not to take on the werewolf by himself. Hell, even if Norton didn't have any supernatural powers, she wouldn't have advised the erstwhile scholar to engage him in a fistfight.

"He's in the holding cells right now. I know this is personal for you, and we'll find some way to make him pay for what he's done, but I need you to understand that he's not to be harmed."

James' mouth drew into a thin line, and the look he shot her burned like hot coals.

"I'm serious, James," she said before he could object. "Norton's the first of his kind we've ever encountered. You're familiar with the theory that each mythical creature embodies a particular trait?"

The scholar nodded curtly.

"Well, I have no idea what trait he represents, but for all we know, he might be our only hope of preserving it."

James' face softened as he considered her words. "That's an intriguing question," he admitted, scratching the stubble on his chin. His scowl faded as academic curiosity took over. "Werewolves have always had an evil reputation – if you ignore the paranormal romances that have inexplicably become popular in recent years. The gods cursed the first werewolf for slaughtering and eating his own son, and the legends grow progressively worse from there on. Of course, sources are so vague and unreliable, it's hard to know what to believe, or even what to conjecture. If I had to hazard a guess though…"

Amari leaned forward, eager to hear his answer.

"Aggression." James nodded to himself, lost in thought. "That's the only thing that makes sense."

Amari lifted an eyebrow. "How did you come to that conclusion?"

James' eyes snapped to hers. "Consider the sample. He tracks Ambrose down across Europe, kills several people for no reason, nearly kills my daughter –" His voice faltered, but he visibly pulled himself together again, and continued: "He is deliberately violent. Hell, if the movies are to be believed, the mere act of transforming from man into wolf is bone-shatteringly brutal. Aggression defines his entire existence."

"You may have a point," Amari said, tapping a finger against her cheek. "Norton is ex-military, after all."

James threw his hands into the air, as if she'd just proven his point.

"But in my experience, the trait isn't always as obvious as you'd expect," the Keeper said. "It could just as well be perseverance, tenacity, dog-headed stubbornness. He's certainly shown himself to be capable of that."

"Whichever it is, the world can certainly do with a little less of it," James muttered.

Amari's eyes widened and she rose to her feet. "Promise me," she said, her voice suddenly cold as steel. "Promise me you will not try to harm him. Under any circumstances."

Her assistant grimaced. "I promise," he finally said, reluctantly.

Amari took a calming breath. "That's what we do here, James. We protect. No matter our personal feelings."

"I understand." But judging by the surly expression on his face, he still didn't like it.

"Come," Amari said, stepping out from behind her desk. "Let's go see him. The sooner you meet him, the sooner you can make your peace."

James nodded unenthusiastically, and the two of them walked towards the holding cells.

Amari's nose scrunched up as she caught a whiff of something pungent, almost like rotting mulch. She looked sideways at James, wondering if she should say something. He kept pace with her, his face clouded in thought. But every time he stepped within arm's reach, the stench wafted her way.

"What am I smelling?" she finally asked, too repulsed to keep quiet any longer.

James looked startled for a moment, and then he patted the pockets of his jacket, searching for something. "Oh, this probably," he said, pulling a strip of discarded basilisk skin out. "I forgot I still had it on me."

"What are you doing with that?" Amari snapped, snatching the skin from him.

The startled scholar stared at her, confused. "I wanted to have a good look at it. Preferably under a microscope. I thought I might determine what the chicken-to-snake ratio is in its DNA."

A flame flared from Amari's palm, and the skin dissolved into a pile of ash. James flinched. He stared at Amari with wide eyes as she wiped her hand against her jeans.

"I understand your professional interest, James, but I can't allow it," she said, continuing along the corridor again. James hurried to keep up. "Creature parts have a habit of finding their way into the wrong hands. I'd rather not risk it."

James' brows lowered into a frown. "Of course. I understand. My background counts against me."

Amari winced. "I'm sorry. Maybe in time…"

"Say no more," James said smoothly, but the frown didn't disappear.

They walked in uncomfortable silence until they reached the holding cells. "He's in the last one," Amari said, relieved at the change of subject.

James visibly steeled himself as he walked past the airavata, absent-mindedly patting a trunk reaching out to him. His gaze was fixed on the cell at the end, his steps slowing down the closer they came. By the time they stopped in front of the cell door, James' shaking hands were clenched into fists again.

Amari peered into the cell. Norton was lying on his back on the pallet in the corner, his arms behind his head and his eyes closed, but she could tell from the way his chest rose he wasn't asleep.

"Hello, pretty lady," he drawled in his deep American twang. He sniffed and opened his eyes, sitting up. "You brought a friend."

"This is James, my assistant. He'll be feeding you until we know what to do with you."

The muscles in his arms bulged as Norton pushed himself to his feet. He strolled leisurely to the cell door, a smile on his lips that didn't reach his eyes. "I remember you," he said as James stepped into his view. Beside her, Amari sensed James tensing. "The professor. Heard you lost your nerve back there in Rome. Must be true if you're hiding behind this one's skirt now."

"You nearly killed my daughter. You tried to kill my son," James said, a red flush creeping across his face.

Norton shrugged. "Your boss wanted to sell me to the highest bidder. Seems only fair."

James lunged towards the cell, but Amari shoved him aside just as Norton's hand grabbed at the air where James' head had been. The man's lips twisted into a growl as Amari clenched her fist and his movements came to an abrupt halt.

The Keeper glared at her captive. "You will cooperate, Mister Norton, or the two of us can make life extremely unpleasant for you. Your choice."

She unclenched her hand and the man stumbled backwards. Shock painted his rugged features. Then his mouth twisted back into a sneer again.

"Whatever you say, sweetheart," he drawled. "But as I understand it, I have rights, even in here. The centaur was very interested to hear about how I was brought here against my will. And injured, to boot." He rolled his shoulder, where a small scar puckered red on his tanned skin.

Amari's teeth ground together. Bloody centaur.

"Home Office," James said cryptically.

Amari quirked an eyebrow. "I beg your pardon?"

"That's my suggestion for his enclosure. I'm sure he'll find the waiting room endlessly amusing."

Amari's lips twitched as she saw Norton's smile falter, but he didn't lose his bluster.

"Whatever you think best," he drawled, drawing closer to the cell door again. "Just don't go to too much trouble. I won't be here long."

"Oh, I wouldn't be too sure of that," Amari

said, stepping in close enough that she could smell the werewolf's stale breath. "I think you're going to be here for a very long time."

She held his gaze until his lips twisted into a snarl, exposing unusually large canines. Amari turned her back on him. "Come on, James. Let's go talk to Flavius about his empty promises."

Amari's skin broke into goosebumps as a howl suddenly rent the air. Around her, a cacophony of trumpeting, hooting, yowling, and hissing rose, until she could hardly hear her own thoughts.

She shot a glance at James. Her assistant looked rattled. She placed a hand on his arm as they walked away. "You handled that well," she said, just loud enough to be heard above the ruckus.

James managed a tight-lipped smile, and Amari made a mental note to ensure she was there the next few times her assistant faced the werewolf. She had a feeling trouble would come from that man's presence in the Repository. She needed to get him out of sight and self-sufficient in an enclosure of his own soon, or who knows what James might do…

✳✳✳

"Ah, Keeper," Flavius said when they found him with one hand lifted as if he was about to knock on her office door. "I came to deliver this." He held a stack of papers out at Amari.

"What is it?" she asked as she took the bundle from him.

"The approved plans for the airavata's enclosure." Flavius smiled officiously. "I took the liberty of reviewing them for you and all is in order. All I require from you is a signature." He offered her a silver pen engraved with his initials.

Amari quirked an eyebrow. "All this paperwork for one enclosure? What about the rest of the proposals I submitted?"

"All in due course, Amari. The Green Grove is nothing if not thorough, as you'll see from the approved specifications. You'll want to initial each page and sign the last one." He looked expectantly at her, still brandishing his pen.

Amari shot James a frustrated glance and her assistant smoothly stepped in. "I'm sure all is in order, but let's give the Keeper a moment to review everything," he suggested. "If you'll join me in the kitchen, Flavius – I'm just about to unpack a consignment of ouzo destined for the nymphs. I'm sure they won't miss a bottle or two if we tasted it first. For research purposes, of course."

The centaur laughed. "Your human beverages all taste like water to me, but I'll consider it my duty to determine if this drink lives up to the nymphs' expectations. After all, the ladies can be quite picky when it comes to the fruits of the vine."

"Indeed," James agreed, looking enquiringly at Amari.

Relieved, she nodded her approval, and then ducked into her office as James led the centaur away.

The stack of papers made an intimidating thump as she dropped them onto her mahogany desk. She sat down, reaching for a pen, and felt a wave of excitement wash over her. Some progress at last!

She flipped through the pages, feeling enthusiasm morph into frustration, until she finally tossed the pen down in disgust. Is this what she had been waiting for for so long? Whoever had written this specification had clearly skipped the research or lost the plot completely. The writer waffled on endlessly about savannah plains, groves of Marula trees and a muddy waterhole – as if an airavata was an African elephant! Where were the lush jungles, the stormy skies, the endless supplies of jackfruit? Where were the animals that would keep it company? How could she possibly sign off on this ill-conceived idea? It was as if they didn't want her to build an enclosure!

Amari slammed her fist against the desk. That's exactly what this was! Just another delaying tactic, another ploy to make her look bad in the eyes of the Council. Well, if they thought she was going to meekly accept their supposed recommendations, they had a surprise coming.

※※※

It didn't take her long to track the centaur down again. She found him in the nymph enclosure, swaying on his feet with a tankard of ouzo in his hands and a bawdy song on his lips. Her assistant sat on the grass, cradling his head in his hands, while a group of dryads were dancing the sirtaki in a raucous ring around him.

Amari marched up to the tipsy senator and planted herself in front of him, hands on her hips. "How could you possibly think that I'd sign off on that document? You said you read it – what made you think the recommended enclosure would be at all suitable for the airavata?"

Flavius blinked a few times, as if he was having trouble focussing. He leaned down to get a better look at her and nearly fell over. Amari grimaced as she watched the quadruped flouncing to keep upright.

"Seemed reasonable to me," he slurred, and Amari took a step away from the reek of alcohol

on his breath. "Big elephant, big open... space."
He hiccupped loudly before taking another swig
from his tankard.

Amari folded her arms across her chest. "After
nearly a month of delays, that's the best you can
come up with?" She shook her head, disgusted. "I
can't believe I bothered to wait for you."

She started walking off, but the centaur
swaggered in front of her, blocking her path.

"Always so serious, Amari. Come, have a drink
with us," Flavius said as a nymph sashayed past
carrying a tray laden with glasses filled with an
opaque white liquid. "We can toast to the airavata's
health in his new enclosure."

"You mean the one I'm going to build right
now? The one that I should have made weeks
ago?"

Flavius pursed his lips. "The one the Grove
recommended, or nothing at all."

Amari scoffed. "The Grove has lost all
credibility. I'll do as I see fit."

She stepped past him, but stopped short as his
hand close around her arm. When she turned, the
centaur didn't look nearly as drunk as he'd seemed
a moment before.

"The one the Grove recommended," he
repeated in a grave voice, his eyes boring into hers.
"Or nothing at all."

Amari glared at him. "Are you threatening me,
Senator?"

Flavius remained tight-lipped, and Amari felt
the hair on the back of her neck stand up. She
shook her arm free of his grip and stormed off.

※※※

Amari patted one of the airavata's trunks
through the bars of its cell door. It had been a

couple of days since her last conversation with Flavius, and she still hadn't created the creature's enclosure. The centaur's unspoken threat weighed heavily on her. He'd been long enough under the mountain – had come and gone in and out of enclosures as he'd pleased – to know most of the inner workings of the Repository by now. Who knew what he could be capable of?

"Amari…" Norton's sing-song voice carried down the hallway. "Amari…"

The Keeper rolled her eyes. She moved on to the colony of blue salamanders. James had filled their bowl of chillies earlier that morning, but it looked nearly untouched. The salamanders lay piled into a heap on top of each other in the cell's corner, clustered together underneath the heat lamp she'd installed. The stripes on their blue bodies shone a pale orangey-yellow.

At the next cell door, the yale bleated happily as she stopped to retrieve a hard-boiled egg from her bag. She stroked the tusked antelope's bristly mane while it greedily gobbled it up.

"Amari…" Norton's voice taunted her again.

Undaunted, she moved on to the next cell, and relaxed as she saw the lamia curled up on itself, its head hidden underneath the layers of its coils. She was supposed to be the Keeper of *all* Exotic Animals, but she'd have been happier if this particular one wasn't her responsibility.

The caladrius was pecking at a half-eaten mango when Amari walked past, stopping to stare briefly at her with one icy blue eye, before attacking its snack again.

In the cell next door, the enormous blue salamander lay on its back, stiff as a rock, its black tongue hanging limply from its open jaws.

Amari swore loudly.

Ignoring Norton's chuckles from the cell

behind her, she wrenched the door open and crouched down on the floor beside the lizard. Cautiously, she touched its blue scales. Her fingers recoiled. The salamander was ice cold.

"Shit," she said again as she rose to her feet. She glanced around the cell, her nose wrinkling in distaste as she noticed the smell. The floor was littered with pepper stalks and runny yellow excrement. She spun on her heels and stormed out of the cell.

"What happened here?" she demanded.

Norton's smile was vicious. "Looks like a case of gross negligence to me," he drawled, clearly savouring her distress. "Doubt the centaur is going to be happy when he hears about this."

"Hear about what?" Amari's shoulders sagged as Flavius trotted into the hallway. The centaur's nose wrinkled, giving his face a pinched expression. "What *is* that smell?"

"See for yourself," the Keeper said, sighing. No point in trying to hide what had happened. Flavius would have noticed the salamander's disappearance eventually, anyway.

Holding a hand across his nose, the centaur peered into the cell. His posture stiffened, and then he spun on his heels. "It's dead!" he exclaimed. "How did this happen?"

"Gross negli–" Norton started saying, before Amari interrupted him.

"A lack of a suitable enclosure, is what's happened! He was too big to survive on chillies alone. He needed a fire to be bonded to. His death is on your head, Flavius. Yours and the Green Grove's."

The centaur's goatee bristled as he glared at her. "I thought the Repository could cure all ailments?"

"Within reason!" Amari said, feeling her blood

pressure rise. "The salamander's essence is tied to his fire. He lost that connection the moment we took him out of the fire salamanders' enclosure and didn't give him a new fire to bond with. No fire, no essence."

Flavius wagged a finger at her angrily. "He shouldn't have been linked to that fire in the first place. If you hadn't taken him into that enclosure, he would still be safe with the clutch in the other cell. No, Keeper, this is on you and you alone. The Grove will hear about this." He shook his fist at her, before storming out of sight.

Amari clicked her tongue. He was right. This was her fault.

Next to her, she heard Norton tutting. "Bad Keeper."

Amari rounded on him. "When are you turning again? At least then I can put a muzzle on you!"

Norton grinned and then lifted his chin and howled. Around her, all the other creatures joined in.

Swearing, Amari stalked off, ignoring Norton's laugher echoing down the corridor behind her.

✵✵✵

"What the…?"

Amari stared at the stream of water flowing down the corridor, soaking into her shoes. An ominous rumble rolled through the air and then, suddenly, it was raining *inside* the Repository. Not far off, the airavata trumpeted loudly. The hair on her arms stood on end, and Amari's face paled as she realised what was about to happen.

Swearing, she jumped as high as she could, grabbing onto a light suspended from the ceiling. A moment later, the corridor lit up as if she'd said the Word to Travel, and the crack of lightning nearly deafened her. The water beneath her feet sizzled and steam rose towards the ceiling.

Amari breathed heavily as she dangled in the air, her shoulders aching from the strain, realising just how close she'd come to being electrocuted.

"James!" she shouted, wondering if it was safe to let go.

"Here!" Her assistant's voice was alarmingly high.

Amari dropped to the ground, her pumps slapping against the water-drenched floor as she sprinted towards the sound of his voice. It had come from the holding cells.

She bolted round the corner and lurched to a standstill, gaping at the enormous five-headed elephant rearing backwards, five pairs of crazed eyes rolling and five sets of tusks swiping like an army of spears.

James, his eyes wide enough to dwarf the cyclops' enormous orb, was on the creature's back, clinging on for dear life.

"Easy, boy," Amari said in a soothing voice, stretching one trembling palm out towards the panicked animal. She just needed to get close enough to touch it. "Easy now."

The airavata's ears flapped threateningly and Amari froze. Another foreboding rumble echoed through the tunnel.

"James," Amari said urgently. "Hold on."

The scholar nodded, his jaw clenched tightly and his white knuckles digging into the folds of skin on the animal's back.

Another crackle electrified the air. There was no time to lose.

Amari dived towards the airavata, ducking as she narrowly avoided being skewered by one of its many tusks. She slapped her palm against the bristly skin on the creature's foreleg, feeling her energy sap as she said the Word. The great beast dropped to its knees and then collapsed onto its side. It was asleep before it hit the ground.

James grunted as he slid from the airavata's back. He looked shaken, but unhurt.

Amari leaned against the stone wall, her knees trembling. "What the hell happened?" she demanded, wiping water out of her eyes.

"I'm not sure," James said, staring at the sleeping creature, its one leg twitching as if it was dreaming about running. "It came storming down the corridor when I came to do the rounds. Somehow, I ended up on its back. It was that or get trampled."

"How did it get out of its cell?"

James shook his head. "No idea. How are we going to get it back in there?"

"It should be released," Flavius said, his nasally voice instantly grating on Amari's nerves like fingers on a chalkboard. She turned to see the centaur surveying the scene, his arms folded across his chest.

The Keeper ground her teeth together. "We've already discussed this, Flavius. I cannot set it free, and I've already sent you my formal objections to the enclosure the Grove recommended. In triplicate."

"And they have been noted. The Grove will respond in due course."

"Then what do you want me to do?" she asked, dangerously close to putting the centaur to sleep as well. That would certainly solve most of her problems, and the repercussions be damned.

Flavius shrugged. "Return it to the holding cell if you must."

"Fine. But we'll need your help." The centaur opened his mouth to object, but Amari cut him short. "Help us move him or help us mop up. Your choice, senator."

Flavius' tale whipped sideways, but he finally nodded. "We'll need something to move him with."

"I have an idea," James said. "But you won't like it, senator."

✖✖✖

It was several hours later by the time the three of them had finally returned the enormous elephant back to its holding cell, James' makeshift stretcher strapped to the centaur's back as if he was a plough horse, and a few more before Amari finally wrung a mop out into the last pail of water. Exhausted, she slumped onto a chair in the kitchen, gratefully accepting the steaming cup James handed her.

She sighed contentedly as the scent of rooibos wafted towards her. "Thank you, James."

"You're welcome," the scholar said as he slumped into the chair opposite her. "The cell door was unlocked."

"Excuse me?" Amari asked, hunching over her cup as if breathing in its fumes could chase away all her troubles.

"It was unlocked, Amari. Not broken down. The airavata didn't escape. It was set loose."

Amari swore silently as she burned her lips on the hot brew. She placed her cup on the table and stared at James. "Why would Flavius do that?"

Her assistant shrugged. "To force your hand? To discredit you?"

"But…" Amari sighed. "Why? What would he gain from it?"

The look on James' face was incredulous. "You've proven unwilling to submit to his demands.

276

If I were him, my next tactic would be to show that you're not a capable caretaker and that the creatures would be safer outside the Repository. That's their goal, isn't it? To have them all set free?"

"I suppose…" Amari replied, rubbing at the vein suddenly throbbing at her temple. "But surely there are safer ways of discrediting me. The Green Grove –"

"*Not* the Green Grove."

Amari's eyes widened. "He means to set the Council against me."

James nodded, grimacing. "Do you have any allies on the Council? Anyone who would vouch for you?"

The rooibos suddenly tasted bitter in her mouth. Judging by the last meeting she'd had with them, the Council was already antagonistic towards her. It wouldn't take much to make them outright hostile. It all suddenly made sense now.

Her assistant was studying her. He nodded, as if he could read her thoughts on her face. "Tread lightly, Amari. It seems like the lamia isn't the only snake in the Repository. If you're not careful, it might catch you unawares."

✳✳✳

Amari winced as she pulled her hand back. She'd knocked so forcefully on the door to Flavius' room that she'd nearly bruised skin. It was not in her nature to play games. She needed to confront the centaur and find out what his intentions were.

The door swung open to reveal the senator, wrapped in his red mantle with a satchel strapped around his torso. Amari's heart lifted. Was the centaur on his way home?

"Ah, Keeper," he said. "I was just about to come see you. I'd hoped you'd be finished with that business with the airavata by now."

Amari folded her arms. "What do you know about the airavata's escape?" she asked bluntly.

The centaur's eyebrows rose in surprise. "Surely you don't think I was involved?"

"Were you?"

"Of course not!" the senator spluttered. "There are protocols to be followed – paperwork to be completed! – before the creature can be removed. I would never circumvent the necessary procedures in such a way."

"Would you do it to discredit me?"

The centaur looked affronted. "Have I ever been anything but frank with you?"

Amari studied the centaur's flushed face, his righteous indignation. Was he telling the truth? She wasn't sure. But if not him, then who? James? He had no reason to set the airavata loose like that. It *had* to have been Flavius. Unless...

There was always the possibility that the missing kitsunes might still be in the Repository. She'd found no trace of them so far, but that didn't mean they weren't there. Riku was clever, and liked to play pranks, and although she trusted him, there was really no telling what agenda he might have now.

Sighing, she dropped her arms. "Alright, I apologise, Senator Regulus."

Flavius grunted, unimpressed. "If I were you, I'd pay closer attention to what my apprentice was doing. The man has an astonishing amount of mythical knowledge, but his reputation is unsavoury."

Amari couldn't argue with that, but she didn't want to admit her doubts to Flavius. Instead, she inclined her head towards the satchel. "Going somewhere?"

The centaur's tail whisked irritably. "Indeed. I

was hoping you would transport me to Rome. The Army of the Green Grove has summoned me to report on the current situation in person. I will have a few choice words to share with Commander Equustos after this."

Amari stifled a sigh. "How long will you be gone?"

"Not long. Two or three days at most. I would like to be back for the full moon, to observe the treatment of the werewolf during his period of change."

Amari groaned. That's all she needed right now. Norton in a fowler, more murderous mood, than he already was. She'd better make sure his cell door was locked tight before the one-time soldier transformed into a raging beast bent on killing them all.

"Alright," Amari said, returning her attention to the present. "Where in Rome would you like me to drop you off?"

"The Colosseum will do. I can make my way from there."

"And in three days' time?" she asked, already relishing the peace his departure would bring her. Perhaps she would have an opportunity to somehow redeem herself in the Council's eyes.

"I will wait for you there again at sunset," Flavius said. "That should be enough time to prepare for whatever the full moon might bring."

Amari nodded. "Senator, before you go…" She hesitated. "I hope you understand that everything I do here is to protect the creatures."

"I believe your intentions are pure, Miss Kerubo," Flavius said, graciously. "But I cannot approve of your methods. The creatures in the Repository are locked away from the world in this prison. Some willingly, I'll admit," he added as she opened her mouth to argue. "But some forcefully, and many are ignorant of their true circumstances. It cannot last. They are owed their freedom."

"What will you do?" Amari asked, again unsure about whether he had set the airavata loose.

"I can only report what I've seen so far to the Green Grove. They will decide how we proceed from here."

"Fine," Amari said. They would never see eye to eye on this. She'd hoped his time in the Repository would have shown Flavius that the creatures were safer here, better off than being hunted and killed for parts in the outside world. She would just have to deal with the Green Grove until the Council ended whatever agreement they had with them.

Flavius lifted his hand in farewell as Amari's whispered Word swept him away.

✕✕✕

The Keeper gasped. There, on a blank piece of paper, was a mark she'd seen written only once before, but she knew immediately what it meant. Her heart was like a drum in her chest as she jumped from her chair and strode over to a bookshelf on the wall behind her desk. It took her only a moment to find Diana's last diary, tucked away between two other books of similar size and shape. She pulled the diary from its hiding place and sat back down at her desk, quickly flipping through the pages.

"This is Diana's diary," Amari said as Ambrose leaned in to have a closer look. It took her a moment to find the page where she had matched up the Words she knew with their written counterparts. Her breath hitched into her throat when she saw the Symbol Ambrose had drawn matching the one on the page. "This!" she exclaimed. "Is this it?"

Ambrose nodded. "That's it, yes. What does it mean?"

"It's the Word I use to travel with," Amari said, her hands shaking. If she could somehow learn how to use the Symbols without knowing their corresponding Words… The thought made her almost dizzy with excitement. "All this time we thought the power lay in the sound, but if this mysterious woman of yours only had to draw it… That opens up a world of possibilities!"

Ambrose's eyes twinkled. "But how does it work? You've told me before that certain words have power, but what makes the magic happen?" He twiddled his fingers in what must have been an impression of someone performing magic. Amari lifted an eyebrow, and he dropped his hands, looking sheepish.

"We only have a few remnants of the First Language available to us," the Keeper said, tracing her fingers across the rest of the Symbols on the page. "Diana dedicated her life to searching for them and learning how they worked. I've gleaned what I could from her diaries, but I'm afraid much is still lost."

"Will you teach it to me?" Ambrose's voice held a hint of a tremor in it, and the intensity of his gaze gave Amari some pause. This wasn't a simple request. This meant something to him.

An indelicate sound escaped her lips. "Not likely."

His shoulders dropped, but he didn't give up that easily. "Come on, Amari," he wheedled. "I already know the Symbol. I've heard you speak the Word many times. It's only a matter of time before I figure it out myself. Do you really want me to experiment on my own?"

Amari frowned. She was about to say no again

when she thought better of it. Ambrose was right, and he was both clever and resourceful. It would probably be in everybody's best interest if she taught him what she knew before he got himself into trouble.

"Fine. Just this one," she said, smiling at the grin splitting his face in two.

Ambrose was a quick learner and Amari was disappointed again that he hadn't taken up her offer of becoming her apprentice when he'd still been afflicted with the asrai's curse, so many months ago. He may not have the vast amount of mythical knowledge his father had, but she trusted him fully, something she unfortunately couldn't say about her current apprentice.

"Don't look so discouraged," Amari said when Ambrose's latest attempt to Travel failed again. His shoulders slumped, and he flopped down into the chair opposite her. "I'd have been very impressed if you'd managed it so easily. Besides, there's something I haven't told you yet."

"What's that?" he asked, disappointment plain on his face.

"The Repository has a powerful Word of protection over it. Only the Keeper can travel in and out of the mountain using a Word. Everyone else needs more conventional means."

"Oh…" Ambrose said, straightening in his chair.

Amari smiled at the look of hope that flashed across his face. "Come," she said, standing up from behind her desk. "I'll go show you where the West Gate is. Maybe you'll have better luck there."

A chime sounded, and Amari stopped mid-stride. She pulled her mobile phone out of her pocket. "Ah, I need to take this," she said, glancing at the caller ID. She frowned. Now this was a number she hadn't expected to see again.

She turned to Ambrose. "Why don't you go see James while I'm busy here? He should be almost done with the morning rounds by now."

As Ambrose closed the heavy oak door of her study behind him, Amari answered the call. "Hello Nadiya. I didn't think I'd ever hear from you again."

✖✖✖

The white light that had taken Ambrose to Dubrovnik had barely faded before Amari went looking for James again.

She found him just as he stepped out of the unicorn's enclosure and Amari had to suppress the surge of anxiety suddenly washing over her. She'd let Una down once before, and the thought of James alone with her left an uncomfortable feeling in the pit of her stomach. She couldn't quite shake the memory of the unicorn shying away from his touch.

"James…" she said, frowning at his startled reaction. One of his hands strayed briefly towards his jacket pocket, but he tried to hide it by running the hand through his hair instead. It reminded her of when he had first come to the Repository, and had kept the little phoenix hidden in his breast pocket.

"Sorry," he said. "I guess I'm a little on edge ever since the incident with the airavata."

Amari nodded. She'd been out of sorts since then too, obsessively checking the lock on every door that she walked past. So far, nothing else had been tampered with. It must have been Flavius…

"First a werewolf, now a chimaera," she said. "What else escaped from the Colosseum that night?"

James rubbed at the stubble on his chin. "It's hard to say, I'm afraid. I'd been out of Marco's good books for a while by that time and didn't have the opportunity to work with the stock anymore." His eyes glazed over as he tried to remember. "The nymphs are accounted for, of course, the five-headed elephant, the baby griffon…" He counted them off on his fingers. "The yale, the salamanders, the white bird, the lamia…" His eyes darted to hers. "The two kitsunes…"

"Two?" So Riku had been there! Had he found his mate and disappeared with her? "Do you know what happened to them?"

James shook his head. "The male helped us escape, but I don't know what became of him afterwards, and the female was Marco's insurance – he wouldn't have sold her. But she's not in the holding cells either, come to think of it."

"How sure are we of that?" Amari asked.

James' eyes widened and he cleared his throat uneasily. "You don't think she's here, do you?"

"I don't know," Amari admitted, wondering why her assistant was suddenly so nervous. A rogue kitsune loose in the Repository was certainly concerning, but hardly warranted this kind of reaction from him. Unless there was more she didn't know. "Is there something you need to tell me?"

James swallowed. "I'm afraid I may have been responsible for her capture." He held his arms up, as if in surrender. "But I didn't know Marco would put her in a cage like that, or use her to manipulate her mate. I just wanted to study her." He hung his head in regret.

"Do you think she might hold a grudge against you?" Amari asked.

James nodded. "It's possible."

"And do you think she could have set the airavata free?"

284

James' gaze flicked to hers. He licked his lips. "Possibly."

"We'd better be extra vigilant then," Amari said. "Shapeshifters have distinctive traits that can give them away, if you know what you're looking for. I haven't seen signs of Riku, but I don't know what to watch out for in his mate. She could be here, right under our noses."

James nodded again, his hand rubbing at his stubbled chin in that way that meant he was intrigued by something again.

Amari cleared her throat. "Speaking of things right under our noses… There's one more creature you haven't mentioned."

James shifted guiltily. "The baby phoenix. You know?"

"There is very little that goes on around here that I don't know about," Amari said, hoping it was indeed true, and suppressing the surge of guilt she felt at snooping in his room. Especially since she'd been so upset with him for entering her study uninvited. "When were you going to tell me about him?"

"I'm sorry, I should have told you sooner." James rubbed the back of his neck. "I knew you'd want to put him in an enclosure, and I just didn't want to give him up yet. I've grown rather fond of the little guy."

Amari sighed. "When he's old enough to take care of himself, he'll have to go into an enclosure, yes. But until then, you can keep looking after of him."

"I suppose that would be for the best," James agreed reluctantly. He rubbed at his chin again. "When I'm done with my rounds, I'll compile a list of the creatures that I can remember Marco having in stock. That should help us determine what went missing. And I think I might have a contact list of his regular buyers somewhere. Perhaps we can persuade them to part with their acquisitions."

"That would be great," Amari said, trying not to let the word 'stock' bother her too much. Then she grimaced. "And while you do that, there's one more person I can go ask about what we might have missed that night in Rome."

✖✖✖

"Keeper." Norton's sing-song voice echoed through the corridor. "Keeper."

Amari stopped in front of his cell, her hands on her hips. The man was visibly hairier than a few days before. His entire body looked like it had a five o'clock shadow, except for the spot on his shoulder where Ambrose had shot him with a silver bullet. Fortunately, the wound had completely healed by now, the skin smooth and unscarred.

"Is there anything you need?" she asked, eyeing him as he scratched at his shaggy arms. "Some flea powder perhaps?"

"When do I get my phone call? I know my rights," Norton said.

Was she imagining it, or were his canines bigger, too? She made a quick mental count and realised with a start that the full moon was the next night. No wonder he was so hirsute.

"You have no rights in here, Mr Norton," Amari said. "You gave up your rights the day you attacked innocent people."

Norton wrenched at the bars of his cell, but the door held fast. "You can't keep me locked in here forever," he growled. "And when I get out, I'll come for you."

Amari quirked an eyebrow. "Threats won't

286

change your situation. You'd better resign yourself to the fact that the Repository is your home now." Norton lifted his head and let out an angry howl. Around her, all the other creatures in the holding cells joined in again. Amari waited patiently until the ruckus had died down and Norton stood panting, glaring angrily at her.

"I can't let you go –" She lifted a finger as he was about to protest again. "But I can do you a deal. It'll be a full moon tomorrow, correct?" Norton nodded angrily. "I'm sure you don't want to be confined to this cell when you change, do you?" He shook his head curtly. "I can build you an enclosure before then. I'll even let you have some input into what you want. All I want in exchange is some information."

"I'm listening."

"Do you know how the airavata escaped the other day? Did you see what happened?"

Norton's toothy smile was predatory. "Of course, I did."

"Well?"

The man folded his tattooed arms across his hairy chest. "I'll tell you, in exchange for my freedom."

"An enclosure is as good as."

"Not good enough." Norton's upper lip pulled into a snarl, revealing his pointed canines. "I'm not an animal to be kept in a cage. Let me out!"

"No." Amari took a step closer, until she could smell his sour body odour. "Like it or not, Mister Norton, you are a mythical creature infused with legendary powers. You belong here."

"Legendary powers," Norton snorted. "I got bit by a wolf. Once a month I get a little moody. Tell me you can't relate."

"We are nothing alike. And referring to your rampaging killing sprees as being 'a little moody' is proof enough that you're not fit for human society."

"Let a judge decide on that."

Amari clenched her jaw. "Are you going to tell me what happened or not?"

Norton only snarled in response.

"Fine," Amari said, folding her arms across her chest. "Then tell me how you became a werewolf. You said a wolf bit you – when did this happen? What were you doing?"

Norton laughed. "I'm not telling you anything until I'm out of this cage."

Amari reached into her jeans pocket and pulled out the bracelet Ambrose had given her. She dangled it in front of him enticingly. "I'll give you this if you cooperate."

A spark of interest flashed across Norton's face, and then he stepped back and sat down on his cot. He closed his eyes, inhaling deeply through his nose. "When I get out of here, I'll come for that too."

The hair on the back of Amari's neck stood on end. She placed a hand on the door and strengthened the Word on it. Full moon or not, the werewolf would not escape from his holding cell.

Her phone pinged and she pulled it out to glance at the display. An email from the Council.

"We're not done talking about this," she said.

"Yes, we are," Norton shot back.

Amari glared at him over her shoulder before she strode off towards her office.

※※※

The Keeper flopped back into the wingback chair by the fireplace, her phone clutched in her hand. A heaviness settled in her stomach as she considered the Council's email. She shook her head. There must be some mistake. Or she must have misunderstood.

Feverishly, she navigated back to the email and reread it, her hands shaking so much she had to put the phone down before she could make sense of the message.

TO: The Keeper of Exotic Animals
FROM: The Council for the Protection and Preservation of Cultural Creatures
RE: Revision of the Policy on the Use of Intrinsic Abilities

Ms Kerubo,

Please note that the Council has discussed and agreed upon an amendment of the Policy for the Protection and Preservation of Cultural Creatures, notably Section 5a: The Use of Intrinsic Abilities.

The revised section is as follows: "The Council hereby approves the sanctioned use of any intrinsic abilities bestowed upon cultural creatures, with the express prohibition that these powers are not dependent upon relics taken from creatures – with the caveat that relics provided willingly shall be acceptable. All intrinsic abilities may be utilised according to their intended use as long as the creature is treated with the rights as described in Section 1c and, if removed from the Repository for the duration of usage, is returned safely and in good stature, forthwith."

This amendment applies with immediate effect.

It has come to my attention that there is currently a caladrius bird in residence in the Repository. You may well be aware of this creature's rumoured ability to heal illness. In light of the revised policy, I wish to put the creature to the test.

I trust you will make the necessary arrangements at your most urgent convenience.

Yours faithfully,
R Drake (Chairman)

Amari chewed on her bottom lip as she contemplated the implications of this message, her heart beating like a drum against her chest. After all these years, the Council had finally decided to cross that line she had been so sure they never would – been assured of, when she had accepted the position. They'd told her – and she'd fervently believed them – that the creatures in her care were inviolate, to be forever kept safe against exactly what the Council was proposing now.

Her eyes roamed over the message for the third time, and she snorted in disgust. "Relics provided willingly," she muttered, closing her email app in disgust. That's how it would start. And soon, who was to say what was provided willingly and what was provided willingly under duress? And who would have access to these so-called 'relics' – nothing more than an inoffensive euphemism for body parts! – other than the highest bidder? The only thing that would now distinguish the Council from a black-market poacher is that they would retain their hold on the creatures forever!

Flavius had been right all along.

But she couldn't just set the creatures free, like he wanted her to. They'd be in danger, and a danger to anyone they encountered. She couldn't just heave the Repository doors open and bid them all be on their merry way. It wasn't that simple.

In her mind's eye, Amari saw Una muzzled in the back of a truck with men wearing blue latex gloves reaching for the unicorn. A shudder ran down her body and she dropped her head into her hands, suddenly unable to keep the flood of emotions from running down her cheeks.

Everything she had worked for, everything she believed in and had fought for – all gone, just like that.

The fire crackled merrily in the hearth as the Keeper of Exotic Animals wept.

※※※

Amari rubbed at her tired eyes as she stepped through the gate and onto the banks of what looked like Loch Ness. She'd had very little sleep the previous night, tossing and turning in her bed, but no matter how much she wracked her brain, she could not come up with a way to prevent the Council from having their way with the creatures in her care, short of barring the Repository doors, that is.

She'd spent the entire day visiting each of the enclosures, making sure their residents were well, wondering how she was going to keep them safe. Keep them from being exploited by the very people who had promised them refuge.

A bitingly cold wind whipped past her, and she wrapped her arms about herself. She stopped at the edge of the lake just as the enormous serpentine body of Kentigern Mor reared up from the water.

"Amari," the dragon rumbled. "You look troubled."

The Keeper frowned. "I'm afraid we've been

deceived, great dragon." The taste of betrayal bitter in her mouth, Amari told him about the policy change and the Chairman's request.

The lake's water churned as the dragon coiled in slow loops, his expression unreadable. Amari had expected him to explode with rage, but instead, he regarded her with a keen gaze. "What would you have me do, Keeper?"

Amari stared at the enormous dragon. "Do?"

"Do you want me to fight, or to submit?"

Amari blinked. Then she shook her head. "I don't know. I don't know what to do." She glanced at him. "What do *you* want to do?"

Kentigern Mor lowered his head down to her level. For a moment, Amari could think of nothing else but the enormous teeth within striking distance of her. She looked into the dragon's stormy eyes and felt the weight of ages press upon her. When he spoke, his voice was like the crack of lightning. "*That* is the question you should be asking."

Then he slipped back into the water, ripples passing through the waves left in his wake as he disappeared from view.

Amari stared out across the lake, grey as the overcast sky above. She didn't have any answers.

But she knew someone who might.

✕✕✕

Diana's diary fell open to the page of Symbols Amari had been trying to decipher. She flipped past it and stared at the blank pages that faced her. She'd been dismayed when she'd first realised that the rest of the diary was unused, but now she stared at those spotless pages with fresh interest.

The Keeper inhaled deeply. A few months ago, when Amari had confronted Reese about the rogue shapeshifter in the Repository, the winged monkey had said something that had been bothering her ever since. She closed her eyes, recalling the vivid blue of his as he'd said to her: "Although she could never prove it, Diana wondered if the Repository was never meant to be the refuge we thought it was." The aged shapeshifter had told her to look to the Council for answers, and it seemed like he'd been right after all.

He'd also said something else to her, much more recently. She'd thought he'd wanted her to find James' little phoenix, but perhaps he had been hinting at even more...

The Word of Revelation flowed from her lips, and Amari gasped as the blank sheets of Diana's diary shimmered. The Keeper's eyes widened as black ink bled across the page, coalescing into Diana's archaic handwriting. Amari's gaze was immediately drawn to a heading at the top, the letters large and somewhat shaky, as if her predecessor had been wracked with emotion as she'd written them:

Who keeps the Keeper?

Amari frowned, bending over the book. Her breathing quickened as she read on:

I have always been under the impression that the work I do here, along with Reese, my faithful assistant, is of the utmost importance. Our sole purpose these many years has been the acquisition of Creatures captured or bred to be sold at market for their parts – not only for the liberation of these astounding Animals, but also for the good of Mankind. For, should a Creature be hunted to extinction, surely the World would lose that Trait, that thread of Magic that binds the very existence of Reality.

To my knowledge, the Repository has always been their Safe Haven, the one place in the World where Creatures are cared for and can live in those Habitats designed according to their specific needs, untroubled and free from the World, but still in it, gifting us with their special Magic by virtue of their existence.

As the Keeper, it is my solemn duty to ensure they are kept in this way and remain free from abuse and misuse.

But, I no longer believe this to be true.

Even in here, are they truly safe?

Feverishly, Amari flipped the page over. She stared at the single sentence hastily scrawled across the sheet:

What have I done?

Amari slammed the diary shut, her heart racing. Diana had known! Shivers ran down the Keeper's spine. A century ago, the legendary Keeper had already feared what Amari had now just realised: that the Repository was the Council's long-term investment. One that was finally about to pay off.

The Councilmembers didn't really care about the creatures! Amari's hands shook as she thought about Marco, the former member who had been selling creatures at the blood moon market in Rome. And Councilmember Bottenfeldt, her disgraced manager, who had secretly traded in creature parts to fund her lavish lifestyle. Even before the policy change, the Chairman had had no qualms about using Asian creatures for his own ends. And it was the Chairman who had brought James to the Repository and who had put forward the motion to allow him to study the creatures in her care.

How could she have been so blind?

The Keeper sat for a moment, stunned into inaction. She jumped as her phone beeped. She looked at the display – it was her reminder to go fetch Flavius.

Sighing, Amari stood up and shoved Diana's diary back into its hiding place on the bookshelf. Then she took a deep breath. This was not a conversation she was looking forward to.

The Keeper squared her shoulders, and then the world was washed in white.

❉❉❉

A howl ripped through the corridors as Amari returned to the Repository, alone. A quick glance at the clock on her phone told her the sun would be down soon. She'd better be there when Norton transformed, just to make sure he wasn't a danger to himself, if nothing else.

But she still had time.

She needed to speak to her apprentice. She needed to find out how much he'd known.

Amari hurried to James' room and knocked on the door. No reply. Her hand lingered above the door handle.

She clenched her jaw. She'd already breached his privacy once before. One more time wouldn't make a difference. She needed to know. The lock clicked open at her whispered Word, and she quickly slipped inside.

Amari gasped. James' room was still as messy as before, but now his collection of jars contained all manner of creature parts – shavings of dryad bark, grey harpy feathers that shone purple where the light caught it, glowing red salamander scales, a milky opaque fluid, and various other bits she couldn't easily identify at first glance.

Heat rushed through her body. Hadn't she expressly forbidden him from taking creature parts? Did the Keeper's authority mean nothing to him?

Thunder crackled, and Amari stiffened. She flinched as an enormous uproar erupted, pierced by an ear-splitting howl. Goosebumps broke out across her skin.

She ran to the door and wrenched it open just in time to see the airavata storm past. She heard shoes slapping against stone, becoming softer as it moved away from her. Thunder rumbled, rolling through the hallway like an ominous portent. The air smelled of sulphur and ozone.

Three barks rang out and was suddenly silenced.

Amari's throat went dry.

Ignoring the rampaging airavata, Amari sprinted towards the holding cells. The commotion had died down, and Amari's entire body shook as she rounded the corner. She stopped in her tracks, unable to prevent a sob from escaping her lips.

All the cages were open, and bodies littered the ground. The yale's throat had been ripped out, and the caladrius bird's snowy feathers were stained crimson. Dead salamanders were scattered everywhere.

Amari dropped to her knees beside the hellhound, tears streaming silently down her face. Blood matted its fur, and the tongues lolled out of two of its heads. The third was a mangled mess.

Swallowing back bile, Amari rose to her feet. She clenched her shaking hands. Where was Norton? She was going to make him pay for this.

The sound of the iron door clanging sent a shot of icy fear down her spine.

He was in the Repository!

The Keeper ran down the hallway and rounded the corner so quickly she nearly slammed into the lamia. The enormous snake reared up, its hood flaring as it hissed threateningly. Amari yelped, skittering backwards.

The lamia's head began to weave and Amari felt the world starting to spin, the edges of her vision becoming fuzzy. With great force of will, she wrenched her gaze from the snake's purple eyes. Behind it, she could see the door leading to the Repository hanging at an angle, deep claw marks scratched into it.

The snake hissed and darted towards her, its fangs dripping with milky venom. Amari dodged, but stumbled to the ground as a sharp pain spiked through her thigh. She cried out and turned to see the lamia's jaw clamped around her leg, its teeth sunk into her flesh.

Terror flared, much like the fire that blossomed from Amari's palms. The stench of singed flesh seared through the air, and Amari gasped as the enormous snake wrenched itself off her, screeching in pain. Sinuous body thrashing, the lamia slithered away and out of sight.

With her vision blurring, Amari fumbled along her thigh until her fingers closed around the fang still embedded in her flesh. Gritting her teeth, she pulled it out and tossed it away from her. She sat on the cold floor, panting.

A howl rang out again, coming from the Repository. Clutching onto the wall, Amari pulled herself to her feet. She swayed, the snake's venom still coursing through her veins. Blinking, she stumbled towards the mangled gate, limping through it, and coming to a stop on the platform overlooking the Repository.

She shook her head, trying to clear her sight. The corners of her vision were still blurry, but she could see better now.

Feverishly, she scanned the enclosures below. There! A streak of black shot past the cyclops pen. The monstrously transformed werewolf was tearing through the Repository on all fours, pursuing its target. Amari's gaze followed its path and her hand shot to her heart as she saw James darting into an enclosure.

Una's enclosure.

"No!" Amari yelled. Adrenaline propelled her forward and she took the stairs down two at a time, heedless of the pain throbbing in her thigh. She staggered through the maze of enclosures, her heart beating in her throat, pushing herself to go faster.

Ahead, she saw the werewolf disappear through Una's gate.

Summoning what strength she had left, Amari rushed after it and into the unicorn's grove. Her breath was ragged as the darkness of the forest enveloped her. The werewolf's howl ripped through the air, and Amari pushed through the tangle of underbrush in pursuit. Branches seemed to grab at her hair, and the mulch underfoot tried to trip her up, but she blundered forwards, letting instinct guide her in the right direction.

She fell into the clearing as if into a nightmare. Moonlight bathed the world in shades of black and grey. It was as if time had slowed to a crawl. James was on the ground where he had fallen. Una, standing protectively over him, was reared up on her hind legs. The werewolf was leaping through the air towards the unicorn, its sharp claws gleaming in the starlit night.

Amari lunged forward, her one hand clenched into a fist. A Word burst from her lips. She saw her will strike the werewolf like a hammer, immobilising it even as its body hurtled through the air. Una lifted her head, her horn shimmering in the pale light. The sickening sound of bone ripping through flesh sent Amari to her feet, retching, as the werewolf slammed into the unicorn.

A gong sounded, and the ground shook as Amari slapped her hands across her ears. Her whole body turned cold.

"What was that?" James asked, pushing himself to his feet.

Amari blinked, feeling like she was drowning, like her limbs were too heavy to move. Stricken, she watched as Una pulled her horn from the werewolf's body and wiped the blood and gore off on the trampled grass. Before her eyes, the werewolf's hair receded and the grotesque limbs twisted back into human form until only Norton was left on the ground, his blood staining the grass a murky red.

Amari couldn't take her eyes off the body. The gong was still ringing in her ears.

Beside her, Una nickered softly and Amari tangled her fingers into the unicorn's silky mane.

"What did you do?" James asked, his eyes bulging at the sight of the dead man. He looked like he might be sick at any moment.

"What I had to," Amari replied. Una was safe. That was all that mattered.

James averted his eyes and spun towards her. His face was pale, but there was a glimmer of something in his eyes. "What was that sound?" he demanded.

Amari's throat constricted. Her hand tightened around the unicorn's mane. When she answered, her voice was barely more than a whisper. "A warning. It means the world has just lost a trait."

Confusion played across the scholar's face, and then his eyes widened as understanding dawned. "And you killed it," he sniggered.

Her gaze whipped to his. The smirk on James' face sent a shiver down her spine. He straightened his shoulders and his posture stiffed. She pulled away from Una as her apprentice's voice took on a new authority.

"Amari Kerubo, on behalf of the Council for the Protection and Preservation of Cultural Creatures, I hereby place you under arrest." Every word was like a slap across her face. "You can stay in your room until the Council has made a decision."

A vice tightened around Amari's heart. She was guilty. She'd killed a creature, and now a trait was lost. The world is worse because of her, and the Council would have no choice but to condemn her. They'd lock her up, far away from the Repository and the creatures she was meant to protect. Who would look after them now? Not the Council. And not this man walking warily towards her, with his bottles of bits and pieces.

Amari took a step backwards, her gaze flitting from James to Una. She took a deep breath.

And then a blinding light scorched the world white.

THE END

(The story continues in *Myth Maker,* the next instalment of the Mythical Menagerie series)

BONUS SCENES

Full Moon Date Night

"There," Cassie breathed, surveying her apartment with satisfaction.

Dozens of candles flickered all around the room, filling the air with the scent of exotic spices – cloves, cinnamon, a hint of cardamom. A path of rose petals led towards the six-seater table, where she'd set it for an intimate dinner for two, her best bone china and heirloom silver glinting in the ambient light. In the kitchen, the timer pinged just as keys jangled at the front door.

Butterflies fluttered in Cassie's stomach as Pavithra walked through the door, still dressed in the stretchy leggings she had donned for class, her yoga mat clutched underneath one arm.

"What's this?" she asked, fumbling with the band that held her long black hair tied up in a loose bun.

"A thank you," Cassie said, swooping closer and pecking her girlfriend lightly on the cheek. "For taking care of me these past few weeks."

A shadow passed across Pavi's face, quickly replaced by a tight-lipped smile. "I'm just glad you're alright." She took a step towards the kitchen, sniffing the air appreciatively. "You cooked?"

"Of course," Cassie said. "Your favourite curry. I found the recipe online. Fully vegetarian, I promise."

"Sounds delicious. And this looks perfect. But do you mind if I take a quick shower first?"

Pavi headed for the bedroom but paused when she reached the window. She stared out, a frown creasing her forehead. She cleared her throat. "You sure you want to do this tonight?"

Cassie crossed the floor to join her at the window. The full moon shone brightly outside. She swept the curtains closed.

"You sound just like Ambrose. I'm fine," she said, a hint of annoyance creeping into her voice despite her best efforts. She could understand her brother's fears, but there was no reason for Pavithra to be paranoid. As far as her girlfriend remembered, her attacker had been nothing more sinister than a mugger with a sharp knife.

Pavi nodded. "I was just concerned the full moon would bring back memories."

"Then we should make some new ones," Cassie shot back, her hands suddenly clenched into fists by her side.

"Fair enough," Pavi said soothingly. "I'll be right back."

Cassie watched her disappear into the bedroom, and then turned towards the mirror hanging over the fireplace, inspecting her face. She didn't look hairy. She grinned, baring her teeth, and nodded at herself. No fangs there. She ran a hand across her cheek. It was smooth, no traces of any scarring left, except for a small silver mark beside her left eye, hardly visible unless one looked closely.

Suddenly, that night flashed before her eyes.

The utter blackness of the alley, her heartbeat drumming in her ears, the stench of stale sweat in the air. Goosebumps lifted on her arms as she remembered the howl that had rent the air – feral, predatory, inhuman. And then the werewolf lunging towards her brother, the spike of fear as she jumped into its path, the sharp pain as its claws raked through her flesh. She shuddered and wrapped her arms about herself as if doing so could ward the memory away from her.

She turned towards the bar and, with shaking hands, poured herself a shot of bourbon. The warmth gliding down her throat settled her nerves somewhat. She poured another shot, lifted it in a toast towards the moon hidden behind the thick curtain, and downed it quickly. Her shoulders loosened a little. Maybe if she had another one, she could forget about that night entirely.

The bottle clinked against the glass, her hands still trembling. And then the subtle scent of cloves caressed the air. Pavi's hand settled on her arm, stopping her from pouring another shot.

Cassie turned towards Pavithra and her breath hitched in her throat. She had changed into a tight top and flowing pants, a beautiful sash thickly embroidered with silver threads tied around her slender waist. Silver cuffs wrapped around her arms and silver earrings glinted from between her black hair. She looked as breathtaking as a Bollywood superstar.

"You won't need that tonight," Pavi said in a husky voice, her eyes dark pools that Cassie could easily drown in.

Cassie put the glass down and coaxed a smile back onto her face.

"No," she agreed. "Not tonight."

ACKNOWLEDGEMENTS

Writing is a solitary endeavour that can only be accomplished with the support of many wonderful people.

A HUGE thank you goes out to my beta readers: Mari Terblanche, Thalia Fourie, and Lynne Jones, who have taken time out of their busy schedules to read my stories, point out their flaws, and help me make it better.

Thank you Claudette and Schalk for cheerleading and motivation!

I would be remiss if I didn't include a shout-out to the Monster Blog of Monsters for helping me spark some ideas for filling the Repository with interesting and amazing creatures. Lamias (shudder). I wouldn't have thought of that one on my own!

Thank you to my husband Gareth, for continued encouragement and support, and for taking care of all the practical parts of day-to-day life while my head is in the clouds, dreaming up adventures for Ambrose and Amari.

And finally, thank you to you, dear reader, for reading this book and supporting this passion of mine. I hope it added a little magic to your life too!

WANT MORE?

Subscribe to Suneé le Roux's email list to receive a free flash fiction in your inbox every month. You'll also receive an exclusive short story prequel set in the Mythical Menagerie universe, only available to newsletter subscribers!

SUBSCRIBE.SUNEELEROUX.COM/KEEPEROFEXOTICANIMALS

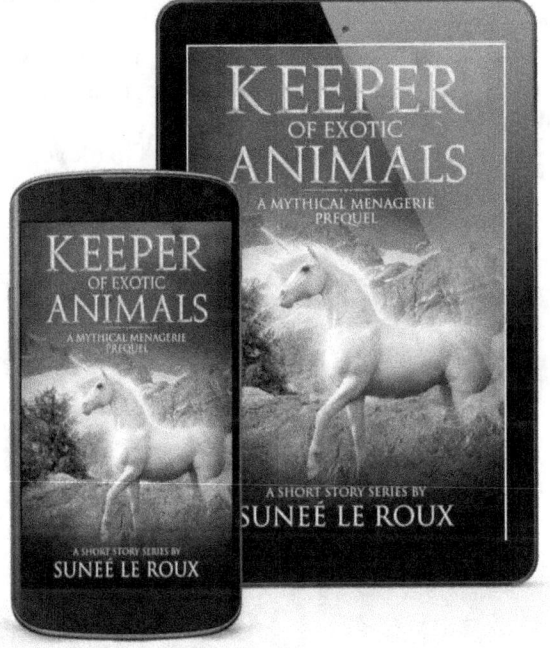

PLEASE REVIEW

If you've enjoyed this story, please consider leaving a review on your online platform of choice and/or on Goodreads. Think of it as word of mouth recommendation. Independent authors such as myself need reviews for visibility and social proof, and to get those algorithms to place my books in the hands of other readers.

It doesn't have to be a long and in-depth review - one sentence, or even just a star rating, will do.

It would mean the world to me. Thank you!

ABOUT THE AUTHOR

Suneé le Roux is a South African author of contemporary and high fantasy stories that blend myth, magic, and adventure. She lives in South Africa with her Welsh husband and their young wizard-in-training.

She loves nothing more than to hear from readers. Connect with her here:

Website: www.suneeleroux.com

Email: contact@suneeleroux.com

Facebook: www.facebook.com/
authorsuneeleroux/

Instagram: www.instagram.com/suneeleroux/

WWW.SUNEELEROUX.COM